SECRETS AND SACRIFICE

A CHRISTIAN ROMANCE BOOK 4 IN THE SHADOWS SERIES

JULIETTE DUNCAN

COPYRIGHT

PRAISE FOR "SECRETS AND SACRIFICE"

"I think this is your best book yet! It's brilliant. I think that although there is a lot about Christianity and prayer, to say nothing about God's love, it is the right amount. It needs to be a central part of this story, or how else could you have told Grace's story?" *Caroline M*

"You have done it again!! This book was absolutely perfect!! The story kept me interested, there was just enough romance in it. The story flowed flawlessly!!!" *Jama C*

"The story is beautiful, everything flows well and the characters all come to life in their own way. Not once was I at a point that I felt I wanted to just scan a section as to get on with the book, I really wanted to read every word." *Deidre V*

"I was hooked right from the beginning when Brianna was in the hospital. The book started out all about Brianna but turned to Grace with her own demons. I love all of the scripture that you add to the book. It makes me realize that God truly is our savior and we are his children that he loves unconditionally." *Carol Y*

GLOSSARY

As **"Secrets and Sacrifice"** is set in Northern Ireland and Scotland, you may come across some unfamiliar words as you read the story. They should all make sense in context, but the following may also help.

UK/Scottish........U.S.

Wig......................A head piece that British judges and barristers are required to wear
Abseiling................Rappelling
Sassenach..............Englishman (derogatory)
Smirr.....................Fine rain
Ceilidh...................A social event with Scottish or Irish folk music and singing, traditional dancing, and storytelling. Pronounced "Kay-lee"
Wellies...................Rain Boots
Burn......................Creek
Curlew...................A large wading bird

CHAPTER 1

*B*elfast 1985

GRACE ROSE, pausing momentarily before marching to the front of the court room. The twelve members of the jury sat in their box, looking weary after a week of listening to the despicable deeds of Donal Patrick O'Malley. Now it was up to her to convince them they should find him guilty of murder.

A hush fell over the court room as Grace cast her gaze over them. She'd prepared for this moment, but would it be enough? Niall would no doubt have a brilliant closing argument. Hers had to dazzle.

Grace took a deep breath to steady herself, but just as she opened her mouth to speak, a tall, thin man with darkish hair, shaved on the sides and spiked on top, entered the room, catching her attention. Grace's body stiffened. *Caleb? No, it can't be. Or could it?* Her brother never came to court, even when she was prosecuting a high-profile case such as this. But it sure looked like him. Grace's heart raced and a feeling of dread flooded her body. He would only come if something bad had happened. Regardless, she'd have to ignore him and focus on the job at hand. Besides, it might not even be him.

Returning her attention to the jury, she began her closing arguments, affording herself the occasional glance at the man. It was Caleb, no doubt about it. His face, normally pale, was deathly white. Something bad must have happened.

Somehow she focused on her speech. She needed to win. No way could she allow O'Malley to walk free after beating his wife to death, but with Caleb sitting in the back, it was a challenge. Finally, she reached her conclusion. "So, members of the jury, after all you've heard, I beg you to find the accused, Donal Patrick O'Malley, guilty as charged. Thank you."

Grace's stomach tightened as her gaze met Caleb's on her short walk back to her seat. She was tempted to go to him, but that would be breaking protocol. She'd have to wait to find out what had happened.

Her head hurt. She'd put everything she had into her speech, and now she felt drained. Normally she could relax a little after her job was done, but now... with Caleb sitting behind her? Impossible.

Bryan leaned over and offered his congratulations. Grace gave him a half smile. Bryan, her trusted assistant and most ardent advocate, would always say she'd done well, even if she hadn't.

Grace inhaled deeply to settle herself as the Judge called for the Defendant's closing arguments. Niall stood, and as he walked to the front of the room, she chastised herself for allowing him to unnerve her. Even after a week of seeing him every day, she failed to treat him like any other man. *Because he wasn't any other man.*

He'd aged a little. Small flecks of grey peppered the dark hair poking out from under his wig, only serving to increase his appeal. He'd also changed. It wasn't just the suit. Or his lean body. There was something else. Grace had seen it from the front of the court room when he'd caught her eye on the first day of the trial. A sadness, and no doubt, she was partly responsible. But it puzzled her—surely three years in London would have given him enough time for him to move on.

He wasn't quite the same man she'd fallen in love with in the heady days of college, but his nearness still stirred something deep inside her.

A tap on her shoulder jolted her, and she looked up into a clerk's concerned eyes.

"Miss, your brother's asking to see you urgently."

Grace spun around. *It must be bad.*

Her stomach churned as she grasped the rail and pulled herself up before making her way as unobtrusively as possible to the back of the room.

Sliding into the seat, Grace grabbed Caleb's thin arm and leaned close to him. She looked into his troubled eyes. "What's happened, Caleb?"

"Come outside, Grace." Caleb took her arm and led her into the foyer as Niall began his closing argument. She shouldn't leave, but this sounded like an emergency, and besides, Bryan was more than capable of taking notes.

"What's wrong, Caleb? It's not Caitlin, is it? Or the girls?" Grace gripped him tighter. "Please don't tell me it's the girls."

Caleb faced her. "If you stop talking, I'll tell you."

Grace pulled herself up. He was right... she needed to stop talking. She was jumping to conclusions. Best get the facts.

"Okay. Who?" Grace's heart beat faster. Was she ready to find out?

Caleb gulped, his protruding Adam's apple bobbing in his heavily tattooed neck.

"Brianna's been found."

Grace's eyes widened and she grabbed his arm again.

"Brianna? Where is she? Is she okay?"

Caleb paused, holding Grace's gaze.

"She can't be..."

"She's alive, Grace, but only just. She was found this morning, unconscious."

Grace covered her mouth with her hand. "I thought you were going to say she was dead..." She let out a huge sigh. Was it wrong to be relieved when your sister had been found unconscious?

"Where was she?"

"In a dingy apartment. Looks like an overdose."

"She promised." Grace huffed and narrowed her eyes. "She promised, Caleb. If only she'd kept her word."

"It's not that simple, Grace. You know that."

Grace sighed heavily. "Yes, I do. Where is she?"

"St. Vincent's. I'm going now. Can you come?"

"Not yet. But I will as soon as I can. Have you called the others?"

Caleb ran his hand along the side of his shaved head. "No—

I only just found out and I came straight here. I'll call them now."

Grace pulled a cigarette from under her robe and lit up. She didn't offer one to Caleb. "She'd better pull through." She took several quick puffs.

"Yes, she'd better. Caitlin's at home praying. She said that's the best thing she can do to help."

Grace rolled her eyes. *That's exactly what Caleb's wife, Caitlin, would do.*

Caleb leaned in and hugged Grace. "Come as soon as you can."

Grace hugged him back and held his gaze. "You're a good brother, Caleb."

As she watched Caleb hurry off, she took several more quick drags on her cigarette before grinding it out in an ashtray on the windowsill.

When she re-entered the court room, Niall was towards the end of his speech. Grace remained at the back to avoid creating a disturbance. It was difficult to focus. All she could think of was Brianna, her younger sister, lying in hospital, unconscious. *What if she dies?* Grace needed to get there as quickly as possible. But what could she do to help? At least Caitlin could pray. Grace couldn't even do that. It didn't matter. Being there would be enough.

GRACE ALLOWED her gaze to follow Niall as he took his seat. Just the look of him stirred her insides. *Why did he come back to Belfast? Surely London would have been more exciting.*

Moving forward quietly, she slid into her seat beside Bryan as a general buzz filled the room.

Bryan lifted his head and looked at her.

"Miss, are you alright?" Bryan's concern for her always warmed her heart.

"Yes, Bryan. Thank you. Just some family issues. I'll be okay." She gave him a weak smile.

Judge Atkinson cleared his throat, and the buzz in the court room died down.

"Thank you, members of the jury. We'll adjourn for now and reconvene at nine o'clock tomorrow for final instructions. Good night, and thank you for your time."

Everyone rose as the Judge stood and exited the room. Gathering her papers, Grace tossed them into her brief case.

"I've got to go, Bryan. But how did he do?" She nodded her head towards Niall who stood with his team on the opposite side of the bench. An unwelcome pang of jealousy stabbed her as a young attractive blond hung on his every word.

"Oh, he did well, as expected, but I think we've got it."

"Nothing's ever definite until the jury comes back. You know that, Bryan."

"Yes, Miss, I do. They can go either way. But if I were a betting man, I'd bet on you."

"Oh Bryan. What would I do without you?" Grace let out a small laugh. "I really do have to fly. I'll see you in the morning."

"Okay, Miss. Good night."

"Good night, Bryan." Grace swept her robe around her shoulders and hurried towards the exit, shooting one quick look at Niall before leaving the room. The blond was standing way too close. Grace sighed dejectedly. *Will I ever get over him?*

Stupid, really. It was her fault they'd broken up. She didn't want to get married. He did. *Too late now.* The blond had her hooks into him.

Grace glanced at her watch. She should change, but no, time was of the essence—she'd go straight to the hospital. What if something happened to Brianna in the time it took to return to Chambers?

As GRACE TURNED into Frew Lane, a biting wind caught her robe and sent it flying. Grabbing it, she pulled it tighter, but as she paused, a deep voice she'd know anywhere called out.

Grace stopped and turned. Niall was jogging towards her. Her heart fluttered. *Drat the man! How does he do that?*

Niall stopped and stood before her, wig in hand, his chest expanding and contracting heavily as he caught his breath.

"Grace, what's happened? I saw you disappear." His warm brown eyes gazed into hers as he touched her arm lightly, threatening to dismantle her resolve to remain aloof. "You don't look too good..."

Grace lowered her eyes. Allowing him back into her life would be asking for trouble. But she could surely do with a friend right now. No. She was strong, and she didn't need anyone. *Especially Niall. Get a grip, Grace.*

She inhaled deeply and lifted her head. "It's nothing, really, Niall. Just a small family matter."

Niall tilted his head, a quizzical look on his way too hand-some face. "Doesn't look like that to me, Grace." He knew her too well. "Where are you racing off to?"

Grace shook her head and pulled her robe higher around

her neck. A light drizzle had begun to fall. People scurried past, hurrying to get home before the skies opened up. Niall opened the umbrella he'd been holding in one hand and held it over her. The gentleman as always.

"Come on, Grace, let's get out of this. Let me drive you to wherever you're going."

Grace stiffened. Should she let her defences down just a little? If she did, would she be able to put them back up again? Or would she succumb to Niall's charms and let all her resolves fly out the window? She looked into the eyes of the only man she'd ever loved and weakened.

Niall's hand rested on her elbow as he guided her towards the car park around the corner, stopping in front of a silver, 1982 Alfa Romeo Spider. Grace cast her eyes over the tiny sports car and approved. She and Niall had always shared a penchant for fast cars.

Niall's seatbelt clicked. As he turned the key, the Spider sprang to life, the roar of the engine thrilling her. He turned and looked at her. "So, where are we off to?"

Grace had to tear her eyes from his before she did something she'd regret. He was way too close for comfort.

"St. Vincent's." Grace's gaze was firmly fixed on the road ahead. "Brianna's overdosed."

CHAPTER 2

*N*iall manoeuvred the Spider into a tight car park and turned off the engine, turning his head towards her.

"I can go in by myself, Niall. You don't have to come."

"I'd like to, if you'll let me."

Grace let out a heavy sigh. "I really am okay on my own."

"I know, but I'd like to be there for you." His steady gaze bore into her, unnerving her.

Grace inhaled deeply. How much longer could she resist him? But she had to. Nothing had changed, and she couldn't, or wouldn't, allow her past to possibly destroy the career of the only man she'd loved. He could have the blond. It would do Grace no good to get entangled with him again.

She pushed her door open. "We need to hurry. She's in the Emergency Department."

"Okay then. Let's go." He jumped out of the car and joined her.

Grace strode as fast as she could in her high heels. Niall easily kept up. She knew exactly where to go... how many times had she and Caleb been through this? Not only with Brianna, but with Brendan, their younger brother, too. What a messed up family they were.

Would Brianna make it this time? Or would she finally succeed with her death wish? It didn't seem to matter how many times Grace and Caleb talked to her about making changes in her life, she never saw them through. Of course, Caleb always talked to her about God. "God can help you, Brianna," he'd always say. Grace would roll her eyes, and then go on to tell Brianna to get a grip on herself. Neither approach had worked. Brianna had a death wish. Grace hoped that today her wish would once again be denied.

"She's in there, Miss O'Connor". The nurse at the reception desk tilted her head towards a curtained off cubicle to the right. Not only was Grace a well-known figure in the Emergency Department, she was often featured on the nightly news. The high profile barrister with the drug addicted sister. Both with secrets they'd hidden since fleeing Aunt Hilda's all those years ago... if ever the media got wind of... no, she wouldn't go there. She'd worked too hard to leave it all behind. And she'd done well for herself. No one would have expected poor, motherless Grace O'Connor to amount to anything. She'd shown them. But Brianna? Different story altogether. Brianna was allowing her past to destroy her.

Grace followed the direction the nurse indicated and paused before entering. What would she find? Each time this happened Brianna looked worse. Grace drew a steadying breath. Time to find out...

Brianna lay in bed with a myriad of tubes hanging out of her nose and arm. Her eyes were closed, but she was breathing. Grace sighed in relief.

Caleb squeezed her arm. "Looks like she's going to make it, Grace." Caleb looked better than he had an hour or so ago. Colour had returned to his face, and his troubled look had eased.

"So glad to hear that, Caleb. What did she do this time?" Pulling her scarf off, Grace placed it on the chair beside her bag and took Brianna's hand.

"Tablets. They've pumped her stomach."

Grace sucked in a deep breath and released it slowly. "Silly girl." A wave of sadness flowed through her. Brianna looked so fragile. Her eye sockets had sunk into her filthy face, and her hair looked like it hadn't been brushed for days, possibly weeks. Grace gently pushed back with her fingertips the strands of hair hanging over Brianna's face. "Why, Brianna? *Why?*"

Grace forced back the tears pricking her eyes. She knew why. But how many more times could they go through this? Something had to change. After all they'd been through, she couldn't lose Brianna now. Her heart ached for the sister she'd shared so much with. Life hadn't been fair to either of them, but for Brianna, it had been worse. She wasn't as strong as Grace, and where Grace had determined not to let her past dictate her future, Brianna didn't have the same resilience or determination.

Grace squeezed Brianna's hand and leaned forward, placing a kiss on her sister's hollow cheek. A tear fell from Grace's eye and splashed onto Brianna's cheek, leaving a muddy streak as it trickled down her face.

A hand on Grace's shoulder jolted her. She remained still, hesitant to move, before slowly lifting her hand and placing it over Niall's. Warmth filled her body. Niall knew how close she was to Brianna. How many nights had they gone out searching for her in the past? How many times had she cried on his shoulder when they'd come home without her?

Grace closed her eyes and steadied herself. Niall's hand on her shoulder meant nothing. It was just his way of showing concern. Nothing more. Nothing less. She couldn't have him, or any other man, in her life. It wouldn't be fair to them. She was better off without them, and Brianna certainly was too. If only Brianna hadn't caught the attention of their cousins. Grace gritted her teeth. What they'd done to her little sister still made her blood boil. She should prosecute them. How many times had she pictured it... bringing those pieces of filth to justice? But if she did, her career would be over... Grace had no doubt Aunt Hilda would expose her secret if she did. And meanwhile, Brianna suffered.

Grace inhaled deeply and rose, letting Brianna's hand slip out of hers. Niall moved back, allowing Grace room to turn. As she did, she lifted her eyes and met his gaze. She swallowed hard. Her heart skittered as she looked into those soft-brown eyes she knew so well. *Why are you here, Niall? After all this time?* She brushed against him lightly as she inched along Brianna's bed towards Caleb, who stood at the end of the bed, arms crossed, legs astride, deep in conversation with the doctor.

"Miss O'Connor." Dr Thompson held out his hand. His face

was serious and his voice less than friendly. He must be getting tired of treating their sister. Grace took his hand and shook it.

"Hello, Dr Thompson. This is Niall Flannery. A colleague of mine." *A colleague?*

The two men shook hands.

"Your sister had a close call this time, Miss O'Connor, but I think she'll pull through. We'll know more in the morning."

Grace glanced at Brianna lying in the bed and her shoulders fell. If only she could wrap Brianna in her arms and protect her from the demons that haunted her. Lying in the bed, she looked so helpless... so thin, so dirty, so unloved. And yet, she'd been such a beauty when she was young, with her russet locks that bounced on her shoulders whenever she ran and her hazel eyes that lit up every time she laughed. Maybe she'd been too pretty. Maybe that had been her downfall.

Grace breathed deeply and gulped. She'd already made her decision. She looked at Dr Thompson and then at Caleb. "I'd like Brianna to come back to my place when she's released. I want to look after her."

Caleb's eyes widened. "We've talked about this before, Grace. How will you cope with your job?"

"I'll cope. I'll cut back my work load. It'll be fine."

"You know what she's like, Grace." Caleb reached for Grace's hand and held her gaze. Her brother's sensitivity was at odds with his appearance. Always had been. She and Caleb had shared the burden of being Brianna's keepers for years, and Caleb had often taken time off from his job at the ship-yards, without pay, to care for her. Brianna had stayed with Caleb and Caitlin and their two young daughters several times, but she'd never lasted more than a few days at a time. It seemed Brianna couldn't handle more than that, and she often disappeared without a word after stealing whatever she could, leaving behind a heart-broken brother, sister-in-law and two little nieces.

"Yes, I do, but I want to do this, Caleb." Grace moved towards Brianna and eased herself onto the bed. Pulling a tissue from a box on the stand, she gently wiped away the dirt caked on her sister's face as she pushed back the tears pricking her own eyes. She would take Brianna home to her apartment and care for her. And once and for all, she'd get Brianna clean.

CHAPTER 3

"*L*et's get a bite to eat, Grace. Would you like to join us, Caleb?" Grace stiffened as Niall placed his hand against the small of her back as they walked along the corridor towards the car park.

What was Niall doing? She hadn't agreed to go out with him, but the thought of going home to an empty apartment didn't appeal. Despite her resolve, Grace's heart beat faster at the prospect of spending time alone with Niall, even though it couldn't lead anywhere.

Caleb ran a hand along the side of his head. "Thanks Niall, but I need to get home to Caity and the girls. They'll want to know how Brianna is. Besides, knowing Caity, she'll have dinner waiting for me."

"No problem, Caleb." Niall flashed him a smile. "Give my regards to Caitlin, will you?"

"Will do. See you in the morning, Grace." Caleb kissed

Grace on her cheek and shook Niall's hand before leaving them and heading off towards his car.

"Well?" Niall tilted his head, a mischievous grin growing on his face as he held the car door open for her. "I know you haven't eaten." One eyebrow lifted, and as much as she tried, she couldn't tear her eyes away from his.

This was happening way too fast. All week she'd tried to avoid him, all the while trying to ignore the fluttering of her heart every time her eyes locked with his, and the stab of jealousy when the blond leaned too close. She angled her head. Weren't they an item? It seemed that way. So what was Niall doing here with her, asking her out for a meal, especially when he knew there was no future for them. She couldn't have made that any clearer when she'd turned down his proposal several years ago. Maybe he was just after a casual fling?

Grace stilled her beating heart. "All right. Let's get something to eat." She slid under his arm and sank deep into the soft leather seat, hoping she'd made the right decision.

The roar of the Spider's engine once again sent a thrill through her body. Niall glanced at her, a wicked grin sitting on his face. He knew her too well. Blow it! She'd relax and enjoy the ride... get her mind off Brianna and the court case for a while. She drew in a breath and laughed as he thrust the gear stick into first and accelerated out of the park a little too fast.

She wasn't surprised when he pulled up outside Molly's Café—their favourite place to chill when they'd been a couple. But they weren't a couple now, and Grace hadn't ventured inside Molly's since the last time she'd been there with Niall, almost five years ago.

Had he chosen Molly's just because it was convenient, or

was he trying to revive their relationship? She'd made it clear she'd never marry. And he'd made it clear if she wouldn't marry him, then it was over... so what was he playing at? Had he changed his mind? And if he had, would she let him into her life again? Her heart pounded. This was all so unexpected and unplanned.

Niall opened the door for her. Grace peeled her long legs out of the car and took his waiting hand. Not that she needed help, but it would have been rude to ignore it.

"Thank you." She flashed him a smile, and then, once steady on her feet, let go of his hand and moved aside to allow him to close the door.

Molly's Café hadn't changed. The heavy timber doors were slightly more weathered, but the cheerful exterior still enticed passers-by to enter. Grace followed Niall as he weaved his way through the scattered tables to their usual booth at the back. They'd always liked sitting here, tucked away from the main area, away from prying eyes. But it was all too familiar.

Grace slid into the seat opposite Niall, tucking her bag beside her. The candlelight accentuated the grey flecks in his hair, giving him a distinguished appearance. She lowered her eyes, needing a moment to compose herself.

A young waitress stood before them with pen and pad in hand. Her dark hair was piled in a loose bun, and her green apron, tied at the waist, sat over a plain white blouse and a short black skirt. She could easily have been the waitress who served them five years ago. "Can I take yer orders?"

Niall looked up and smiled. "Not quite ready, sorry. Could you come back in a few minutes?"

"Sure." She gave the table a quick wipe and then scooted off to the next table.

"What would you like?" Niall's voice was so smooth, so familiar.

Grace gulped and picked up the menu, saying, "I'm not sure yet," as she opened it, thankful for the distraction.

She decided on a Chicken Parmigiana, and he chose a Beef and Guiness Pie.

Once their orders were placed, Grace decided enough was enough. She wouldn't let Niall's presence affect her any more. She'd converse with him as if he were any other person she was having a meal with.

Grace lifted her gaze and held it steady. She could do this. "What brought you back to Belfast?"

Niall wrapped his hands around his coffee mug. "I was wondering when you'd ask that." He met her gaze, his expression growing serious. "Father had a health scare recently. He asked me to come back and help so he could reduce his work load. Doctor's orders." He raised his eyebrows. "So here I am."

Grace straightened and leaned forward.

"I'm sorry to hear that. Is he all right?" She didn't like to think that Randal Flannery, a successful barrister known for his skill and tenacity and his passion for helping the downtrodden, would be out of action for long. She enjoyed the time she met him as opposing counsel.

"Yes, but he has to take it easy if he wants to avoid a full heart attack. You know how hard he works."

"Yes, I do." *But don't we all?*

Niall looked down at his mug. "I'm sure he'll be fine. But he won't like not being at work."

"It might do him good, though." Grace sipped her gin and tonic as her thoughts turned to Niall's parents. Niall's mother, Leah Flannery had always welcomed Grace warmly. In many ways, Leah was the mother Grace yearned for after her own mother died when she was twelve and she and Brianna were sent to live with Aunt Hilda. Leah Flannery was everything Aunt Hilda wasn't. Cheery, happy and kind. Aunt Hilda was stern, cold and demanding. The memories of Leah's warmth towards her tugged at Grace's heart strings, and her voice softened. "How's your mother?"

Niall's eyes lit up and he let out a small laugh. "As busy and involved as ever. I don't know where she gets her energy from."

"I'm glad to hear that. Your mother's a wonderful woman." Grace blinked back tears. "You're very lucky."

"I know." Niall paused, his gaze locked on hers. "But I also came back because of you."

Grace froze. *Had she heard right? Niall came back because of her? Why would he do that when he knew she'd never marry him? Plus, wasn't he with the blond? She needed to find out...* "I thought you were with that blond?"

Niall laughed. "Absolutely not!"

Grace raised a brow. "She looks at you as if she owns you."

"I'm not sure why. I'm definitely not interested in her."

Grace wasn't sure if she was relieved or not.

Leaning forward and keeping his gaze steady, Niall took her hand in his slender one. His eyes were filled with a curious, deep longing, and she fought to control her swirling emotions. "All the time I spent away, I couldn't get you out of my mind. I haven't dated anyone seriously since you, Grace, and seeing you again this week has made me want you more than ever."

Grace let out a shaky laugh. "Niall... don't."

"It's true. We weren't just lovers, we were best friends, and I've missed you so much." His brown eyes didn't waver as he laced his fingers with hers, they just grew softer and needier.

Why was he doing this? He was right—they'd been best friends before they became lovers, and it had taken everything she had to turn down his proposal. What girl in her right mind wouldn't want to marry Niall Flannery? But she'd had no choice. Her past, if ever it came to light, would ruin not only her career, but his as well if they were married. There was no way she could do that to him.

He squeezed her hand. "Can we start again, Grace?"

Grace bit her lip. Why was he putting her through all of this again? He wasn't after just a casual fling, he wanted to revive their relationship, and she couldn't do it. As much as she wanted to, she couldn't. Nothing had changed.

The waitress appeared and placed their meals in front of them, but Grace's appetite had fled. She downed her gin and tonic and asked for another.

Niall was still waiting for an answer. She had to tell him... it was no use prolonging it. She drew a breath. "I can't do this, Niall. Not now, not ever. I'm sorry." She gulped.

A muscle in his jaw twitched as he held her gaze. "I don't understand."

She shook her head. "I just can't do it. I'm sorry." She couldn't hold his gaze any longer. "I need to go. I'll call a taxi."

As she stood, Niall gripped her hand. "Grace, don't do this."

The desperation in Niall's voice almost made her change

her mind. How she hated hurting him like this again, but it was for his own good—he just didn't know it.

"I have to. I'm sorry." Pulling her hand away, she threw her wrap over her shoulder, raced outside and hailed a taxi.

WHEN GRACE ENTERED her apartment a short while later, she headed straight to the drinks cabinet and poured herself a double. Trapped by the secrets of her past, she was defeated. She felt bereft and desolate. Leaning against the cabinet, she squeezed her eyes shut as her heart ached with the pain of lost love.

If only Niall hadn't returned. She'd been doing fine... work had been her solace. But now she'd have to build her walls higher. She drew a long, slow breath and downed her drink before collapsing on her bed.

CHAPTER 4

The following morning, Grace entered the powder room at the court house and placed her brief case on the floor. Leaning into the mirror, she inspected her face. She looked better than she felt. The eye drops had worked their magic and her eyes had cleared. She splashed her face and patted it dry with a paper towel before reapplying some face powder and lipstick. Tucking a stray hair under her wig, she studied herself again. She would pass, but only just.

Lifting her chin, she drew a deep breath and re-joined her team in the foyer.

Bryan gave her a warm smile. "Better?"

"Yes, thank you, Bryan." She returned his smile.

Five minutes later, Grace took her seat beside Bryan and forced herself to not even glance at the opposing counsel's seats. Niall would be there by now, and she couldn't risk catching his eye.

Judge Atkinson entered and everyone stood. Grace made

herself focus. As well as dealing with Niall's presence, Caleb's phone call earlier that morning weighed on her mind, but she'd have to deal with Brianna's release after the judge had finished his summing up and the jury had been instructed.

Only once during the Judge's summary did Grace steal a glance at Niall. She shouldn't have. The uncomfortable ache in her chest returned at the mere sight of him. Her eyes blurred with tears and she tore her gaze away, forcing all thoughts of what might have been away and focusing instead on the judge.

It didn't take long, and in less than thirty minutes, Grace was heading back to Chambers with Bryan.

~

NIALL FELT an acute sense of loss as Grace walked out of the court room. He still didn't understand. She had no one else in her life—he'd checked, but Grace had never given him the real reason why she couldn't marry him. He let out a heavy sigh. He'd hoped fleeing to London after she'd turned him down, instead of taking the job with his father's firm in Belfast, would have got her out of his mind, and his heart, but seeing her over this past week had confirmed to him that he still loved her. He'd just have to convince her of that and do everything in his power to win her back.

~

GRACE CHECKED her schedule and rearranged a few things. She would have to return to court as soon as the jury came back, but that could be days. She got the impression they might be split. She and Niall had both done a good job. Donal O'Malley was guilty, no doubt about it, but had she done enough to convince the jury? Niall certainly had done a good job of attacking her argument and casting doubt. Time would tell. But right now, Brianna needed her.

When Grace entered Brianna's cubicle a short while later, Brianna was sitting up in bed. Her hair was still a mess, but at least her face was clean. "Hey-ya." Grace leaned down and kissed Briana's cheek, brushing the unruly hair off her face.

Brianna's expression remained unmoved.

Grace sighed. This was going to be an uphill battle. She felt like shaking Brianna. Why couldn't she just kick the habit and get on with life? Grace hated weakness in people, but this was her sister, and if anyone knew what Brianna had been through, it was her. But still, why couldn't she just sort herself out? It was so frustrating.

Sitting beside Brianna on the bed, Grace took her sister's cold, bony hand. "How are you feeling, Bibi?"

Brianna gave a slight shrug and turned her head away.

Grace bit her lip and glared at her. "Brianna, look at me."

Forcing herself to remain calm, Grace waited.

Brianna slowly turned her head towards Grace and lifted her dull, lifeless eyes. "Go away, Grace. You're wasting your time."

Grace clenched her fist. She wasn't going to let Brianna have her way. "No, I won't go away, Brianna. I don't care what you say... I'm not going to let you do this again. You're coming home with me, and I'm going to look after you."

Brianna jeered at her. "To your fancy apartment? Yeah, right. What would your neighbours think? I don't think so,

Grace. Just let me be." Turning her back on Grace, she slid down the bed and curled up, pulling the blankets around her neck.

Grace seethed. She felt like yanking the blankets off Brianna and shaking her. How dare she talk to her like that? "I'm not going anywhere, Brianna. I've made up my mind." It would be so easy to walk out and leave Brianna to her own demise. Grace was sure that's what Brianna wanted, but she couldn't do that. Having looked out for Brianna her whole life, she wasn't prepared to let her go now.

The doctor entered the cubicle and picked up Brianna's chart. After giving Brianna a quick check, he told Grace Brianna was clear to leave.

After the doctor left, Grace rubbed Brianna's arm. "Okay, time to go, like it or not."

Brianna grunted and slowly pulled herself up. "Why can't I go to Caleb's?"

Grace gagged at Brianna's stale breath. "Because you're coming with me." Obviously Briana would have preferred to go home with Caleb, *but tough.* This time she was coming home with her, and this time, she'd get off those drugs if it killed Grace in the process. Caleb was too soft. Brianna needed someone who'd tell her how it is and not just tell her she needed God.

"Let me brush your hair before we leave—it looks like a rat nested in it." But Brianna's hair was so matted that Grace couldn't get a brush through it, instead, she tied it up with a hair tie she found in her purse. "We'll have to sort it when we get home."

After signing the necessary paperwork, Grace led Brianna

to her car and helped her in. It wasn't a long drive to her downtown apartment, and within half an hour she was helping Brianna settle into her room.

"There are more blankets if you need them. And the bathroom's just through here. But first, let's give you a wash and sort out that hair."

"It's fine the way it is, Grace."

Grace's blood boiled at the defiance in Brianna's expression. She put her hands on her hips and stared Brianna down. "It is not fine the way it is, Brianna. You probably have bugs, let alone the fact you can't get a brush through it. I'll run a bath and we'll get you clean at least, but then we have to do something with it."

She gave Brianna no choice, and as she sponged her sister's emaciated body, her heart almost broke. What had happened to her beautiful little sister? It was all Da's fault. If he hadn't deserted their Mam, leaving her to raise eight young children on her own, Mam wouldn't have run herself into the ground and died so young. And then she and Brianna wouldn't have been sent to Aunt Hilda's. How Daniel and Caleb had ever forgiven Da before he died was beyond her.

"There… better?" Grace poured warm water down Brianna's back and then rested her hand on her bony shoulder.

Brianna nodded slowly.

Tears rolled down Grace's cheek as she leaned forward and hugged her sister. "It's going to be all right, Bibi. We're going to get you fixed."

BRIANNA SLEPT FOR FIVE HOURS. Grace looked in on her every

ten minutes or so. She couldn't relax. What was she going to do with her? If they stayed here in the apartment, Brianna would pack up and leave within days, as she always did at Caleb and Caitlin's. They'd tried putting her into a rehab facility several times, but she'd never lasted. Brianna needed a change of scenery. A complete change. Grace started to formulate a plan. As soon as the jury came back and delivered their verdict, she'd take Brianna on a road trip. They'd drive to the sea. Let the wind and the fresh air blow away all of Brianna's troubles. Yes, that's what they'd do.

Caleb thought it a grand idea. "Why don't I put in for holidays and Caitlin and I and the girls can join you?"

Grace's heart fell. How could she tell Caleb she wanted to do this on her own without hurting his feelings? She just had to tell him. "I'd like to spend time alone with Brianna first, if that's okay with you, Caleb. But maybe you and the girls can join us after a while? Once Brianna's stable?"

Caleb pursed his lips but eventually agreed. "We'll pray for you."

"Thanks Caleb." She couldn't tell him she didn't need his prayers when she'd just told him she didn't want him on the trip.

She hugged him when he went to leave. "You're a good brother, Caleb. The best." She smiled warmly into his face and their shared history flashed through her mind. Apart from Brianna, Caleb was the sibling she knew the best, and the one she could depend on if ever she needed anything. She just needed to do this trip without him.

"And you're not too bad yourself, sis." He winked at her as he pecked her on the cheek and disappeared down the hallway.

CHAPTER 5

*B*rianna reluctantly allowed Grace to cut her hair and treat it with bug shampoo. She also allowed Grace to dye it her natural russet colour. She looked in the mirror and didn't recognise the person looking back.

Grace had made her eat small regular meals, and she'd already put on some weight. She hadn't left Grace's apartment since the day Grace had brought her here. The few times she'd asked Grace to let her go out, Grace refused. Apart from jumping off the balcony, there was no way out. She felt like a prisoner.

For the first day or so, they'd spent most of their time watching television. Grace tried to get her talking, but she didn't feel like it. She'd slept a lot, but whenever she was up she couldn't relax. Grace wouldn't let her have a drink, although she was allowed the occasional cigarette. Big deal. What she wanted, *needed*, more than anything, was a hit. Grace had told her she was to go cold turkey. She'd done it before and hated it.

As each day passed, Brianna craved her drugs more and more. Her body went into withdrawal. She felt sick. She threw up. She shivered. Grace bathed her body with cool damp sponges. She lashed out at Grace. Scratched Grace's face. Threw objects around her room. And threw herself onto the bed and screamed.

On the third night, when her body was wracked with cramps, she thrashed her arms about and pummelled Grace's chest. "I can't do this, Grace. Let me go."

Grace caught Brianna's arms and held them above her head. Finally calming, she sobbed into Grace's chest.

"You're almost there, Bibi. You can do this." Grace rubbed Brianna's back and pulled her close. Maybe she could, but she hated it. Why couldn't they just let her be?

THE JURY RETURNED four days after they were dismissed. Grace had Caitlin on call to sit with Brianna while she was gone, and within the hour of receiving the phone call, Grace was wigged up and sitting in court beside Bryan. To be honest, she'd almost forgotten the case was still in progress. She'd hardly given Donal O'Malley a thought since she'd taken Brianna home. And she'd tried not to think about Niall. But there he was, with the blond still looking like she owned him. Grace turned her head away quickly when Niall caught her looking at him, but one moment was enough. Her heart still refused to listen to her head.

Judge Atkinson entered and everyone rose. Donal O'Malley was expressionless as the jury's foreman read out the verdict of guilty. Bryan grabbed Grace's arm and squeezed it. Grace glanced once again at Niall. The blond had her hand on top of his. It was over, and she'd won. She should have felt relieved, elated, but instead, she felt nothing.

Becoming a top barrister had always been her dream, and how hard she'd worked to get there. But now she felt empty. Had it really been worth all the effort? Maybe if she'd spent more time with Brianna rather than studying and working so hard, Brianna might not have ended up in the gutter. At the time it seemed the right thing to do, but now? She was looking forward to the break. Would she miss the court room with all its pomp and ceremony? Would she miss the kick she got from standing in front of a packed court room making witnesses and defendants squirm? Probably, but right now she didn't care. She said goodbye to Bryan and shook Niall's hand as protocol demanded, trying to avoid his eye, but when he slipped an envelope into her hand, she glanced up and met his gaze. He didn't say a word, just looked at her with soft brown eyes that almost made her resolve fly out the window. She gulped and turned away. She didn't trust herself to speak.

WHEN GRACE RETURNED to her apartment, she opened the door quietly and tip-toed inside. Caitlin was sitting on the couch flipping through a magazine and looked up as Grace put her briefcase down.

"How is she?" Grace whispered as she glanced towards Brianna's room and slipped her jacket off.

"She slept the whole time." Caitlin's jolly face seemed to be getting rounder by the day. "Not a peep out of her."

"That's a relief. Coffee?"

"Yes please, that would be lovely." Caitlin eased herself off the couch and joined Grace at the breakfast bar. "When are you planning on leaving?"

Grace stood with her arms folded, leaning back against the counter. "Now the case is over, tomorrow, I hope. Brianna's really fidgety, and I need to get her out of here as soon as I can. We could even leave today." Grace felt brighter at the thought.

Grace had rarely talked to Caitlin on her own. Usually Caitlin was with Caleb, and she let Caleb do most of the talking. But Grace knew Caitlin to be a caring wife and mother, and a devout Christian. Maybe that was one of the reasons Grace had avoided being with her on her own. She'd heard Caitlin had a knack of getting under people's outer layers, breaking through the walls they'd put up. Grace had many walls, and she didn't want Caitlin, or anybody else, getting under, over, or through them.

"Where are you thinking of going?"

Grace lifted two brightly coloured mugs from the cupboard. "We might head north, and then go along the coast, and see what happens after that. Neither of us has seen much of the country, so we'll just take a day at a time."

"Sounds super. Brianna must be looking forward to it."

"Yes, she is, surprisingly. Milk? Sugar?"

Caitlin settled herself onto a stool. "Yes, please. Three sugars."

Grace raised an eyebrow. *No wonder she's stacking it on.*

Caitlin didn't seem to notice. "Have you ever thought of going to Danny's place?"

Grace's head jerked up. "Danny's place?"

"Yes, I thought Caleb would have mentioned it."

Grace joined Caitlin on another stool. "He may have, but I probably didn't take much notice." She always stopped listening whenever Caleb started talking to her about what Daniel and Lizzy were doing since it usually included something to do with the Bible College where they worked, and she simply wasn't interested. The only time she'd ever really listened was when Caleb told her about her new little niece and nephew. And that was over a year ago.

"Well, I think it would be perfect for Brianna. He and Lizzy are managing this place where young people go if they're struggling to fit in or can't stay out of trouble." She paused and took a sip of her coffee. "It's not rehab, and it's not a college—I guess it's somewhere in between. They've had a lot of young people through already with quite a lot of success. The students, as they call them, work for half a day, and then they have lessons for the other half and evening, all the while living in community with counsellors on hand, twenty-four seven." Caitlin's eyes twinkled as she spoke, and her second chin wobbled.

"I guess it's a church run place?" Grace had no doubt, but asked anyway.

"Yes, it's sponsored by the college Daniel worked at. Caleb and I also support it financially, as do a lot of others. It's a great ministry, and I think it'd be perfect for Brianna." She placed her chubby hand gently on Grace's wrist. "Think about it, Grace. I'm sure they'd welcome both of you." Caitlin stopped and laughed. "I didn't mean you as a student... they'd welcome you as a guest!" She let out another chuckle.

Such a jolly person, and she means well, but no, I won't be taking

Brianna there. "Thanks for the information, Caitlin. I'll keep it in mind." Grace finished her coffee just as Brianna appeared in the kitchen.

"Hey, Bibi, how are you feeling?" Slipping off her stool, Grace hugged Brianna and kissed her forehead.

"Okay, I guess. Did you win?"

Grace's head jolted up. *The case... she'd forgotten already...* "Yes, we won. It's all over now, and we can head off as soon as we're ready. Do you want a drink?"

"Yes please."

"How are you, Brianna? Doing better?" Caitlin reached out and squeezed Brianna's arm gently as Brianna took a seat beside her.

"I'm getting there, but Grace has kept me locked up." She shot Grace a less than kind look.

"It's worked though, Brianna. You haven't taken any drugs since you were taken to the hospital."

"I almost died, though." She pouted, but took the mug of steaming hot coffee Grace handed her.

"You might have died if I hadn't brought you here." Grace raised her brow.

"I see you two are going to have a fun trip—you sound just like my two! Always bickering." Caitlin let out a jolly laugh. "Anyway, I'd better be off. Ladies luncheon at church today." She paused and looked at Grace. "Guess you don't want to come?"

Grace shook her head. She was right.

"No harm in asking." Caitlin chuckled.

"Sorry. Maybe another time." She was just being polite. She would never go to a ladies luncheon at church. "Thanks so much for coming today." Grace leaned forward and kissed her on the cheek.

"My pleasure, and have a wonderful trip, the two of you." She gave Brianna a huge hug and bustled out the door.

"Phew, I'm glad she's gone." Brianna settled into one of Grace's leather arm chairs with her mug of coffee, tucking her legs underneath her.

"She means well."

"I guess so, but she's so gooey and squidgy."

Grace laughed. "That's one way to describe her!"

Brianna rolled her eyes and joined in with Grace's laughter. It was so good to see the real Brianna finally emerging from the depths of darkness.

"So Bibi, do you want to leave today?" Grace sat down opposite her with another mug of coffee.

Brianna stopped laughing and locked eyes with Grace. "You mean I finally get to leave here?"

"It was for your own good, Bibi. I didn't do it for fun, you know." Grace held her mug with both hands and let out a sigh.

"I understand, and thank you, Grace." Brianna's eyes watered. "I mean it. I can't promise to stay off the stuff forever, but I'll try. I just hope you know what you're letting yourself in for."

Grace shrugged. "I'm tough. I'll cope with whatever."

CHAPTER 6

*G*race packed quickly. Brianna had very little, so Grace lent her what she could, and promised to buy whatever she needed along the way. There wasn't much room in Grace's sports car anyway.

Grace was tempted not to take the envelope Niall had given her, but against her better judgment, tossed it into her bag. She'd read it later, although it would do her heart no good.

They headed north out of the city. Brianna's body visibly relaxed when Grace took the A2 and not the M2 towards Londonderry. Neither she nor Brianna had been back to Londonderry since they'd fled Aunt Hilda's house when Brianna was four months pregnant. The memories were too painful, and neither girl dared look down that road.

It was a warm day, and Grace had the roof down. She wore a bright red scarf to help keep her hair in place, but as she'd cut Brianna's hair so short, Brianna had no need of one. She did give her a pair of Oroton sunglasses, though. Grace glanced at

Brianna as she accelerated onto the open road and smiled. She hadn't seen Brianna looking so relaxed for a long time.

It was impossible to talk, so Grace just enjoyed being out in the country. It had been way too long. She and Niall used to go for long drives on weekends. In fact, his parents lived just off this road. She peered down Derry Lane as they flew past the intersection, and she just made out the roof line of the large country manor Randal and Leah Flannery had lived in their entire married lives. Thinking of them made her glance at her bag holding Niall's envelope. He probably had nothing new to say... she should have left it behind or tossed it in the bin. But it was a link... a little part of him she could hold close to her heart.

The afternoon drew in, and as they hadn't booked anywhere, Grace slowed down at the next town they came to. The small village of Lorne hugged the banks of the Glendun River, and two pubs, a church, and a few shops lined the road. Signs advertising the local Bed and Breakfast places were scattered here and there. The pubs looked less than inviting, not somewhere to take Brianna on their first night. One of the Bed and Breakfast places would be better.

"Which one, Bibi?" Grace pulled the sports car to a stop as they looked at the signs. Neither one stood out, but as Brianna didn't have any preference, Grace chose the more expensive one. She had plenty of money, and it should be the better of the two.

A short, round lady bustled down the stone steps, bordered on either side with overflowing brightly coloured flowers, and greeted them. She wore a grey, knee-length skirt and a pink twin set with two strings of fake pearls draped around her chubby neck. Her face was round and kindly, and her greying hair was swept up in an old fashioned bun.

"Welcome, ladies! My name's Maeve, and I'm happy to see you both. Come on in and I'll show you to your room." She stopped suddenly. "Did you want one room or two?"

Grace glanced at Brianna. She was hanging back, and her face was blank, as if it was all too much for her. Grace held out her hand and pulled her along. "One room, thanks, Maeve." Grace gave the woman a warm smile. "I'm Grace, and this is my sister Brianna."

"Nice to meet you both. And where have you come from today?" Maeve bustled ahead, but stopped at the top of the stairs to catch her breath. "Oh my goodness." She patted her chest. "These steps seem to be getting steeper every day."

Grace let out a small laugh to be polite. "Just from Belfast. We had a late start."

"Oh, and where are you heading?"

"We're not sure yet. We'll just drive and see where the road takes us."

"There are some lovely wee towns further north if that's what you're looking for."

"Thanks, we might check them out."

"And now, here's the best room for you. It opens out onto the garden and you can take your tea out there if you like."

The room, halfway down a dimly lit hallway adorned with black and white family photos, reminded Grace of a number of similar rooms she'd stayed in with Niall, except of course those rooms had a double bed. Grace's throat tightened at the memory.

Maeve continued talking. *Did she ever stop?* Grace turned

her head. Brianna had paused in the hallway and was looking at the photos. Grace reached out her hand and motioned for her to follow.

'There are more blankets in the cupboard if you need them. And there's a private bathroom just through here." Maeve half opened a door on the far wall of the room. "What time would you be wanting breakfast?"

"Eight o'clock would be perfect." Grace smiled politely.

"Are you right for dinner? If not, I could rustle something up."

"That's very kind, thank you, Maeve, but we might just pop back into the village and see what we can find."

"The Green Leprechaun does meals until nine—that's probably your best option. I wouldn't recommend the Derry Arms —a bit rough for two young ladies like yourselves."

"We can look after ourselves, can't we Bibi? But thanks, Maeve. We might check out the Green Leprechaun."

Grace paid for the night and then closed the door, letting out a huge breath as she flopped backwards onto one of the beds.

"I didn't think she'd ever stop talking." Brianna walked over to the double doors leading out to the garden and looked out. "Feels strange staying in someone's home."

Grace sat up. "Maybe we should have stayed at the hotel. Will you be okay here, Bibi?" Grace stood and slipped her arm around Brianna's bony, fragile shoulder.

Brianna shrugged. "It's too nice for the likes of me."

"Oh come on, Bibi. Stop it!" Grace turned Brianna around to face her and placed both her hands on Brianna's shoulders. She lifted Brianna's chin with her finger and looked into her sister's hazel eyes. "Enough of all that nonsense. This holiday is about spoiling you and getting you better, so get used to it."

"I'm more at home on the streets—you know that." Brianna shook Grace's finger away and looked around the room. "All this frilly stuff." She reached out and fingered the lace edged lamp shade on one of the bedside tables. "I've never seen so many pillows and cushions in all my life. And all these flowers —they'll do my head in."

"Oh Bibi! Just relax and enjoy it! Come outside and we'll sit for a while. I'll make us some tea."

Grace put the kettle on and made a pot of tea while Brianna continued to inspect the room, commenting on everything from the heavy floral duvets on each bed, to the highly perfumed soaps and shampoos in the bathroom.

Grace carried the tray with the teapot, two dainty porcelain china cups and saucers, matching side plates with a homemade scone each, and tiny pots of strawberry jam and cream outside onto their private terrace. Despite the chill in the air, the late afternoon sun peeked in through the vine covered trellis, creating an inviting and warm sitting area. Grace felt right at home, but Brianna shivered as she perched on the edge of a cushioned cane armchair.

"Bibi—just relax and enjoy. Here, let me pour." As Grace poured tea into the dainty cup with delicate pink roses painted on it, she glanced at Brianna's stony face and sighed.

~

BRIANNA STARED at her tea cup. A set, just like this, sat on a shelf at Aunt Hilda's in that horrible, dingy kitchen that reeked of greasy mutton and stale tobacco. Brianna's heart pounded like it did when her body was waiting for a hit.

She stood, bumping the table and spilling the tea. She didn't care. She ran inside and flung herself onto the bed. This was a big mistake. Why had she let Grace talk her into it? She didn't belong in places like this… she was a drug addict, and she needed a hit, not a cup of tea in a cup she couldn't even hold without getting her fingers stuck.

The bed creaked as Grace sat beside her. Brianna turned her head away. *Why can't she let me be?*

"Bibi, what's the matter?" Grace stroked her hair, just like she used to. But that was years ago. Tears pricked Brianna's eyes as a weight settled on her chest. Where could she start? Everything was the matter. She pushed Grace away and curled into a ball.

Grace leaned over her.

Brianna kicked her away. "Go away, Grace." Tears choked her voice and she could hardly breathe.

Grace grabbed her and held her. Brianna struggled. She didn't want Grace's sympathy. She fought against her, but Grace was too strong and she finally gave in, sobbing uncontrollably into Grace's chest.

"Oh, Bibi." Grace's voice was soft and caring. Brianna hated it. If only Grace would let her be.

Brianna's sobs slowly subsided. Grace dried her face with a tissue, but kept one arm around Brianna's shoulder.

"I can't do this, Grace." She could barely speak.

"Yes you can, Bibi. Look at me." Grace tipped Brianna's chin and held her gaze. Grace's eyes were moist. "I'm here for you. Whatever it takes, okay?"

Brianna drew a shaky breath. She didn't want to do it. That was the problem. She needed drugs because they helped her forget. There was nothing Grace could do that would wipe her memory of those horrid years. Memories that tormented her night and day. Only the drugs sent them away.

Grace tucked a lock of hair behind Brianna's ear. "I'll find those boys and prosecute them."

Brianna slumped. How many times had she thought about tracking them down and making them pay for raping her when she was just fifteen? But Grace had told her she probably wouldn't win, and it might just make it worse, so she'd tried to forget. It was no use. Besides, the thought of facing them in court made her ill.

She lifted her gaze. "No, Grace. I don't want you to."

Grace nodded slowly. "You know I'm prepared to, Bibi, if you want me to?"

"I just want to forget, Grace. That's all I want to do."

"You've got so much to live for, Bibi. You could be anything you want. A nurse, you could go to University, you could work in an office, you could be anything you want."

Brianna's eyes moistened. "How could I do that, Grace? I didn't even finish school."

"Yes, but you can study, just like I did. I can help you. Think about it? It might help you forget."

Brianna shrugged. How could she study when she could barely read?

"Come on. Let's clean up and get some dinner." Grace gave her a big squeeze and then stood.

Brianna let out a deep sigh. *Everything's so simple for Grace, but she doesn't have a clue.*

CHAPTER 7

*L*ater that night, after Grace and Brianna had been out
for dinner at The Green Leprechaun, a lively little
place with great food, and Brianna was tucked up in
bed, Grace reached for Niall's envelope. All day she'd been
tempted to open it, but had stopped herself each time she'd
reached for it, reminding herself she was trying to forget
him. But try as she might, she couldn't get him out of
her head.

The light from the bedside lamp was dim, but Niall's handwriting was as strong as ever, and she could make out the
words easily. She bit her lip as she read.

Grace,

I'm so sorry for putting you under pressure the other night. We're
soul mates—you know that. We can't turn the clock back, but I would
love to be your friend if you'll let me, and to be there for you when-
ever you need someone to talk to. Obviously, I want more than that,
but if you won't marry me, at least be my friend?

Call me if you need anything at all. Wherever you might be, whatever the time of day or night, I'm only a phone call away.

I love you, Grace, and I always will. Nothing will change that.

Forever yours,

Niall

Grace flopped against her pillow and held the notepaper to her chest. Part of her wanted to tear up the letter and throw it in the bin. But Niall was right—they were soul mates. Despite the years of separation, there was a bond between them, and her heart still quickened at the very thought of him.

She picked up the letter and re-read it. Her thoughts filtered back to the day she met him... her first day at Belfast University. She wore a long wrap-around Indian style skirt, black knee-high boots, and a blue denim jacket. Niall was wearing skinny jeans and a blue, hand-knitted cardigan. Her first thought was that someone special had made it for him. She laughed when she discovered later that the special person was his mother.

They sat beside each other in their first lecture—Introduction to Law. As he chatted with her, it became apparent he was from a well-to-do family. His father was a high-profile barrister, as was his father before him, and there was never any question about Niall following in their footsteps.

Grace was tempted to make up a story of her own. How could she tell Niall that she'd worked by day and studied by night just to get into University? Or that she was supporting her younger sister whose two-month old baby, a result of being raped by her cousins when she was only fifteen, had just died? Grace gulped. *Or that she herself had blown up ten innocent people when she was only sixteen?* He'd never believe her... In the end, she told him she'd decided to study Law because she'd seen too many violent crimes go unpunished, and she wanted to do what she could to change that. She'd gone home that day with the brown-eyed Niall Flannery on her heart and her mind. And that's where he'd stayed for the next five years. Until the night he proposed.

Brianna stirred. Grace quickly folded the letter and placed it in her purse. She should throw it away, but she couldn't. She switched off the light and hoped Brianna would settle. All afternoon and night Brianna had been restless. Was it a mistake to take her away? Would it be too much for both of them? Grace hoped not, but doubt flooded through her as Brianna writhed around in bed.

Grace finally climbed out of her own bed and climbed in with Brianna, wrapping her arms around her and pulling her close, just like she used to do when they were first sent to live with Aunt Hilda.

Brianna settled for a short while, and then woke with a start, jerking to a seated position.

"Where am I?" The fear and desperation in Brianna's voice tore at Grace's heart.

Grace flicked on the light and sat up. Sweat dripped from Brianna's brow, and her bed clothes were damp. Her face was twisted with anguish.

"It's okay, Bibi. I'm here." Grace wiped Brianna's brow. "Were you having a nightmare?"

Brianna nodded and fell back onto her pillow, curling into a ball and sobbing. Grace lay back beside her and held her tight, all the while uttering soothing words until Brianna's breathing slowed and she fell asleep.

Grace was almost asleep when Brianna jumped out of bed and began rummaging through her bag.

"What are you doing, Bibi?" Grace climbed out of bed and tried to pull her back.

Bibi brushed Grace's hand away. "Leave me alone. I need a hit."

Before Grace could stop her, Brianna upended the bag and began tossing items all around the room.

"Stop it, Brianna." Grace's voice was a firm whisper, but panic was setting in. Brianna couldn't give in now.

"Don't stop me, Grace." The determination in Brianna's face frightened Grace, but she had to stop her. No way could she let Brianna go into town on her own in the middle of the night.

"No, you're not going anywhere. Stop it now." Grace's pulse raced as Brianna struggled with her. Brianna jerked one hand free and slapped Grace across her face. Grace gasped and her hand flew to her smarting cheek. How dare Brianna hit her! Who did she think she was?

An urgent knock on the door was enough to distract Brianna long enough for Grace to gain the upper hand. "Is everything all right in there?" Maeve called out in a concerned voice.

"Yes, thank you, Maeve. Everything's fine." Grace put on her most convincing voice as she held her hand over Brianna's mouth and tried to keep her still.

"Okay then, dear. If you need anything, let me know."

"Thank you. We will."

As Maeve's footsteps receded, Brianna's body slumped and Grace loosened her hold. Wrapping her arms around Bibi, she pulled her close. "We'll get through this, Bibi, you'll see."

Grace's heart tore in two as Brianna sobbed uncontrollably into her chest.

THE FOLLOWING MORNING, Grace had trouble waking Brianna in time for breakfast. In the end, she decided to let her sleep and told Maeve they'd eat in their room. A weaker person would have given in to Maeve's inquisitive glances, but Grace held her ground and didn't say anything other than her sister was still sleeping.

While Brianna slept, Grace took her tea and toast outside and sat in the gazebo. Feeble rays of sun warmed her body as she flicked through the local newspaper Maeve had provided, but her mind was on Niall's letter. Even though she'd only read it twice, the words were etched in her memory and played over in her mind. What she wouldn't give to have him here right now.

Grace glanced towards the room where Brianna still slept. How long would it take for Brianna to be free from her addiction? Grace longed for her little sister to be whole again. She leaned back in her chair and her thoughts drifted to a happier time... the time before Mam died.

Even though they were poor, they'd been such a happy family in the years after Da left. Brianna had always been the fun-loving girl, whereas Grace had been the studious one, but despite that, the two girls had been thicker than mud. The day they got sent to Londonderry to live with Aunt Hilda was etched in Grace's memory. The day of Mam's funeral was cold, wet and miserable. The eight children lined up beside her grave and one at a time threw a handful of dirt on top of the coffin lying in that horrible, deep hole. The minister prayed for Mam's soul, but that was the day Grace told God she would never talk to Him ever again, and she hadn't.

Brianna cried the whole way to Londonderry, and when they were met at the bus stop by Aunt Hilda and Uncle Dougall, Brianna hid behind Grace. They were put in the back room that was no bigger than a broom closet. In fact, Grace initially thought that's what it was. It had no heating, and in winter, she and Brianna clung to each other at night to stay alive.

In all the years they lived there, not once did they feel welcome. They were treated as the poor cousins who'd been taken in and were told they should be grateful for a roof over their heads. *Grateful?* The dogs were treated better than they were.

Grace looked up as Brianna appeared in the doorway, her hair dishevelled and dark circles hanging under her eyes. Grace's heart broke. She held out her hand. "Come and sit."

Brianna took Grace's hand and sat beside her. Grace poured her a cup of tea, and placed it in front of her.

"I'm sorry for last night." Brianna's voice was raspy and faint.

Grace pushed back the tears pricking her eyes. "It's okay, Bibi. We can do this." She gave Brianna an encouraging smile, but wondered if she really believed what she'd said. "It looks like a nice day for a drive along the coast. I thought we could head to Cushendall, but we can just see how far we get."

Brianna shrugged. "Whatever you think."

Grace bit her tongue. It'd be nice if Brianna for once

showed some enthusiasm. Maybe once they were back on the road she'd brighten a little.

It didn't take long to finish breakfast, shower and pack. Maeve wore an inquisitive look as they said good-bye, but Grace pretended she didn't notice. As Grace started the engine and pulled back onto the main road, she glanced at Brianna and hoped they'd have a good day.

CHAPTER 8

Five days later, Grace stopped the car on top of a cliff. "Well, go on then. Jump." Grace's nostrils flared as she spat the words at Brianna.

Brianna turned in her seat and reached for the door handle. A gust of wind blew the door back as she tried to open it. She wouldn't let it stop her. Gripping the door with both hands, she pushed it open and climbed out. Another gust of wind whistled past, almost knocking her off her feet. She steadied herself and inched closer to the edge.

Below, angry waves crashed onto the rocks, sending sprays of water into the air. She could taste the salt on her lips. Sucking in a breath, she glanced back at Grace. Her heart was racing. Could she really do this? For the past two days she'd been telling Grace she just wanted to end it all, but now, could she really do it?

It had been over two weeks since her last hit. Surely she was getting to the point where she no longer craved a high, but in the meantime, it was torture. Grace had no idea. Telling her to be strong wasn't enough. Grace had nothing to offer her, and Brianna didn't have Grace's strength or will-power. Never had. Never would.

Grace hadn't been able to save her before, and she couldn't save her now. There was nothing to live for. Nothing. She may as well jump. The nightmares were killing her. Her head ached constantly. Her body was tired. No, she had nothing to live for.

Inching closer to the edge, she lifted her chin. She wouldn't look. She'd just step forward, and then it'd all be over. No more nightmares. No more memories. She'd be free from them all.

"Bibi, don't do it." Grace grabbed her from behind.

"No! You can't stop me." Brianna struggled, kicking and elbowing Grace. Sobs choked her throat and she could barely speak—she just wanted to end it all, why couldn't Grace let her be?

She tried to free herself from Grace's hold, but she was no match for Grace. A heaviness grew in her heart and she collapsed onto the ground. Grace crouched beside her and hugged her. Brianna curled into a ball and wept. She wept for the baby she'd loved and lost. She'd never expected to love him, but when Aedan was born, waves of love and pity flowed through her from the moment she held him.

She didn't even know who his father was—it could have been either of them. Being born prematurely, Aedan had been given a fifty-fifty chance of living, but despite the odds, he survived. Brianna brought him home to the apartment she and Grace lived in, and for two months, she cared for her son. Lying on her bed, she often held him close while he slept. He needed her, and she needed him. But then he got sick.

That night, Brianna woke to Aedan wheezing. She jumped out of bed and shook Grace. Panic set in. "We need to get Aedan to the hospital, Grace." Quickly dressing, she bundled Aedan in a blanket and raced out the door. Grace hailed a taxi. Brianna's entire focus was on coaxing Aedan to breathe, but his tiny body shuddered with every weak breath he took. His face paled to a bluish tinge, and then he stopped breathing.

There was nothing the doctors could do. He'd developed pneumonia and his weak lungs couldn't handle it. She blamed herself. If only she'd looked after him better. If only they'd had better heating. It wasn't Grace's fault... she'd done her best to provide for them after fleeing Aunt Hilda's, but she was only seventeen and her meagre wage from working at the hotel barely paid the rent. If only Aedan had lived, things would have been different.

A seagull cried overhead, jolting her out of her memory.

"Come on Bibi, we need to go." Grace helped her to stand. The wind had eased, but heavy clouds had rolled in from the sea and rain was falling. She hadn't even noticed.

What was ahead for her? She'd come so close to ending it all, but what now? There was no end in sight—nothing was going to change. *She needed a hit.*

GRACE BREATHED a sigh of relief when she finally got Brianna back in the car. This time she thought Brianna might really do it. In some ways, it would have been easier if she had. How was she going to help her? Grace didn't want to admit defeat, but she had no answers. It would only be a matter of time before

Bibi stole money off her and disappeared. She couldn't watch her twenty-four seven. Then what would she do? Start all over again? Grace felt ill at the thought.

Why couldn't Brianna just leave it all behind her and get on with life? Grace took a moment and settled herself before starting the engine. Turning to look at Brianna, her heart softened and she reached out and squeezed Brianna's hand. Tears welled in Brianna's eyes. Grace handed her a tissue. "It'll be all right, Bibi. Not much longer now." But Grace didn't believe it, so how could she expect Brianna to?

Grace stared out at the dark rolling sea. Out there somewhere was Scotland. On a clear day, Grace had been told you could see it. Maybe she should take Brianna to Danny and Lizzy's place after all. Maybe they had some answers, as long as they didn't try to push God down her throat. She'd give it some thought.

Days passed. Grace and Brianna drove through town after town. They visited castle after castle, drank copious amounts of coffee and spent hours upon hours walking and driving, but one day, when Grace came out of the shower and found the contents of her purse strewn all over her bed and Brianna missing, she'd had enough. She quickly dressed and threw their bags into the car and raced out to find her. It wasn't hard. She headed straight for the local pub. Brianna was there. She hadn't bought any drugs, but it was only a matter of time.

Grace forced Brianna into the car and headed straight to Caleb and Caitlin's.

IT WAS ALL ORGANISED. Brianna had the required medical

assessment and got accepted into the Elim Community Centre, the place Danny and Lizzy managed, and within a week, Grace was standing at the airport with Brianna saying goodbye to Caleb and Caitlin. She'd half expected Niall to be there. Scanning the departure lounge, her heart fell. He wasn't there. But why would he be? She hadn't even told him she was back in Belfast after the trip with Brianna. She could have called him, but if she was ever going to be able to forget him, she had to force herself to not even think about him.

"Come here, sis," Caleb pulled her into his arms and hugged her tightly. "We'll be praying for you both."

Grace cringed. She didn't need Caleb's prayers, but hugged him anyway. "Thank you, Caleb." She smiled into his eyes. Caleb meant well, and if he was happy praying, who was she to stop him?

He gave her a kiss and let her go when final boarding was called. She picked up her carry-on luggage and walked slightly ahead of Brianna, giving a final wave before she entered the plane.

Grace turned to make sure Brianna was still following. They'd come this far, she couldn't let Brianna bail on her now. She was there, but she wore a vacant look on her face, as if it was all too much for her. The past week, since the day Brianna had almost jumped, she'd been quiet and withdrawn, as if she didn't care whether she lived or died, and although it'd been easier on Grace, it had also made her angry. Grace had often felt like shaking Brianna and yelling at her. Okay, she'd been through a lot, but why couldn't she just pull herself together? Grace didn't understand.

Brianna shrugged and raised her eyes just enough to meet

Grace's gaze. Her eyes were dull and lifeless. Grace had thought flying for the first time might have excited her a little, but no... seemed she didn't care about anything. Grace was starting to doubt whether anything or anyone would ever get through to her. Danny and Lizzy were Brianna's last options. If they couldn't help her, Grace had no idea who could.

CHAPTER 9

*E*lim Community Centre - outside Fort William, Scotland

"COME ON, Daniel, we don't want to be late." Lizzy drummed her fingers on the door-frame of her husband's office and glared at him. What was he doing at his desk again?

Daniel glanced up and met Lizzy's gaze. "I'm coming—give me a minute." He quickly finished what he was doing and closed his notebook before grabbing his jacket from the back of the door. He placed a kiss on Lizzy's cheek and flashed her a cheeky grin. "What's the matter, love?"

Lizzy humphed, but found it impossible not to return his disarming smile. She couldn't stay angry with Daniel for long, and he knew it. "Nothing, I just want to be early for once in our lives, that's all. And we need to leave before the children come back from their walk."

"Well come on then, let's go." He grabbed her hand and led her out of the house to the waiting van.

As they drove down the rough track leading to the small highland village of Glen Brannie, Lizzy snuggled closer to Daniel and placed her hand on his leg. Mist still covered the top of Ben Nevis, but there was hope the day would be fine and sunny. Lizzy rarely went anywhere these days without their three young children, and rarely did she and Daniel leave the Community alone, so this was a special treat. Not that she minded sharing her husband with the staff and students of the community. She was still in awe of the way God had blessed them.

Nobody had expected their marriage to last. She'd been distraught after Mathew, the handsome student minister she'd loved dearly, broke their relationship without explanation. Daniel had come into her life when she was the most vulnerable and had swept her off her feet and helped her forget about Mathew. *For a time.* It wasn't long before Lizzy knew she'd made a mistake by marrying Daniel. She didn't know him, and when he started drinking and mistreating her, all she could do was trust God to sort out her mess. And sort it He did. God had blessed them abundantly since the day Daniel gave his heart to the Lord following a car accident that almost took his life. Three beautiful children, a wonderful job they could never have dreamed of, and a ministry that gave hope to those who found themselves struggling with life, just like Daniel had. And now they had the opportunity to minister to Daniel's two sisters.

Lizzy's heart warmed as Daniel skilfully weaved the community van along the track that wasn't much wider than the tracks on the surrounding mountains that only the sheep and goats could navigate.

She'd only met Grace once when she and Daniel and baby Dillon went to Belfast for Daniel's Da's funeral just over three years ago. Grace had built so many walls around her, it had been difficult to talk with her, but by the time the week was over, Lizzy felt that she'd connected with Grace just a little, and she and Daniel had hope that one day, Grace might reach out to them. And that day had arrived.

Brianna she had yet to meet. Daniel had told her a little about their early years before all the children were separated following their Mam's death, but he didn't know Brianna as well as he knew Grace. He was nervous about meeting them, even though he said he wasn't. All week he'd been on edge, not his normal, cheery self. He'd cleaned the room they'd set aside for Grace three times. "She won't be happy if there's even a speck of dirt, Lizzy. You've seen her apartment." And he'd gone over the basic programme Brianna would be starting as soon as she arrived no fewer than ten times. Normally, whenever new students arrived, they'd go through a week of settling in before joining in with the main programme, but Daniel wanted to review the whole process. Not because the existing strategy wasn't working, just because it was his own sister who was coming.

She'd told him to stop it and trust God to touch their hearts. They'd prayed for both Grace and Brianna every morning and every night since the day they received the phone call. But Lizzy couldn't blame him for being anxious. Caleb had told them that Brianna was a mess and Grace wasn't much better—she just didn't know it.

"How are you doing, Daniel?" Lizzy turned her head and smiled at him. His dark hair was still as curly and unruly as ever, but she wouldn't have it any other way.

"I'll be better once they're here, Liz. I bet they're nervous too. They have no idea what they're coming to." He chuckled as he changed down a gear to turn onto the A82 towards Inverness. "I can just see Grace's face when she sees the place. She might turn around and leave straight away."

"Stop it, Daniel. It'll be fine. You're underestimating her. She's made the decision to come because she cares about Brianna, so she'll handle it. It's not that bad, anyway."

"It's not that great, either, Lizzy. You know that."

She raised her brow. "It's better than when we came..."

"Yes, but it's not what you'd call a fancy manor house."

"No, but it's warm and welcoming, and that's the most important thing. She'll be fine, Daniel. Stop worrying."

Daniel let out a slow breath. "Okay, love. I'll try." He reached down and squeezed her hand.

"I wonder how the kids are."

"Now you're the one worrying."

"I'm not worrying."

"Yes you are."

She chuckled. "Maybe just a little. I hope Mia's coping with Dillon. He's being a very cheeky four-year old of late."

"She'll be fine with him, Liz. It's only you he misbehaves for."

Lizzy let out a sigh. "I know. I guess it's normal."

"And Mia's great with the twins, so don't worry about them, love." Daniel shot her a smile that gave her confidence that everything would be okay with her not there.

He was right. Mia, the young woman they'd employed to be the children's nanny was the eldest of six children and had a wonderful way with their three. Lizzy had nothing to worry about. Still, they could be a handful at times.

For the remainder of the hour and a half trip to the airport, Lizzy and Daniel chatted about anything and everything, and enjoyed their brief time together knowing that as soon as his sisters arrived, everything would change.

~

BRIANNA GRABBED Grace's hand as the plane accelerated and began racing down the runway. Her heart pounded and she couldn't move. She was going to die, she knew it. Strange, because when she'd decided to jump off the cliff just a week or so ago, she wasn't nearly as frightened as she was now. Why had she let Grace talk her into this? She braced herself as the plane began to lift. How was it possible for something this big to stay in the air?

Grace squeezed her hand. "It's okay, Bibi. This is normal."

Normal? Who for? The noise was too much. She was going to vomit, or pass out. She closed her eyes and rested her head against the seat, all the while gripping Grace's hand as the plane banked left, and then right before steadily climbing. Her breathing slowed as the plane levelled, and she dared open her eyes. She had the window seat, but she hadn't looked out, until now. Her eyes widened as she took in the city of Belfast. It was so little from up here. And the fields spread out like patchwork. Who would have thought? She couldn't tear her eyes away—this was magic. She should have looked earlier. She'd survived, and it was amazing. Not until land was replaced by sea did she tear her eyes away and settle in her seat.

"See, I told you you'd be fine." Chuckling, Grace patted Brianna's hand.

"It's way better than I thought." Brianna relaxed in her seat, but when the pilot announced they'd be landing in Inverness in less than twenty minutes, she tensed again. "I don't want to do this, Grace."

Grace sighed. "Do what, Bibi?"

"This." She stared Grace down.

Grace didn't flinch. "It's too late, Brianna. Daniel and Lizzy will be waiting for us."

"I'll just stay on the plane. You can't make me get off."

"You can't do that. You have to get off."

Slumping in her seat, Brianna pursed her lips and folded her arms. *Just watch me.*

GRACE FELT THE SAME, although she couldn't say so to Brianna. What had made her agree to this nonsense? How could Danny and Lizzy do what she herself hadn't been able to do? Brianna didn't want to change. How many chances had she had over the years? Caleb and Caitlin had gone out of their way on numerous occasions to help her, but she'd only thrown it back in their faces each time. How many times had they picked her up off the streets and taken her to hospital and then to rehab? None of it had made any difference. Brianna always returned to the gutter.

Grace sighed. Maybe she should have been brave enough

years ago and reported those cousins to the police rather than be intimidated by Aunt Hilda's threats to disclose what she knew about the bombing. If Grace had been brave enough, maybe Brianna's life would have turned out differently. But so would have hers. Grace gulped. It wasn't too late. Maybe she should do it and face the consequences, even if that included prison, which no doubt it would if Aunt Hilda followed through with her threats.

It would be Brianna's word against the cousins, but surely Grace's testimony would hold more weight now than it would have years ago. Her stomach tightened. *But not if she was charged with murder.* Aunt Hilda would say that Brianna had encouraged the boys, but it was the opposite. Both she and Brianna hated Uncle Dougall and their cousins. No way would Brianna have encouraged them. She'd just been more trusting than Grace, and she'd paid the price.

The more Grace thought about it, the more determined she became. Proving the two of them guilty of rape would surely free Brianna once and for all from her demons. She'd start the ball rolling as soon as she could. It would mean going back to Londonderry with Brianna, but she'd do it if it put an end to Brianna's problems. And Aunt Hilda's threats? Well, so what if she did have the piece of paper she said she had? It proved nothing. Any good lawyer would get her off, and if they didn't, she'd go to prison so Brianna could be free. Grace closed her eyes as a cold chill ran through her body. *If she was really prepared to do it, why hadn't she done it already?*

The flight attendant tapped her on the shoulder. "Seat up, miss." Grace's eyes shot open. She nodded and then straightened her seat. She took a deep, slow breath and turned to look at Brianna. Her seat was already upright, and her hands were clenched and her eyes squeezed shut. Was she nervous about landing, or about meeting Danny and Lizzy? Or both? It was all a mistake. She shouldn't have brought her here.

Brianna didn't move from her seat until the flight attendant told her she had to get up. They were last off. Brianna dragged her feet the whole way. She vomited in the toilet, and Grace had to drag her along. If there was any way to turn around, Grace would have taken it. They paused before taking the final step. Turning to face her, Grace lifted Brianna's chin and forced her sister to make eye contact. "We won't stay if you don't want to. Okay? We'll go back whenever you want."

Brianna's eyes widened. "Are you just tricking me?"

Grace sighed. "No, I mean it. You say the word, and we'll leave."

Brianna narrowed her eyes. "So why can't we leave now?"

Grace sucked in a breath. "Just give it a go, Bibi. You never know. It might just work."

She rolled her eyes. "I doubt it."

Grace stepped forward and hugged her. "Come on, let's go."

CHAPTER 10

*G*race squeezed Brianna's hand and drew a deep breath as she and Brianna stepped into the Arrivals Hall. Scanning the waiting faces, she easily spotted Daniel and Lizzy. Daniel had put on a little weight since she'd last seen him, the day he and Lizzy sailed back to England after Da's funeral, but apart from that, he still wore that cheeky grin and she'd know him anywhere. Lizzy, on the other hand, had changed a lot. Her hair was cut shorter into a bob. It suited her. And she'd lost weight. *Must be all the running around after those children.*

There were hugs all round, but Brianna held back. Lizzy seemed to understand and just gave her a warm smile. Daniel put both his hands on Brianna's shoulders, his face splitting into a wide grin. Grace winced. Brianna hated being the centre of attention. But something was happening as Brianna met Danny's gaze, as if scales were falling from her eyes and she was remembering her big brother whom she hadn't seen since she was shipped off to Aunt Hilda's at age ten. Tears rolled down Brianna's cheeks.

Grace forced back tears of her own.

"Brianna—welcome! It's grand to see you after all this time." Danny's eyes sparkled. He leaned forward and kissed Brianna, pulling her into a gentle hug. Brianna hugged him back. Grace couldn't believe it. But then, this was Danny. She should have known that if anyone could get through to Bibi, it'd be Danny.

Then Danny turned to Grace. She'd been determined to remain aloof, but his infectious grin disarmed her, and before she knew it, she was stepping into his arms and hugging him like a long lost brother. When he released her, she wiped her eyes before hugging Lizzy.

"Welcome to bonny Scotland, both of you!" Danny took Brianna's bags while Grace took her own and followed him to an old white van with "Elim Community" printed along the side.

Danny must have noticed Grace's raised brow. "Sorry about the van, Grace... I know it's not quite up to your standard, but it gets us around." He winked as he unlocked the vehicle and began loading their luggage.

She certainly wouldn't be seen dead or alive in a van like this at home. But what did it matter? She wasn't at home.

"Sit up front with me, Grace." He opened the door for her and motioned for her to get in. Grace glanced at Brianna. Lizzy seemed to have taken her under her wing. Grace smiled to herself as she climbed into the front and sat beside Danny.

"Well, this is grand, this is. Three lovely ladies to keep me company." Daniel flashed a smile at Grace and then at Lizzy and Brianna in the back as he clicked his seatbelt and started the engine.

Laughing, Lizzy leaned forward and gave him a flick on his shoulder. "Behave yourself!"

"Always!" He chuckled as he pulled out of the car park and onto the main road.

"So Grace, how's Caleb?"

"He's fine, as usual." She turned her head. "He wanted to come."

Danny shot her a quick glance as he slowed for a red light. "Why didn't he? Would have been grand to see him."

Grace blew out a breath. "I didn't want him to."

Danny's brows puckered. "Why?"

Grace glanced quickly at Brianna. Amazing... Lizzy was chatting to Brianna as if she was a normal person. Grace leaned closer to Danny. "It would have been too much for Brianna. Caleb's a bit intense sometimes."

They locked eyes for a moment. Danny understood.

Grace settled back in her seat. "What's the place like, Danny? Caleb didn't tell us much, apart from saying it's in the middle of the Highlands."

"Well, he got that right." Danny chuckled. "We are a bit isolated, but that's a good thing."

"Don't you miss the city?"

He shook his head. "Not at all. Wait until you see it, Grace. It's magic."

A comfortable silence fell between them for a few minutes. Grace looked out of the window and took in the sights of the city—the steep spire of the cathedral, the old-fashioned stone buildings, the dark waters of the Moray Firth, and the sprawling mountains in the distance. It wasn't that different from some of the towns she and Brianna had driven through, except that she half expected to see a piper in a kilt on every street corner they passed.

Danny interrupted her thoughts as he changed down gears to take a corner. "So, how are you really, Grace?"

The question caught her off-guard. Danny was often direct with his questions, so she should have expected it. Her immediate response was to say she was fine, but if she were honest, she was nothing of the sort. The last few weeks with Brianna had shown her she didn't have a clue how to help her sister, let alone herself. But she wouldn't admit that to Danny. "I'm fine."

Turning to meet her gaze, Danny raised his brow. He didn't believe her, but she wasn't prepared to say anything further.

A short while later, Danny slowed the van as they entered the small town of Drumnadrochit on the western side of Loch Ness, and pulled over in front of a row of shops. "Lunch-time, ladies... all out!"

Grace chuckled. Her brother was a charmer, always had been, always would be, so it seemed. His love of life was infectious, and Grace couldn't help but warm to him.

Grace slipped her arm loosely around Brianna's waist as they followed Danny and Lizzy into a café where they were greeted by a short, friendly, middle-aged lady who spoke with a broad Scottish accent. Grace could barely understand a word she said.

The lady directed them to an old wooden table near an

open fire-place. Being summer, the fire wasn't lit, but Grace could imagine how cosy it would be in there when it was.

The lady handed menus out to each of them. When she left, Grace opened hers and gagged. Half the menu was filled with Haggis in all different variations. She lifted her gaze to Danny, who was sitting opposite her. "You won't get me eating Haggis, so don't even try."

Danny chuckled. "You don't know what you're missing out on."

Lizzy laughed as she reached out and tapped Grace's wrist. "Don't worry, Grace. I haven't tried it yet, and I don't intend to."

Danny shook his head in mock disgust.

"I don't care." Lizzy glared at him and lifted her chin before bursting into laughter.

Grace relaxed. It was fun being with these two, but she had to be careful. Last time she let them get too close and they'd almost broken through her walls... she didn't want that to happen again.

"Well, I think I'll have the soup of the day." Lizzy placed her menu on the table and sat back in her chair.

"That'll do me, too." Grace turned to Brianna. "Bibi, what do you want?"

Grace's heart fell. Bibi had that overwhelmed look on her face again. Of course Brianna wouldn't know what she wanted... she'd have no idea what all the menu items were. Grace's voice softened as she lowered her face towards hers. "Would you like the soup, Bibi? It's potato and leek."

Brianna nodded, but her eyes were dull and unresponsive. Maybe this wasn't going to work after all.

"Well, I'm going to have the Guiness pie," Danny said, leaning back in his chair and rubbing his tummy.

Grace raised her brow. *So that's how he's put on weight.*

They ordered their meals and Danny and Lizzy began chatting, obviously trying to make both her and Brianna feel comfortable. But their lives were so different to her's and Brianna's. They had no idea. They chatted about the children, which Grace knew was normal, but really meant nothing to her and Brianna. Children were just messy little creatures who put grubby hands on walls and ran around and screamed. But she had to listen and feign interest.

"Dillon's such a little monkey. You wouldn't recognise him, Grace. He runs around all day." Lizzy chuckled. "He doesn't stop, does he, Daniel?" She touched Danny's arm lightly and looked at him with such love and devotion shining from her eyes, it almost made Grace envious of what they had.

"I think they'll need to tie him to his chair when he starts school. If they can catch him!" As Danny laughed, his blue eyes sparkled and Grace could see how much Dillon meant to him.

"The twins try to keep up with him, but their little legs don't go quite as fast." Lizzy laughed as she pulled some photos from her purse and held them out to Grace and Brianna. "This is James and Clare, they're almost eighteen months, and here's Dillon. A little bigger than the last time you saw him, Grace." A proud smile sat on Lizzy's face as she glanced up.

Grace looked closer at the photos. The resemblance between James and Danny was remarkable. Clare was shorter than James, but had the same facial features she herself had at that age. Caleb had given her copies of the few family photos he'd retrieved from the house after Mam died. Not that she looked at them often—just occasionally when she'd drunk too much and hankered back to happier times. She was sure that if she pulled out the photo of her and Danny at about the same age, they could almost pass for James and Clare.

Grace's shoulders sagged as a deep sadness flowed through her. She'd never thought about having children. Just like she could never marry, she could also never have children. It wouldn't have been fair to bring them into the world when her past could be discovered at any time and she could be sent to prison for the rest of her life. Her fate had been sealed the day she went to that bus-stop. No use getting sad about it now. What was done was done.

Grace pushed it all aside as she always did and looked up, giving Lizzy the best smile she could manage. "They're lovely, Lizzy. You must be so proud."

Lizzy nodded, her face breaking into a beaming, beautiful smile. "They're such a blessing, Grace, and we love them to bits. Daniel dotes on all three of them, but little Clare is daddy's girl, isn't that right, Daniel?" Lizzy leaned into Danny and looked up into his eyes as he wrapped his arms around her.

"She reminds me of you, love." He kissed the top of Lizzy's head and pulled her close.

Grace's eyes moistened. She quickly passed the photos to Brianna and ran her hand over her eyes, hoping nobody noticed. She'd never know the love Danny and Lizzy shared. If only she and Brianna hadn't been sent to live with Aunt Hilda, everything would have been so different. It wasn't fair.

THEIR MEALS CAME and before long they were back in the van heading south to the Elim Community Centre. With every mile that passed, Grace became more certain that she and Brianna would be heading home as soon as they arrived. They didn't belong in the Scottish Highlands with a bunch of Christians. Only madness had made her think this was a good idea.

CHAPTER 11

*G*race had no idea what she was coming to. She'd imagined a cold, crumbling castle standing amidst a barren, wind-blown moor, but as they rounded yet another bend, her eyes widened. Instead of a crumbling castle, a solid, sturdy stone mansion, covered in creeping ivy, and surrounded by the most beautiful flower garden she'd seen in a long time, came into view. Spirals of smoke drifted lazily into the pale blue sky from a number of chimneys scattered along the roof line.

The house sat on the shore of Loch Linnhe. A small jetty ran out into the water from in front of the house, and a number of row-boats and canoes bobbed up and down in the gentle waves. Why hadn't Danny told her it was so beautiful?

Danny winked at her. "Like it?"

Grace chuckled. "It's stunning. How did you end up in a place like this?"

"I'll tell you one day, if you want to listen." His voice grew serious.

Grace groaned. She knew what he'd say... *God gave it to us...* and she didn't want to hear that rubbish. "I think I'll pass."

"No problem." He brought the van to a stop in front of a smaller stone building to the left of the main house. Long and low, it too was edged with bright, colourful flowers, giving it a very warm and homey feel.

Danny smiled broadly as he opened the door for Grace and then for Brianna and Lizzy. "Welcome to Elim Community."

Three young children burst through the front door of the house and ran towards them. The older one, who Grace assumed was Dillon, was wearing a cowboy outfit and ran around pretending to shoot them all. The younger boy, James, tried to keep up with him, but the little girl went straight to Danny and grabbed his leg. Leaning down, Danny picked Clare up and gave her a big cuddle.

"Hey there little one. Daddy's missed you." As he kissed her, Clare threw her arms around his neck, but when he propped her in his arms and stepped closer to Grace and Brianna, her thumb flew straight to her mouth. "Look who we've got here, Clare. This is Auntie Grace, and this is Auntie Brianna. Say hello."

Clare clung to Danny and buried her head in his chest, but peeked out through her fingers. She really was a daddy's girl.

"They're not going to bite you, Clare."

He tried to pry her head from his chest without success but then just shook his head.

Dillon raced past just then and Danny grabbed hold of his jacket, bringing him to a sudden stop. "Whoa there, Dillon.

Settle down—we've got guests. Come and say hello to your aunties."

As Dillon looked up, Grace sucked in a breath. Dillon had Danny's eyes and cheeky grin.

He gave them a quick once over, said hello, and then escaped his father's hold and raced off again.

James stopped beside Lizzy and put his arms up. Lizzy bent over and picked him up and carried him over to Grace and Brianna. He was tongue-tied, just like his sister.

"I don't know what's got into them, they were so excited before." Lizzy sighed and rolled her eyes. "Anyway, let's go inside and I'll get you a cup of tea." She settled James onto her hip and directed Grace and Brianna inside.

Grace stood in the entry and gazed around her. "This is lovely, Lizzy." The whole place was homely, from the rich rugs on the timber floors to the bright curtains on the windows— the exact opposite of Grace's apartment, which was functional, chic and modern. Danny and Lizzy's house was a family home full of character and love.

"Thank you, Grace. We didn't know if you'd like it or not." Lizzy laughed and glanced at Danny, who was following behind with their bags. "Come into the kitchen and I'll make that tea."

Grace and Brianna followed her down a short hallway into a warm, spacious room. A large wood-burning stove with pots and pans hanging above it from hooks attached to the ceiling sat on the far wall. A heavy timber table and a kitchen dresser covered in all sorts of bits and pieces took up the rest of the space, but Grace's eyes were drawn to the view out the window above the sink. The mountains Grace had admired earlier hovered in the distance behind the loch, but in between the house and the loch, a wooden table with bench seats sat amidst a meadow of daisies. It was beautiful.

"Coffee or tea?" Lizzy asked as she placed James onto one of the chairs and gave him a colouring book and some pencils.

"Coffee, thanks," Grace replied.

"Coffee for me too, please."

Grace's eyes widened. Brianna spoke. *Amazing.*

Grace's eyes widened further as Brianna picked up a pencil and began colouring with James. Never in her wildest dreams had Grace expected Brianna to do such a thing. Who would have thought?

"Would you like to see your room, Grace? I can show you while the kettle's boiling." Lizzy twirled a finger through her hair as her eyes darted to Brianna and back.

Grace got the message, and followed Lizzy back down the hallway and into a clean and tidy room filled with two single beds and an old timber dresser. A bunch of freshly cut flowers sat on the dresser, filling the room with a sweet perfume. Cream fluffy towels and flannels sat on the end of each bed. The room had the same outlook as the kitchen. She'd like lying in bed and gazing out at those mountains. Maybe she could consider climbing them one day. She blinked. Since when did Grace O'Connor climb mountains? She chuckled to herself. It must be the highland air getting to her.

"This is lovely, Lizzy, thank you." Without thinking about it, Grace reached for Lizzy's hand and squeezed it. When she realised what she'd done, she quickly withdrew it.

"Our pleasure, Grace. Danny and I really hope you enjoy your stay." Lizzy's smile was genuine and warm. "You know, ever since Danny found out you were coming, he's been so excited, and a little nervous." Lizzy let out a small chuckle as she sat on the bed and motioned for Grace to join her. Her expression grew serious as she met Grace's gaze. "Is there anything we need to know about Brianna?"

"How long have you got?" Grace raised her brow, but then realised she shouldn't be flippant about such a serious matter. "Sorry... she's a drug addict, Lizzy, but you already know that. Just be careful—she'll steal and lie if she's desperate. Keep a good eye on her." There was so much more she could say, but really, that was enough.

"We've had others like her through here, so we know what to expect. We'll do our best for her, Grace." Lizzy took Grace's hand and squeezed it. Tears pricked Grace's eyes. She was sure Lizzy and Danny would do the best they could for Bibi, but would it be enough? And would she even stay?

Whistling sounded from the kitchen. Lizzy released Grace's hand and hurried back to the kitchen. Grace followed. Brianna was still colouring with James, and a smile grew on Grace's face. Danny arrived with Clare and placed her beside James. Dillon was still running around, but stopped when Lizzy offered him cake.

"Now sit down and eat quietly with your brother and sister," Lizzy said as she placed three plastic plates on the table with a slice of homemade chocolate cake on each. She made coffee and tea, and then placed a larger plate on the table with the remainder of the cake.

"I love this place, Danny. Did you do it all yourself?" Grace asked as Danny took a seat at the head of the table, on either side of Clare and Dillon.

Danny laughed. "No. We had a lot of help from the boys."

"The students, you mean? How many are there?" Grace glanced away and smiled at Lizzy as she took a small slice of the cake she was passing around.

"It varies. Right now we have seven boys and six girls—including Brianna. But we've had up to twenty."

"That's a lot. You must have other people helping?"

Lizzy nodded enthusiastically as she gulped down a mouthful of tea. "We're lucky to have some highly qualified and experienced staff members. I hope you don't mind," Lizzy glanced at Grace and then at Brianna, "but we've asked them over for supper."

Grace glanced at Brianna to check her reaction. Brianna hardly flinched and just kept colouring. *Why would they do that, and on our first night? She really didn't need to meet the staff, but seemed she'd have no choice.* Grace forced a smile. "That will be lovely, Lizzy."

"They're keen to meet you both. It's always good when family members come to visit. Danny and I haven't had any family here since my parents visited a year ago."

Grace sipped her coffee. "Your parents must have enjoyed seeing their grandchildren."

Lizzy sat beside Grace and picked up her cup of tea. "Very much so. And the kids absolutely adored having them here. The twins were only babies, but it was still wonderful. And such a surprise... my father was always so formal and standoffish, but you should have seen him down on the floor giving horsey rides to the twins! They wouldn't leave him alone." Lizzy leaned back in her seat and smiled. "And Mother, well, she was the one who got our garden sorted." Lizzy chuckled.

"I'd always wanted a house with a lovely garden, and now I have it."

"You must get snow here in winter. What do you do then?"

"Oh, Mother showed me how to keep the seeds and bulbs to plant in early spring, and it worked! I was so surprised when the first shoots came up. In fact, we had a party to celebrate!"

The chatter continued around the table, but Brianna didn't join in. Instead, she hid herself in the colouring book, just lifting her head occasionally. At least she was still here, that was something, but Grace got the feeling she wasn't okay. She knew her too well. Grace pushed back her chair. "I think we might freshen up before dinner, if you don't mind."

Lizzy jumped up. "Oh, I'm sorry. You both must be tired. Feel free to take a bath or a shower, and have a rest if you like. Dinner for the adults isn't until seven, so there's plenty of time."

"Thanks." Grace smiled at Lizzy as she placed her hand lightly on Brianna's shoulder and motioned for her to follow.

When Grace and Brianna were on their own in the bedroom, Grace sat beside Brianna on one of the beds and put her arm around her. "What's up, Bibi? Something's wrong. What is it?"

Brianna shrugged and hung her head. "They're all so nice. I won't fit in."

"Oh Bibi, don't feel like that. They're family, and they want you to feel welcome." Grace lifted Brianna's chin and turned her face towards her. Brianna's eyes were filled with tears. Grace pulled her close and hugged her, brushing her hair with her hand. "I'm sure it'll be okay, just give it time.

But I'll keep my promise and take you home if you want to leave."

Brianna didn't reply. Instead, she pulled away and curled up on the bed, hugging a pillow to her chest as she closed her eyes.

As Grace looked at Brianna's pitiful frame, hopes of ever getting her well faded and despair for her sister's future grew.

CHAPTER 12

*A*n hour or so later, Grace managed to get Brianna showered and dressed, and they headed back towards the kitchen. The rest seemed to have done Brianna good—at least she was prepared to leave the room and come for dinner. The sound of a piano playing drew them into a cosy living room where Lizzy sat at a piano beside Dillon. He was propped on a cushion so he could reach the keys, and he looked so cute. And could he play! He and Lizzy were playing together, and whilst Lizzy was the better player, Dillon was doing a great job for a four-year old.

Grace and Brianna stood at the door listening until Lizzy must have sensed their presence and turned around.

"Don't let us stop you," Grace said. "You're both great!" The cheeky smile on Dillon's face made Grace laugh. "I don't know how you got him to sit still for so long, though."

"That's part of the bargain. If he wants to run around like a tornado, he also has to do piano lessons. No lessons, no play.

It's that simple, isn't it, Dillon?" Lizzy ruffled his hair and he nodded eagerly, looking up into his mother's face with a cheeky grin, just like his father's. Lizzy and Danny were so lucky to have such lovely children. Who would have thought that her brother, Daniel O'Connor, ex-alcoholic, would turn out to be such a model husband and father, and manager of a place such as this. Amazing.

"We were just finishing up anyway. It's almost bed time for the children. Come and tuck them in with me." Lizzy stood and closed the piano lid, and then led Grace and Brianna into the children's bedrooms. Dillon ran ahead, grabbing Grace's hand and dragging her with him.

"Come on, Auntie Grace, you can read me a story."

Grace shuddered, but chuckled at the same time. What could she do? She didn't have a choice.

Lizzy sprinted after him and grabbed his pyjama top, managing to stop him just before he reached his room. "Whoa there, Dillon, slow down. You'll pull your auntie's arm off!"

Dillon had his own little room next to the twins' room, and he pulled Grace in there and directed her to sit on his bed while he chose a book from his bookshelf. His floor was covered with toy trucks and cars. Dillon jumped onto the bed and presented her with his book of choice. Grace groaned. Of course it would be a Bible story book.

She rarely read to Caleb and Caitlin's girls, but when she did, they usually chose Bible stories too, and Grace always struggled to read them, mainly because of the memories they brought back. Memories of happier times when Mam was still alive, and she'd gather the children around at bedtime and read to them all. Mam loved her Bible stories, but what made it worse, she actually believed them. Mam had a simple faith, and it annoyed Grace. God hadn't saved her in the end, so what use was He? Surely if He loved her like Mam said He did, He would have healed her, and then they all could have stayed together as a family, and she and Brianna wouldn't have gone to Aunt Hilda's. And Brianna wouldn't have been raped by her cousins, and Grace wouldn't have...

"Are you going to read it, Auntie Grace?" Dillon's little voice interrupted her thoughts.

"Yes, I'm sorry, Dillon." Grace quickly opened the book and began reading, pushing her memories away.

When Grace reached the end, Dillon promptly asked if she could read another.

"I don't think so, I think it's time for bed. I can hear your Mum finishing up with the twins. Do you need to clean your teeth and go to the toilet?"

Dillon pushed his bottom lip out. "I don't like cleaning my teeth."

"You need to look after them or they'll fall out."

His little face lit up. "That's what Da says."

Grace sucked in a breath. Dillon's reference to Da brought a sudden memory of her own Da. That horrid man who'd caused all their problems. Just as well Danny was nothing like him.

Just then, Danny appeared at the door and Dillon jumped up and ran into his arms. "Daddy, you made it!"

"You bet I did, little man." Danny spun Dillon round and then plonked him down on the bed beside Grace. "Have you been good for Auntie Grace?"

"I'm always good."

Danny laughed. "Yes, right… and did she read to you?" Danny glanced at Grace and winked at her.

"Yes, she read me Noah's Ark."

"That's about the hundredth time you've had that book read to you. Maybe you should pick a different one tomorrow night."

"But it's my favourite, Daddy."

"Yes, I know, and it's a grand story. Anyway, I believe it's bed-time, so off you go. Toilet, teeth and bed."

"And prayers."

"Yes, and prayers."

"Can Auntie Grace pray with me?"

Grace stiffened. *Please don't ask me to do that…*

Danny glanced at her, briefly meeting her gaze. "I'm sure Auntie Grace would love to pray with you, Dillon. Wouldn't she?"

Grace narrowed her eyes and glared at Danny. He knew she wouldn't want to pray. The hide of him to put her on the spot like that! As much as it irked her, she'd have to go along with it to keep Dillon happy, so she put on a happy face but spoke through clenched teeth. "Of course I'll pray with you, Dillon. Just as soon as you've cleaned your teeth and been to the toilet."

In the next room, Lizzy was doing much the same with the twins. Brianna was with them, and Grace had heard James ask if she could read to them, but Lizzy had stepped in and said maybe Auntie Brianna could read to him another time. Thank goodness Lizzy seemed to understand where Brianna was at.

Dillon cleaned his teeth in record time and was back in the room waiting for Grace to say prayers with him. Danny had gone into the twins' room, so Grace had no option but to get down on her knees beside Dillon, but there was no way she was going to steeple her hands like he was doing.

"Will you go first, Auntie Grace?" He looked at her with his sweet innocent face, almost melting her heart. How had she gotten herself into this position? Grace O'Connor, barrister, atheist, murderer, kneeling on the floor with a four-year old, praying to a god she didn't believe in?

She couldn't do it. "Why don't you go first, Dillon?"

"Okay." He squeezed his eyes shut and began. "Dear Lord Jesus, thank you for bringing Auntie Grace to stay with us. And the other Auntie, I can't remember her name. Mam says she needs Your help, so Lord Jesus, can you please help her? I'm sorry for being naughty for Mia today, and please help me to have a good sleep tonight. Thank you for loving me, and for giving me my Mam and Da, and James and Clare. I love them lots. Amen." He looked up and smiled. "It's your turn."

Grace gulped. How could she pray? She'd vowed she'd never talk to God again after Mam's funeral. And she hadn't. But this little four-year old had put her on the spot, and she'd have to break her promise. "Okay, close your eyes."

She gulped. This was not going to be easy. "Dear God. Thank you for Dillon, and for his love of life. And thank you for bringing me here so I can spend time with him and with his mum and dad. Watch over him tonight as he sleeps, and let us have a good day tomorrow. Amen."

Grace quickly brushed unexpected tears from her eyes, but not quickly enough.

"Are you crying, Auntie Grace?" Dillon's little face peered up at her.

"No." She brushed the last tear away and sucked in a breath. "Come on, let's get you to bed."

"I need my animals. I take three to bed... Mouse, Rabbit and Fred. Here they are." He put the three stuffed animals under his blankets and snuggled down with them. "Good night Auntie Grace. I love you." As he smiled up at her, tears pricked her eyes again.

She bent down and kissed him on the cheek. "I love you too, Dillon. Night night. Sleep tight."

"Good night."

She stepped back and tip-toed out of the room, flicked the light switch, and bumped into Danny just outside the room.

"You did good, Grace. Dillon's taken with you." He squeezed her hand as he whispered. "I knew he would be."

Grace shrugged. "I don't know why."

"I told him you're a very clever person and that you wear a wig when you're at work, and that you're my little sister, just like Clare's his little sister." Danny stepped towards her and hugged her before drawing back and meeting her gaze. "And that did it for him, Grace. You're now his favourite Auntie."

Grace couldn't help it. She blinked back unwelcome tears that sprang to her eyes as mixed emotions assailed her.

Danny brushed her tears away with his thumb and drew her close. "It's so good to have you here, Grace." His voice was soft and caring, and she knew he meant it. But drat the man. He had a knack of getting through her carefully constructed walls and exposing her inner feelings, and she couldn't allow that to happen.

Grace sucked a deep, slow breath and regained her control. "Thanks Danny, it's good to be here."

"Come on now, supper must be almost ready, and there are people waiting to meet you."

Grace groaned. A nice quiet evening with Danny and Lizzy would have been preferable. Now she'd have to put up all her defences since no doubt all the people waiting to meet her and Brianna were Christians. And that was not something she looked forward to at all.

CHAPTER 13

*G*race followed Danny down the hallway into a larger room she hadn't noticed before. Tucked away at the other side of the kitchen, it served as a dining room and lounge room all in one. Brianna was already seated on the edge of an old brown leather couch, looking very uncomfortable. Lizzy, perched on the arm of the couch beside her, was talking to another shorter, chubbier young woman who wore a pleasant smile. Brianna looked up as Grace entered the room and shot her a plea for help.

As Grace stepped closer to Brianna and Lizzy, a man, possibly in his early forties, entered from the door at the far end. Her heart skipped a beat. Acutely conscious of his tall, athletic physique, her eyes were drawn to him like bees to a honey pot. His smile was wide and warm as Danny clapped his arm around the man's shoulders. "Ryan, great to see you. Come and meet my sisters."

Grace quickly pulled herself together as Danny steered

Ryan towards the group at the couch, but she couldn't stop the ripple of excitement that flowed through her as his brilliant blue eyes met hers.

Danny smiled as he made the introductions, seemingly unaware of the undercurrents flowing between her and this hunk of a man. "Grace, Brianna, meet my good friend and co-worker, Ryan MacGregor. Ryan, these are my sisters, Grace, and Brianna."

Grace raised her brow slightly as she took Ryan's outstretched hand, which was firm, warm and masculine.

"Nice to meet you, Grace." His voice was just as warm as the touch of his hand. With a name like MacGregor, she'd expected a broad Scots accent, but instead, he spoke with an English one. She was almost disappointed.

"And nice to meet you too, Ryan." Her voice was low and husky as she held his gaze.

"I've heard a lot about you, Grace." His blue eyes sparkled, and his hand remained in hers slightly longer than would normally be expected on occasions such as this.

"All good, I hope?" She gave a small laugh.

"Of course. Danny wouldn't have a bad word to say about anyone." Ryan elbowed Danny gently in the ribs and chuckled.

"I can always count on you to build me up, Rye old man." Danny gave Ryan a playful punch on the arm.

Grace laughed at their friendly banter. Supper with the staff might be fun after all.

Still very much aware of Ryan's presence beside her, Grace tore her eyes away and glanced at Brianna as Ryan shook her hand. Grace winced as Brianna only managed a cursory smile.

Brianna certainly gave the impression she didn't want to be

here, but then, Danny and Lizzy would be used to that, from what Lizzy had said.

The chubby young woman, who was introduced as Emily, sat beside Brianna and began chatting when Lizzy excused herself.

Grace returned her attention to Ryan, quirking her eyebrow. "And what do you do here?"

Danny squeezed her shoulder before Ryan could answer. "I'll leave you to it, sis—I need to help Lizzy." He promptly disappeared into the kitchen, leaving her alone with Ryan.

Amusement flickered in Ryan's face. "I'm in charge of the outdoors programme."

Of course... that would make sense. "What types of things do you do?"

He shrugged. "Depends on the season, but in summer, like now, we do all sorts... mountain climbing, hiking, abseiling, rafting, rowing, and in winter, tobogganing and cross-country skiing, but there's also an indoor gym, so most of winter's spent in there."

Grace angled her head. "The students get to do all that?"

Ryan nodded. "Yep. It's often the first time any of them have done anything like this, so it can be a real challenge for them, but they usually love it once they get over their initial fear." He smiled at her, sending another ripple of excitement flowing through her. "Can I get you a drink, Grace?"

"Thought you'd never ask. Gin and tonic, thanks."

Ryan laughed as if he was sincerely amused. "You won't get one of those here, Grace, sorry. It's soft drink or punch."

She let out a frustrated sigh. She should have realised. Of

course they wouldn't serve alcohol here... what was she thinking? She drew in a breath. "Guess I'll have a punch."

He steered her towards a table where a punchbowl sat and poured two glasses before handing her one.

"First time in the Highlands?"

She nodded.

"I can take you into the mountains one day if you'd like."

She raised a brow. "Hiking?"

"We can drive if you prefer." His eyes twinkled.

She chuckled. "Driving sounds good... let me think about it." She took a sip of her punch.

Stepping closer, he lowered his voice. "Danny told me a little about your sister. She's come to the right place."

Grace rubbed the back of her neck and blew out a breath. "She doesn't want to be here."

"Most of the new students say that when they first arrive, but it usually just takes a day or two, and then we can't get them to leave!"

Grace shrugged. "Guess we'll see."

"Come on, supper's served." He cupped her elbow with his hand and directed her to the table, where he pulled a chair out for her before taking a seat next to her.

Brianna sat on the opposite side of the table between Emily and Lizzy. Danny sat to Lizzy's right, and then another older woman, who introduced herself as Rosemary, sat on his other side. Rosemary had a broad Scottish accent, and taught sewing and piano. She also oversaw the female students' general welfare and was the first person they should see if they had any issues or concerns. Emily was in charge of the kitchen and other domestic duties. The last person at the table was David, Rosemary's husband. Like Rosemary, David also had a broad Scottish accent. He was in charge of the Bible school, and also oversaw the male students' welfare. Grace learned during the course of the evening that Lizzy also taught basic literacy skills in the school, as often students arrived without being able to read or write, but the one who surprised Grace the most was Danny. He taught classes in basic Christianity.

"So who funds all of this?" Grace asked Ryan during a break in the meal, which was being served by two of the students. It was a blunt question, but someone had to be paying for it all, and Grace was curious. The students obviously weren't paying.

Ryan chuckled before sipping his drink and leaning closer. "A lot of people wonder that... David and Rosemary own the property, and a number of interested people provide financial support, and I've got my Army pension, so we get by."

"You were in the Army?" Grace's eyes shot open.

"Yes, for just over twenty-two years." Grace did a quick calculation. That would make him in his early forties, depending on when he joined.

"Where did you serve?" She held her breath.

Ryan angled his head. "You really want to know?"

Grace nodded. She didn't, but she couldn't help herself. She had to know... what if he was in Londonderry when the bomb went off?

"Well, the British weren't involved in Vietnam, thank God, but I was in the Aden Conflict, and then I got tangled up with the Troubles in Ireland in the late sixties and early seventies."

Grace felt the blood drain out of her face. Her heart raced and she bit her lip. She had to get a grip on herself. She couldn't allow even a smidgen of concern to show. Besides, he was probably in Belfast, not Londonderry.

"And I was in Malaysia, and also the Falklands." He leaned closer. "Best not make this public, but I was in the Special Forces."

Grace's eyes widened. Why was he telling her all of this? And why would a man like Ryan, who'd obviously seen so much action, choose to come and work in a place like this, with a mob of drug addicts and drop-outs? It didn't make sense. Surely he'd be bored stiff. She would be. She was already missing the challenge of the court room, and that was nothing like the adrenalin rush she imagined Ryan would have gotten from being in the field.

"So how are you finding it here? It must be tame after what you're used to." She tried to keep her voice calm, natural.

"Yes, it is, but the thrill of helping these kids, and seeing them face challenges they've never dreamed of facing before, is worth it. It's such a rewarding job, especially when most of them come to know God."

Grace blinked. *God?* Surely this burly ex-Special Forces soldier didn't believe in God? Surely after all the evil and hatred he would have seen, he'd be more cynical about God than ever. But here he was, talking about God as if it was the most natural thing in the world. Something told Grace that Ryan meant it, and just like Lizzy and Danny, his faith would be utterly genuine.

Dessert was served, saving Grace the need to provide some kind of answer to Ryan's last statement. *For now.* If she got the chance to spend more time with him, no doubt it would come up again, and she'd have to have a response ready.

Following dessert, Ryan pushed his chair back. "Sorry folks, I'm going to have to leave you. Early start in the morning and all." He smiled at everyone, and then leaned closer to Grace, whispering in her ear, "Let me know when you want to do that hike." And then he was gone.

The evening was finished as far as Grace was concerned. She had no inclination to strike up a conversation with any of the others, especially the older couple who she guessed could be quite boring, especially after Ryan. Who wanted to talk about Bible school, sewing and piano? Or cooking or domestic duties? No, the only person of interest here was Ryan. Apart from Danny and Lizzy, of course.

"I think I might head off, too if you'll excuse me." Grace wiped her mouth with a napkin and pushed her chair back. "It's been a lovely evening, thank you all." She nodded to each person in turn, and then made eyes at Brianna.

"I need to go to bed, too." Brianna took the hint. She stood and thanked everyone, before leaving with Grace.

Grace turned as Lizzy caught them just outside the kitchen. Grabbing both their hands, Lizzy gave them a warm smile. "I hope you both sleep well. Let me know if you need anything."

"Thanks, Lizzy. I'm sure we'll be fine." Grace returned her smile. "Thanks for a lovely evening."

"Our pleasure, Grace. I'm so glad you enjoyed yourselves." Lizzy leaned forward and hugged and kissed them in turn before saying goodnight.

ONCE IN THEIR ROOM, Brianna climbed into bed fully dressed.

"Are you okay, Bibi?" Grace eased herself onto the bed and brushed the hair off Brianna's forehead with her fingers.

Brianna sighed and closed her eyes. "I'm tired. And I'm sick of talking. That's all they seem to do." Her voice trailled away as she rolled over and faced the wall, curling into a ball as she always did, as if she just wanted to hide from the world.

Grace leaned over and hugged her. "It'll be all right, Bibi. Just get some sleep." She rubbed Brianna's back gently until her breathing slowed and her body relaxed.

Grace tip-toed away and prepared for bed, but as she lay in bed, sleep eluded her as her mind drifted back to the day that had haunted her for so long. She'd only been sixteen. Young and rebellious, and looking for a cause to follow. Something that would relieve the boredom of life in Londonderry...

CHAPTER 14

$\mathcal{L}$ ondonderry, 1969

"FERGUS HAS AGREED to meet you after school," Grace's best friend, Samara whispered to her one boring Wednesday lunchtime in the school cafeteria.

Sixteen-year old Grace's face lit up at the prospect of something new happening in her life. Aunt Hilda treated her and Brianna like they were servants, not relatives, and Grace was sick of it. She didn't care if she got into trouble for being late to do her chores. Samara had been telling her about Fergus for some time, and finally she was getting the chance to meet him. Not that she believed for a second that was his real name. But that only added more to the intrigue and mystery.

"That's great, Sammy. Will you be there too?"

"Yes, I'll come. Meet me at the main gate and we'll catch the 3.11 into town."

Grace smiled at her. "I'll be there."

As they alighted from the 3.11 in downtown Derry and made their way first along Bishop Street and then through a rabbit warren of narrow alleys full of overflowing rubbish cans, stray cats and ancient crooked buildings, Grace's heart beat with anticipation. Finally she was getting a chance to do something exciting. Ever since she and Brianna had come to live with Aunt Hilda and Uncle Dougall after Mam died, she'd been longing for some excitement to replace the everyday drudgery of life in the tiny house in the suburbs of Londonderry.

The Troubles had begun a year ago, but having been kept on such a tight leash by Aunt Hilda, Grace hadn't seen any of it first hand, although, explosions and gunfire could often be heard in the distance, and occasionally, helicopters would fly overhead. But she wanted to see it for herself. And now she was sixteen, she was prepared to stand up to Aunt Hilda and get a life.

Sammy finally stopped in front of a nondescript door in a narrow alleyway and knocked three times. A voice from inside called out some unintelligible word, and Sammy replied with the word 'potato'. Seemed it was the word the person inside was looking for, because the door creaked open. Grace squinted. The shades were drawn over the solitary window, and she gagged at the smell of stale cigarettes and beer. Steeling herself, Grace followed Sammy inside. Sammy stopped in front of a table littered with wires and cables and bits of tin and metal. On the other side of the table sat a man with a big bushy beard and a cap drawn low over his eyes.

"Fergus, this is my friend, Faith."

Grace clenched her hands and inched closer to Sammy and the table. Her heart raced. Now the moment was here, could she really go through with it? What would Sammy think if she pulled out now? No, she had to hold herself together and go ahead with this meeting and prove to Fergus that she was capable of doing what was required.

Fergus leaned back in his chair, folded his arms, and sized her up.

Grace bit her lip to stop it quivering.

"So, Faith, what makes you think you might be of use to us?" His voice was deeper than she'd expected, and slightly gravelly, as if he was trying to disguise it.

Sammy pushed her forward. Grace swallowed hard. "Well, sir, I believe in the cause, and I'm smart, and I'm quick." Her voice was less confident than she'd hoped it would be.

"Smart, huh? Mary here has told me you're top in your class. Bit of a whizz kid."

"I don't know about that, sir, but I think I've been blessed with a decent brain."

Fergus continued to study her. Grace forced herself to stand still, although she was itching to turn around and flee.

"Mary said we can trust you. She'd better be right." He paused, as if he was weighing up whether he really could trust her or not. He lit a cigarette and blew smoke out of the corner of his mouth. The glow from the cigarette highlighted the red in his beard. Grace jumped as he leaned forward and folded his arms on the table. "You'll have two classes, and after that you'll be given your first assignment. You're not to say a word to anyone. Mary's already been chastised for talking to you." He glanced at Sammy. "We normally do our own recruiting."

Grace gulped. "Thank you, sir." She got the feeling that something was going on between the two of them and she felt sick in her stomach at the thought of it. Sammy had never said anything directly, but a few things she'd said now made sense. *How could Sammy do that?* Fergus was a disgusting creep.

"One thing, don't call me 'sir'."

"Okay, thank you, sir. Sorry, *Fergus*." Grace needed to get out before she vomited. She was panting, and couldn't steady her breathing.

"Read this and memorise it. You've got ten seconds and then I'll have it back."

Grace took the paper and read it carefully. Details of her classes were scrawled in untidy capital letters. She committed them to memory and handed the paper back. Fergus lit a match and held the paper up, making sure it was alight before tossing it in the bin.

"That's all. Good afternoon, ladies." He glanced at Sammy and ever so slightly nodded his head at her. Was Sammy planning on coming back later? What excuse did she give her Mam for being out so often? Grace gulped. Did she really know what she was getting herself into?

Once back outside in the alleyway, Grace gulped in lungfuls of air and steadied her breathing. If only she'd pulled out then... but she couldn't lose face with Sammy, and so she pretended she was impressed with Fergus, and feigned her excitement about the classes.

The following day she told Aunt Hilda she was going to

101

Sammy's place after school to work on a joint assignment, but instead she went to her first class. Being clever, Grace picked up the art of bomb making very quickly. But what interested her the most was finding out which wire to pull out so it wouldn't go off. She couldn't ask directly, but by the time she'd completed her second class, she'd worked it out herself. And with that knowledge, she left the class with details of her first assignment scribbled on a piece of paper.

～

RIGHT FROM THE moment the girls arrived, Hilda resented them. She'd never wanted to take the girls in, but Dougall had spoken and she had no say in the matter.

"They're just poor wee little lassies without a Mam or a Da, Hilda, love. We have to offer them a home." He wrapped his stinking arms around her and breathed his foul breath on her, and then told her he'd earn extra money so they could afford to feed and clothe them. What a fool she'd been to believe him. Whatever extra money he might have earned, he spent at the pub on the way home. She never saw a penny of it.

She rarely spoke to the girls, apart from giving them chores to do. The boys resented them too, and made faces at the girls, especially the youngest one who was much quieter than the older one. She sat in the corner and sucked her thumb even though she was ten when they arrived. She wet her bed every night too. Hilda made the older girl wash the stinking bedding. Why should she have to do it?

But Grace was the sly one. She was too smart for her own good, and Hilda despised her even more with every day and year that passed. She knew Grace was up to something when she was quieter than usual one morning at the breakfast table. She'd grown into quite a striking teenager, and Hilda had noticed Dougall's not so discreet interest in her. But what did she care? She couldn't stand the man touching her anymore, so if he was able to satisfy his needs with this young hussy, she should be grateful. But the airs and graces that girl put on! Who did she think she was? She should leave school and get a job, that'd bring her back to earth, but Dougall wouldn't allow it. "She's the clever one, Hilda, love. She can become anything she chooses. Leave her alone."

But Hilda kept watch, and this morning she had a feeling she was onto something. After the girls left for school, she quietly opened the door to their tiny back room and closed it behind her. No one was home, but still, it paid to be careful. She scanned the room. Rarely had she come in here, just on the odd occasion when she had extra jobs for them to do, but then she'd only stand in the doorway. The room was barely big enough for the two girls.

As she eased her large frame onto the bed, it squeaked and sagged in the middle. At least the bedding was clean. On the faded timber bookcase, a lone photo sat in front of a row of books. Hilda reached for it and studied it. The woman must be their mam. She held a babe in her arms, and was surrounded by seven other children ranging in ages from about two to early teens. Hilda peered closer. It must have been taken not long before she died. She picked out Grace and Brianna and was tempted to tear the photo up. Instead, she replaced it carefully.

Her gaze moved slowly around the room. There had to be

something. The girls were surprisingly neat. But then again, they didn't have much to be untidy with. Her gaze settled on a notebook on the desk. She picked it up and flicked through it. Nothing. Then a scrunched up piece of paper in the bin caught her attention. Hilda leaned over and picked it up. She smoothed out the creases and tried to read the few words that had been written in neat handwriting. She wasn't that literate, but could make out a few of the words. *'Friday 13th November Stop 20 4pm'*. Somehow she knew this was what she'd been looking for. She shoved it into her apron pocket, and after standing, smoothed the bed covers and backed out of the room with a smile on her face. She'd catch that young hussy out once and for all. Studying with Samara, sure. *And the Queen's my mother.*

ALL DAY AT SCHOOL, Grace couldn't concentrate. She glanced at the clock on the wall every few minutes. Every now and then Sammy kicked her and she turned her attention back to the algebra she was supposed to be doing, or the Shakespeare she was meant to be reading. Finally, the bell rang, and Grace quickly packed her books into her backpack. Her stomach convulsed. She just made it to the toilet block before vomiting violently into the bowl. Anyone who saw her probably thought she was pregnant. But that was impossible. Despite all Uncle Dougall's attempts, she'd never once given into him. Her acrid tongue and sharp words had somehow kept him at bay. But it had backfired, and he now paying Brianna attention.

Grace wasn't sure if Brianna was strong enough to hold him off much longer. But that was the least of her concerns right now. She stood slowly and wiped her mouth. Sweat dripped off her forehead despite the chill of the day.

"Grace, are you okay?" Sammy called from the other side of the door.

Grace inhaled slowly and forced herself to reply. "Yep, coming." Sammy didn't know today was the day. Nobody knew, apart from her and Gregor, her teacher. *And Fergus, no doubt.*

"I've got to go home today, Sammy," Grace said when she finally opened the door. "I just remembered Aunt Hilda needed me to do extra chores this afternoon. Sorry." She planted a smile on her face and hoped she hadn't given anything away. "I'll catch you Monday, if not before."

Sammy narrowed her eyes but didn't say anything. She probably guessed, but what did it matter? "Okay then, see you Monday." As she began to walk away, she stopped and turned. "Come over tomorrow if you want."

Grace lifted her hand and smiled. She could see it in her eyes. Sammy knew.

Left on her own, Grace returned to the toilet cubicle and opened her back-pack. So many times she'd played this over in her mind, but now she had to do it for real. Carefully lifting the device she'd made during her class out of her back-pack, Grace set the timer for four p.m. Less than thirty minutes to get to the bus stop, plant it, and get out of the area. Before replacing the package in her back-pack, Grace did one more thing. She carefully picked up the white wire, but instead of connecting it to the terminal, she left it hanging. Maybe she'd be excused for not tightening it up properly since it was her first mission. But Grace doubted Fergus would let her off that easily… she'd be expelled from the group, but she couldn't do what they were asking. She'd just have to suffer whatever penalty he doled out if he realised what she'd done.

CHAPTER 15

lim Community, 1985

GRACE SPRANG UP IN BED. Her heart pounded like a hammer drill and sweat dropped from her forehead in beads, landing on her already sodden bed clothes. Where was she? She held her hand to her chest and calmed her breathing. The first rays of daylight peeked in through the window. In the other bed, Brianna stretched and turned over. Grace remembered. She was at Danny and Lizzy's, and meeting Ryan must have triggered that horrible memory.

If only she hadn't gone to the bus stop that afternoon, everything would have been so different for both her and Brianna. The bomb shouldn't have gone off. Her stomach convulsed again just recalling the images of bodies flying through the air. And the noise. It shouldn't have happened.

How had she made the mistake? She knew which wire to leave off. She knew what she was doing. It was quite simple. But somehow she'd made an error. A fatal error. How had she lived with herself all these years knowing she'd killed all those innocent people?

She'd been a hundred yards away when the bomb went off. She stopped and turned as if it was all happening in slow motion. Her heart stopped beating for what seemed ages as people ran all around her trying to get as far away as possible. Someone pulled her along, but she kept turning her head to see what was happening. Within seconds, sirens screamed as response teams raced to the site. Soldiers intermingled with Police as the area was cordoned off, and then Grace was pulled around a corner and could no longer see the devastation she'd caused.

"Best get home quickly, miss," a man said. She had no recollection of what he looked like; the only image in her head was of bodies lying on the ground amongst the debris, along with the memory of the smell of the smoke and dust that stung her nostrils. She could never forget.

She found the nearest train station and ran into the toilets where she retched violently into the putrid bowl until nothing was left in her stomach. How long she remained there she had no idea. Finally, she cleaned herself up and made her way home.

Aunt Hilda wasn't in the kitchen. Strange, since she was always there. Grace breathed a sigh of relief and went straight to her room, closing the door behind her. Brianna lay on the bed, curled in a ball and sobbing. Her clothes were ripped and strewn over the edge of the bed and the floor.

Grace's heart pounded again. Throwing her bag down, she bent over Brianna, turning her over slowly. She peered into Bibi's eyes. "Bibi, what's happened?" Grace could barely speak.

Brianna's sobs increased, and Grace gently pulled her up and hugged her until she settled. Grace had a feeling she knew what had happened. Uncle Dougall had finally had his way. Her blood boiled. She'd report the brute to the police. But when Brianna finally spoke, and whispered "the boys", Grace could hardly believe it. She pulled Brianna closer and hugged her tighter.

"Both of them?" Grace asked quietly.

Brianna nodded.

Grace's chest heaved with anger. If only she'd come straight home from school, this wouldn't have happened. "I'm going to report them."

Brianna shook her head. "No…please don't." Her voice was barely a whisper.

"Why not, for heaven's sake? They've raped you, Brianna!"

A fresh round of sobs assailed her, and Grace pulled her close once more. "Well, I'm going to tell Aunt Hilda for a start." Grace gently laid Brianna back on the bed and tucked a blanket around her. "I'll come back and clean you up in a minute."

Grace left the room and strode into the kitchen. This time Aunt Hilda was there, and she had a smirk on her face. Grace's blood boiled. She strode straight up to her and stood over her. She was already a foot taller than her aunt. "Do you know what your boys have just done?" She didn't recognise the voice coming out of her mouth, it was so determined and full of hate and anger.

Aunt Hilda didn't reply, but she held her ground and met Grace's angry gaze.

"Well, do you?" Grace stepped closer. "I'll tell you what they've done. They've just raped Brianna, that's what. And I'm off to report them."

Aunt Hilda laughed. "You do that, missy, and I'll tell them who planted that bomb."

Grace sucked in a breath and stopped dead. She stared at Aunt Hilda. How did she know? Grace's whole world crumbled. They couldn't stay here a moment longer.

She gave Aunt Hilda one final stare and then turned and fled.

"Come on Bibi, we've got to get out of here." She helped Brianna up, quickly cleaned her, and helped her dress.

"What's happened, Grace? Why do we need to go?" Brianna's voice was weak and weary.

"Trust me, you don't want to know. We just need to get out of here." Grace pulled a bag from under the bed and quickly threw in as much as she could. Changing out of her school uniform, she climbed into a pair of jeans and put on her thickest shirt and jacket. "Okay, let's go." As she pushed Brianna out the door, she glanced in the bin. A heavy weight landed in the pit of her stomach. The scrunched up piece of paper she'd tossed away in disgust wasn't there.

She swallowed hard. It was too late. They snuck out the back door and into the narrow lane-way that ran behind the houses. Darkness had set in along with the chill of the night. Grace had no idea where they'd go. They just had to get as far away as possible. *And quickly.*

Dogs barked as they passed behind each of the neighbouring houses. Grace wished they'd stop. Would Aunt Hilda come after them? Or worse still, would she send the boys? Grace's heart was already thumping, but the thought of facing those two disgusting vile creatures made her blood boil. She dragged Brianna along with her until they reached the end of the lane. They headed the opposite way they'd normally go, and weaved in and out of the lanes running through the area until they reached the main road out of town. Grace put out her thumb and hoped they'd be picked up by someone quickly, praying that whoever picked them up wouldn't take advantage of two young girls out on their own on a cold winter's night.

Brianna stirred, bringing Grace back to the present. Brianna rubbed her eyes as she pulled herself up onto her pillows.

"Good morning, Bibi. Did you sleep okay?" Grace forced herself to sound normal.

Brianna shrugged. "Same as usual."

"I know, Bibi." And Grace did know. Neither of them had had a good night's sleep since that fateful day. They were each tormented by their own demons, they'd just handled them in different ways. Grace became so obsessed with study she stayed up late each night cramming for her next exam. Brianna turned to drugs. But now Brianna had the opportunity for a fresh start, and Grace hoped she'd grasp it with both hands. For both their sakes.

"I don't want to do this, Grace." Tears rolled down Brianna's cheeks.

Grace slipped out of bed and climbed in with Brianna, wrapping her arms around her like she used to do. "Give it a chance, Bibi, you've got nothing to lose."

As they lay in each other's arms, Grace tried to erase from her memory the horror of what she'd done, but it was no use. She knew she'd be tormented forever. It was her punishment.

A SHORT WHILE LATER, once they'd woken again and freshened up, Grace and Brianna made their way down the hallway to the kitchen where the children's happy voices could be heard.

Grace peeked in before entering. Dillon's little face lit up as he caught sight of her. He hopped out of his chair and ran over to her, hugging her around the middle.

"Steady on, Dillon," Lizzy called out from her seat opposite James and Clare. "Give your auntie some space."

"It's okay, Lizzy." Grace smiled at her as she leaned down and hugged Dillon.

Dillon grabbed Brianna's hand, and walked between the two of them to the table. "You sit here, Auntie Grace, and you sit here, Auntie…" He glanced at Brianna before looking to his mother.

"Brianna," Lizzy said.

Dillon turned his focus back to Brianna. "Bianna."

Everyone laughed. Dillon's face dropped.

Grace gently hugged the little boy. "It's okay. Dillon. I call her 'Bibi'. I'm sure she won't mind if you call her that too."

"Auntie Bibi." He flashed a charming smile at Brianna.

Brianna's lips lifted at the edges into a small smile. Even Brianna couldn't help but warm to this little boy.

As Grace and Brianna took seats on either side of Dillon, Lizzy stood and collected the children's dirty breakfast dishes and carried them to the sink. "What can I get you for breakfast? There's cereal and toast, or I can cook eggs... whatever you like."

"Just toast and tea for me, thanks Lizzy," Grace replied. She could never stomach breakfast. What she needed was a cigarette and a stiff drink.

"Same for me, thanks," Brianna added quickly.

"Did you sleep well? I hope the beds were comfy." Lizzy popped two pieces of bread into the toaster and turned on the kettle.

Grace blew out a breath and smiled. "The bed was great, thanks. Took a while to get to sleep, but that's normal." *So normal that I haven't had a good night's sleep since before that horrible day...* Just as well she'd learned to survive on next to no sleep.

"The mountain air should fix that pretty quickly." Lizzy flashed her a quick smile as she grabbed the toast. Smoke drifted into the air and the smell of burnt toast reached Grace's nostrils. "Just as well I don't do most of the cooking here." Lizzy tossed the burned pieces into the bin and started again.

After breakfast, Mia, the children's nanny, came to take the children outside. "Come and play with us, Auntie Grace and Auntie Bibi," Dillon called over his shoulder as Mia led them out the door.

Grace laughed. "Maybe later, Dillon. Have fun!"

Once on their own, Lizzy poured herself another cup of tea and sat down, letting out a contented sigh.

"They're lovely kids, Lizzy." Grace smiled warmly at her. She really meant it.

"Thank you." Lizzy returned Grace's smile. "They can be hard work sometimes, but we love them to bits." She took a sip of her tea and placed her cup on the table. "So, Brianna, are you ready to see your new quarters?"

Brianna's face paled. Grace squeezed her hand. "She'll be fine, Lizzy." Grace turned her head and gave Brianna an encouraging smile. "Won't you, Bibi?"

Brianna's shoulders slumped. Grace drew a slow breath. This was Brianna's last chance to start a new life. She had to take it. She narrowed her eyes at Brianna and pursed her lips. "She's ready."

CHAPTER 16

*B*rianna's heart thudded as she walked between Grace and Lizzy along a gravel pathway leading to the students' quarters in the huge stone mansion. Never in her wildest dreams had she imagined she'd be living in a place like this, but would she fit in? She doubted it. It was too nice a place for the likes of her. She was more at home in a gutter or a dingy apartment than a grand place like this.

Lizzy directed them towards a side door made of heavy timber. The door stood open, and they followed Lizzy up a spiral staircase. Brianna paused half way to catch her breath.

"Are you okay, Bibi?" Grace stopped behind her.

Brianna nodded. She held one hand against her chest and took several deep breaths. A pleasant aroma wafted down and tickled her nose. She'd expected the mansion to smell like some of the buildings she'd lived in, dank and musty, but this smell was different... it was nice. She drew a deep breath and continued on.

At the top of the staircase, a bunch of fresh flowers sat in a beautiful painted vase on a highly polished timber dresser. That's where the smell came from. Brianna's gaze turned to the area to the right of the staircase. A bookcase filled one wall, and an old piano another, but her attention was caught by the three over-sized couches covered with lap rugs and brightly coloured cushions, and the large coffee table sitting between them. A pile of magazines sat on one corner of the table, and on another corner, a pile of board games. Another smaller bunch of perfumed flowers sat in the middle, making it cosy and inviting.

The couches faced a large open fireplace, and Brianna could imagine herself curled up on one of those comfy couches, flicking through a magazine in front of a roaring fire. There was something about this room, and a sense of serenity flowed through her. Three large, religious posters hung on the far wall. She didn't have many thoughts either way about religion, but she hadn't seen much good come out of it. Grace, on the other hand, never hesitated to tell anyone who'd listen that she didn't believe in a God who'd let the mother of eight young children die an untimely death. If pushed, Brianna tended to agree.

"Ah, there you are." The kindly lady from last night bustled towards them, reminding Brianna a little of that lady at the first place she and Grace stayed at on their trip, but this lady seemed much nicer. Before Brianna could remember her name, the lady held her arms out and drew Brianna to her ample chest. "Ah Brianna, lassie, so good to see you. I hope you slept well." When she released Brianna, the smile on her face was as warm as her voice.

"Yes, thank you." Brianna's voice quivered, and she struggled to say anything more than that, but she liked the lady even though she spoke funny. The lady then hugged Grace and Lizzy with just as much warmth as she'd hugged her.

"How are you, Rosemary?" Lizzy returned the lady's smile.

Rosemary. That's her name...

"Oh, I'm fine, lassie. How are your wee bairns this morning?"

"As active as ever, but they're off with Mia for the day."

"And what a jolly lassie she is. But come, we need to show Brianna around." Rosemary took Brianna's hand and patted it while she talked. "As you can see, this is the female students' lounge area. There's a television in the corner, but the reception's bad and so it barely gets used. But don't worry, lassie. The girls find they don't miss it—there's plenty of other things to do.

"This hallway leads to the girls' dormitory." As Rosemary led the way, she continued chatting. "The kitchen and dining room are downstairs, but the classrooms are further along this hallway, in the front of the building. I'll show them to you later." Stopping in front of a closed door, Rosemary squeezed Brianna's hand. "This is where you'll be staying." Her double chin wobbled. "There's room for four girls, but there's only three at the moment, including you."

Brianna's heart raced. What if they didn't like her?

Grace's hand settled on her back and Brianna relaxed a little.

As Rosemary opened the door, Brianna's eyes widened. She'd expected to see double bunk beds, or at least a row of single beds close together, much like they'd grown up with, but instead, there were four separate areas, each with their own single bed, dresser and wardrobe. Each bed was covered with a soft, thick duvet, and more pillows than she'd know what to do with. On top of each dresser sat a lamp and more fresh flowers. The room was lovely. Tears flooded Brianna's eyes. She hadn't felt comfortable in Grace's modern apartment, but here, in this warm, friendly room, maybe, just maybe, she might be happy.

"This is your bed over here, Brianna." Rosemary directed her to the area in the far left hand corner. Brianna gasped as she gazed out at the mountains that seemed so close she could almost reach out and touch them. She stepped closer to the window. In front of the mountain was a lake with row boats tied up to a wharf. This was a dream, surely. It couldn't be happening to her. She pinched herself to make sure it was real.

Grace stood behind her, placing her arm around Brianna's shoulders. "It's lovely, isn't it, Bibi?"

All Brianna could do was nod as more tears slipped down her cheeks.

Rosemary handed her a tissue. "There, there, lassie. It has that effect on all of us." She chuckled. "The other two lassies are eager to meet you. They'll be back from morning duties shortly, but let's have a cup of tea and a chat while we wait."

"I'll leave you to it, Rosemary." Lizzy leaned down and placed a kiss on Rosemary's cheek before turning to Grace, arching an eyebrow towards the door. "Come with me?"

Brianna's eyes shot open. As much as she liked Rosemary, she didn't want to be left alone with her. She held her hand out to Grace and pleaded with her eyes for Grace to stay.

Grace held Brianna's gaze for a second, but then tore it away and looked at Lizzy. "Yes, I'll come with you." She placed Brianna's bag on the bed and then stepped closer to Brianna, brushing the tears off her cheek with her hand. "You'll be fine, Bibi. I'll be back soon." She squeezed her hand, and then turned and left with Lizzy.

Brianna crumpled. How could Grace just leave her like that? Tears stung her eyes again, and her bottom lip quivered.

Rosemary closed the gap between them, drawing Brianna into a hug, and smoothing Brianna's hair with her hand. "You'll be fine, lassie. The first day is always the hardest." Her voice was soft and kind. Rosemary pulled a white, scented handkerchief out of her pocket and gave it to Brianna.

Brianna sniffed, then blew her nose. She drew a steadying breath and lifted her head slowly to meet Rosemary's kind gaze. She managed a small, tentative smile. "Thank you." Her voice was no more than a whisper.

"You're more than welcome, lassie. Come now, leave your unpacking until later. Let's go and have that cup of tea."

Rosemary guided Brianna into another room at the far end of the hallway, passing two more rooms along the way that Rosemary told her were the other girls' rooms. "We have beds for twelve girls altogether, and this my office."

Brianna followed her into a room that looked more like a sitting room than an office. A small desk sat in one corner, but two comfy looking couches, positioned at right angles and both with a view of distant mountains, grabbed Brianna's attention.

"Take a seat, Brianna. I'll put the kettle on." Rosemary

opened a cupboard and pulled out a kettle, two large mugs and a tea pot. She placed three heaped teaspoons of tea leaves into the pot before joining Brianna on the opposite couch.

"So, what do you know about the place, Brianna?" Rosemary gave her an easy smile as she perched on the edge of the couch.

Brianna shrugged. "Not much."

Rosemary chuckled. "Well, you're in for a treat." Her face expanded into a beaming grin. "There are so many things to do here. It's a wonderful place to learn new skills. Most of the girls love the cooking lessons, and some prefer gardening to piano, but there are so many options, and you can try them all to start with and see what you prefer."

The kettle whistled and Rosemary bounced up and turned it off. She poured the steaming water into the teapot, and then placed a colourful tea cosy over it, just like Mam used to do. The sudden memory brought tears to Brianna's eyes. She rarely thought of Mam, but when she did, she always grew sad. She missed Mam so much. Why did she have to die? She brushed her tears away quickly with the handkerchief before Rosemary could see them.

Rosemary poured two mugs of tea, placing them, along with a jug of milk and a sugar pot, on a small table between them. As she looked up, her expression changed. She sat beside Brianna, placing her arm around her shoulder. "What's wrong, lassie?" Her voice was gentle and soft.

Tears returned to Brianna's eyes. She clenched her hands and tried to squeeze them back. She wasn't a cry baby. What was she doing? She sucked in a breath and gulped. "It's nothing."

"Ach, lassie, if you don't want to talk, that's fine, but something's unsettling you, I can see it in your wee, bonnie face." Rosemary spoke in a gentle voice with a lilting Scottish burr, and as she brushed Brianna's face lightly with her warm fingertips, tears streamed down Brianna's face.

Sniffing, Brianna lowered her eyes and balled the handkerchief in her hands. "Mam had a tea pot and cosy just like yours."

"How old were you when she died?"

Brianna sniffed again. "Ten."

Rosemary pulled her close and rocked her. "Poor wee lassie." Her voice was soothing, like the sound of a dove cooing to its young. "There's no need to talk about it now, lassie, but when you're ready, I'm a good listener."

Brianna was tempted, but she wasn't ready. Straightening, she blew her nose and slowly lifted her eyes to Rosemary's. "Thank you."

"You're welcome, sweetheart. Would you like some shortbread? Handmade by the girls, and it's very good." Rosemary held the plate out to her.

Brianna took a piece and nibbled it. Rosemary was right, it was really good.

"Do you like cooking, Brianna?"

Brianna blinked. "I've not done any, so I don't know."

"Would you like to learn?"

Brianna blinked again. "I've never thought about it, but maybe."

Rosemary smiled as she took a bite of shortbread and settled back further on the couch, balancing her cup and saucer with one hand. "I think you'll like it here, Brianna. It's a place where hurts from the past can be slowly healed. Daniel will give you a full run down on the programme this afternoon with the other new students." She glanced towards the door as two girls stopped in the doorway. One was thin and had shoulder-length brown hair and very narrow, arched eyebrows. The other girl had dark hair and pale skin, and a heart tattooed on her neck. Rosemary's face expanded into a beaming smile as she extended her hand to the two girls. "Come in, lassies, and meet your new room-mate."

The two girls stepped into the room. Rosemary put her tea cup down and patted spots on either side of her on the couch. As the girls sat, Rosemary placed her arm around the thin girl on her left. "Brianna, this is Maggie. Maggie comes from London, and has been with us just under a week."

Maggie gave Brianna a half smile and fiddled nervously with her hands.

Rosemary then placed her arm around the other girl, the dark-haired girl with the tattoo. "And this is Susan, and she comes from Glasgow. She's been here just under a week as well."

"Hi-ya." Susan sounded just like Rosemary, and her smile was warmer than Maggie's.

"Hi." Brianna gave a small smile before lowering her eyes.

"I've been telling Brianna a little about the place, and she's seen your room, but hasn't unpacked yet." She patted both their legs. "Why don't we head back there and I can leave you girls to help Brianna settle in before you meet with Daniel?" Rosemary smiled at them both, her double chin wobbling as she turned her head.

The two girls agreed and they stood, waiting for Brianna to do the same.

Brianna swallowed hard. She was just getting used to being with Rosemary, and now she was expected to spend time with girls she didn't know. She wasn't ready for this, but seemed she had no choice.

"Where are you from, Brianna?" Susan asked in her Scottish burr as they walked along the hallway together.

"Belfast." It was all Brianna could manage.

"You're going to love it here. It's such a cool place, and the people are great. Wait…" Susan turned and placed her hand on Brianna's shoulder. "Daniel's your brother, isn't he?"

Brianna's shoulders slumped. She didn't want to be known as the manager's sister, but it seemed everyone knew already. She sighed. What did it matter? "Yes, but I hardly know him. Last time I saw him, I was ten."

"Really? Wow!"

They reached the room before Susan could say more. Rosemary glanced at her watch as she stopped in front of them. "Okay girls, you've got half an hour before you need to meet Daniel down in the meeting room." Turning to Brianna, Rosemary rubbed her arm. "Are you okay, lassie?" Her eyes were soft and warm as she met Brianna's gaze.

Brianna sucked in a breath. Was she okay? She really didn't know, but surprisingly, in the few short moments she'd spent with Susan and Maggie, something had clicked with Susan in particular, and for the first time in a long time, Brianna thought she might end up having a friend. She nodded, giving Rosemary the biggest smile she'd given anyone in a long time. "I think so."

"That's grand, lassie." She pulled Brianna in for another hug before releasing her. "I'll see you there soon. Have fun!" She turned and bustled down the hallway, leaving the girls alone with each other for the first time.

CHAPTER 17

For the next half hour, Susan and Maggie helped Brianna unpack and set up her area of the room. Brianna discovered that Susan had been trying to kick her drug habit for the last two years without success, and it was her mother who'd heard about the Elim Community and arranged for her to come. She'd been clean for three weeks, and was eager to be clean for the rest of her life. Maggie's problem was different. She'd been brought up in foster care all her life, and didn't seem to fit anywhere. A care worker from the local parish recommended the Elim Community to her. Brianna found herself opening up with the girls. She told them she'd been on drugs since she was sixteen, and that it was her sister who'd brought her here in the hope of getting her clean. She didn't tell them about being raped or losing her baby. Some secrets were just too deep.

"It's time to go," Susan said as she glanced at the clock beside the door. "We can help you finish later, Brianna."

The girls headed along the hallway and down another spiral staircase similar to the one Brianna had gone up earlier. Brianna had no idea where they went after that. The building was full of narrow hallways that twisted and turned and went up and down, but finally they arrived in a room that looked much like a classroom, except that the chairs were placed in a semi-circle and not straight rows. Daniel looked up as the girls entered.

Brianna hung back, but Susan grabbed her hand and pulled her in. Brianna's heart raced again. What was she doing here? This was crazy. Brianna O'Connor in a classroom, with Daniel, her brother, as teacher? She shook her head and blinked. She must be dreaming. But no, Daniel strode over to her, and taking one of her hands, kissed her on the cheek. Her face grew warm. Why would he embarrass her in front of everyone like that?

He smiled easily, and his eyes sparkled. "Brianna, great to see you." She felt like hiding. He then turned to Susan and Maggie. "And good to see you both." He gave them a warm smile but didn't hug or kiss them. "The boys are on their way, but in the meantime, take a seat."

Just as they were sitting, two young men entered. Brianna's eyes popped. *Brayden McCafferty! What's he doing here?* The boy all the girls crushed on in school... the boy everyone expected to go places, to be someone. She peered at him... *yes, it's him, but he's different.* His eyes were dull and lifeless, and his head hung low, but she would have known him anywhere. Every night in that horrid room Aunt Hilda had called their bedroom she'd dreamed about him as she and Grace huddled together to keep warm, but now he was in front of her, all she wanted to do was hide.

"Boys, come on in." Daniel waved Brayden and the other young man in and clapped both of them on the back.

As Daniel introduced everyone, Brianna's heart pounded. What if Brayden recognised her? What would happen then? But there was no recognition in his face. Brayden didn't remember her. Brianna breathed a sigh of relief.

Grace had said that their brother had a way with people. Brianna wasn't sure what Grace had meant by that until now, but when Daniel stood in the front of the room, all eyes were on him. Even Brayden's.

He cleared his throat. "Well, good morning, everyone." His eyes and voice were bright. "Most of you have been here for a few days already, and I hope you've started to settle in, but now you're all here, it's time to kick off properly. Welcome to Elim Community, a place of hope and new beginnings." He paused and caught each student's eye as his gaze travelled around the room. "We've all messed up. You and me, both. I've been where you are today, and okay, I'm not perfect by a long shot, just ask my wife, but I can assure you that my life now is so much better than it was just a few years ago. What we have here in this community is a place where you won't be judged. You'll be offered hope, love and understanding, and you'll have the opportunity to learn skills that will help you live a more fulfilling life than you've ever dreamed possible." Daniel took a mouthful of water, and pulling his chair closer to everyone, leaned forward.

As Brianna listened to Daniel, she caught a little of his infectious enthusiasm. Her heart quickened. Maybe, just maybe, this place might hold the answers to questions she didn't even know she was asking.

Daniel angled his head. "What makes us different from other places you might have been to? For a start, you're living in a beautiful mansion in the Scottish Highlands. That has to be different." He chuckled. "But apart from that, being away from the city and your normal environment helps give a different perspective on life. How many of you have ever sat on the top of a mountain you've spent all morning climbing and gazed out into the distance in awe?" He waited, but no one claimed they had. In fact, they all shook their heads. "How many of you have rowed along a loch in the early morning when the water's so still and glassy you can't tell where the loch ends and the mountains begin?" They all shook their heads again. "And how many of you have had someone you can talk to who'll listen without judging or trying to tell you what to do?" His voice had an infinitely compassionate tone, and all eyes were fixed on him.

"You've all come here because you've tried other places or programmes, but nothing so far has worked. You're still struggling with your demons, whatever they are, and you've come here, possibly as a last resort." He smiled. "We don't offer any guarantees, but we know that if you're committed to turning your life around, it's more than possible to do that here. We're a Christian community, but we don't force religion down your throat. We expect you to go to classes where you'll have the chance to find out what Christianity is all about, but then it's up to you to make the decision. You won't be judged either way. You'll also meet with either David or Rosemary at least once a day to chat about how you're doing. They're great people, and you'll find them both easy to talk to." He took a sip of water. "Our programme also includes outdoor and indoor activities, such as hiking, rowing, abseiling, sailing, metal work, carpentry, gardening, cooking, piano lessons, painting... basically whatever you want to learn, you can learn here.

"We also expect students to work for several hours a day to help cover their board. Apart from daily chores, we have several small businesses running, and you'll be assigned on a roster basis to help out with each of them in turn." Daniel paused, letting his gaze travel around the students again. "So, you'll be kept busy, but what you get out of this place will depend on how much effort you put in. I have great hopes for all of you." He smiled at them before glancing towards the door. "And now, here are David, Rosemary, Ryan and Emily. Let me introduce each of them properly."

The four staff members briefly spoke as Daniel introduced them one at a time. When Rosemary stood and smiled at Brianna, warmth trickled through Brianna's body.

"Okay, then," Daniel said once the staff members had finished. "Lunch, and then you get to choose an activity. Ryan's running a beginner abseiling class, and Emily's holding a cooking class. Shepherd's Pie's on the menu, and I believe we'll be eating that for dinner."

Emily nodded.

"And then after that, you'll have some free time, and after dinner we'll have our first class. Sound good?" Daniel glanced around the group as he stood.

Everyone nodded, apart from Brayden.

"What are you going to choose, Brianna?" Susan asked as they walked to the dining room together.

That was a good question, but since she had no idea what abseiling was, there really wasn't an option. "Cooking."

Susan smiled broadly and linked her arm through Brianna's. "Me too."

Maggie walked ahead with Rosemary, and Brianna felt a pang of jealousy run through her.

The afternoon passed, and Brianna enjoyed her first cooking class ever. Emily was a patient teacher, and Brianna was proud of the pie she'd made—she hoped everyone would like it. During her spare time, she finished unpacking and settled into her room.

Later, sitting in the classroom and hearing Daniel talk about God and Jesus, it was like a switch flicked in her mind. Daniel said to forget all they'd heard and been taught about religion. Jesus had come to offer peace, hope and forgiveness, and all the fighting over religion just showed how many people had missed the true message. Over the coming weeks they'd be studying the Gospel of John, but any questions they had along the way would also be addressed. They all left with their very own copy of the New Testament.

Brianna glanced at Brayden as the students shared supper after class. The other boys chatted together, but he barely said a word. *What happened to you, Brayden McCafferty?*

MEANWHILE, Grace spent the morning with Lizzy and helped with her jobs, all the while keeping a lookout for Ryan. Her pulse quickened when she caught a glimpse of him just before lunch as he jumped out of his truck and sprinted into what Lizzy told her was the meeting room.

"I saw you looking at him, Grace." Lizzy's face twisted in an amused grin, and her eyes sparkled.

"No I wasn't." Grace turned quickly and composed herself.

"I hope you do better than that in court." Lizzy chuckled. "Still no one special in your life?"

Grace shook her head slowly. *There never will be...*

"He's a nice man. You should get to know him."

Letting out a sigh, Grace's shoulders slumped. But Ryan had been a soldier and had probably killed a hundred times more people than she had. Maybe she could risk it. She drew a breath. "We'll see."

CHAPTER 18

One morning, several days later, Grace was sitting outside in the garden wrapped in a blanket, trying to read a John Grisham thriller she'd found amongst all the Christian books on Lizzy's bookshelf, but she was finding it hard to relax, and was wishing she was back in the courtroom. A movement distracted her, and looking up, Grace saw Brianna coming towards her with a smile on her face. Putting her book down, Grace held out her hand. "Hey, Bibi, this is a nice surprise. How are you?" Pulling Brianna onto the seat beside her, she gave Brianna a big hug.

"Good. Really good." Brianna's eyes were brighter than Grace had ever seen them. Even her voice sounded more alive.

Grace smiled into Brianna's eyes as she brushed some hair off Brianna's forehead. "That's great. What have you been doing?"

Brianna let out a small chuckle. "I've been learning how to cook." Her eyes sparkled as she held out a covered plate. "I made an apple pie this morning, and I brought you some." The proud smile on Brianna's face brought tears to Grace's eyes. Was this the same girl she'd left in Daniel's care just three days ago?

"It smells wonderful!" Grace lifted the cloth and took a peek.

Brianna smiled, her eyes glistening. "I've done some painting too, and I've been canoeing on the loch. I didn't even fall in."

Shaking her head, Grace laughed. "I don't believe it."

"Here's something you really won't believe." Brianna's expression grew serious and she glanced down at her hands before meeting Grace's gaze. "I've been taking the Bible classes Daniel runs, and he's amazing. You should hear him."

Grace stiffened. "Don't tell me they've brainwashed you already?"

"No, Grace. It's not like that, really. There's no pressure. We're allowed to make our own minds up, but I'm starting to understand about God, and how He can fix my life if I let Him. I've still got a lot to learn, but so far it makes sense."

"Well, it's great to see you so excited." Grace smiled at her but let out a sigh. *At least she's off the drugs, for now...* "You know I don't believe in all that, but if you want to, that's up to you."

Brianna grabbed Grace's hand. "You should come to one of Danny's classes and see for yourself."

Grace pursed her lips. "I don't think so, but thanks."

"Tomorrow Ryan's taking us hiking, and he said to ask if you wanted to come."

Grace's eyes widened. *He hadn't forgotten.* "Who's going?"

"All the new students. There's five of us—three girls and

two boys. Oh, I forgot to tell you—one of the boys was in my class at school, but he doesn't remember me." Brianna's smile slipped. "He's not doing too well."

"But you are, Bibi, and that's all that matters." Grace squeezed her hand.

Sighing, Brianna glanced down at her hands. "Yes, I know, but everyone else is doing well, apart from him." She looked up, her face brightening. "Danny's coming too."

Grace ran her hand through her hair. "I'll think about it." But she'd already made up her mind. She'd go.

"We're leaving at nine if you decide to come." Leaning forward, Brianna gave Grace a hug. "Thanks for bringing me here, Grace."

Tears stung her eyes. Was it possible that Bibi was finally getting clean? Straightening, Grace smiled into Brianna's eyes and tucked a stray lock of hair behind her ear. "I'm glad you're happy here, Bibi. I really am."

Brianna nodded and gulped. "See you in the morning?"

"Maybe."

A spark of hope grew inside Grace as Brianna walked away with a spring to her step. It had only been a few days, but already Brianna was a changed person. *But would it last?*

Lizzy poked her head out the kitchen door. "Lunch is ready, Grace."

"Coming." Grace folded the blanket, picked up her book and headed inside. The children were already seated at the table, as noisy as ever.

"Come and sit here, Auntie Grace." Dillon jumped up and grabbed her hand, pulling her towards the seat next to him.

Grace laughed as she let Dillon drag her along. How could

she resist his charm? He was just like his father. "Have you had a good morning?" Grace asked as she sat beside him.

"Yes, we played lots of games and we did some painting. I did this one for you." He jumped off his seat again and scrambled through a box of bits and pieces, finally pulling out a folded piece of paper which he handed to her.

Carefully opening it, Grace swallowed hard. Dillon had painted himself holding her hand. "It's lovely, Dillon. Thank you." She swallowed again as she gave him a big smile. "I'll take it home with me and put it on my wall."

"Really?" His whole face lit up.

Grace nodded. It might not fit her decor, but it would take pride of place in her living room.

"That's enough now, Dillon." Lizzy placed a tray of sandwiches cut into triangles on the table.

"He's fine, Lizzy. Let him be." Grace chuckled as she folded the painting and slipped it into her book.

"We did some too." Little Clare spoke timidly, her big round eyes serious as she looked at Grace.

"Did you? You'll have to show me."

Clare nodded as she stuck her thumb in her mouth.

Lizzy joined them at the table, and reaching out her hands, took hold of the boys' hands. "Let's give thanks before we eat."

Having been there three days already, Grace was used to this, so she took Dillon's other hand and gently plied Clare's thumb from her mouth, and bowed her head while Lizzy gave thanks. It was a pointless routine, but she had no choice.

Lizzy raised her head and began placing sandwiches on the children's plates. "Please help yourself, Grace."

"Thanks." Grace smiled and reached for a ham and tomato sandwich.

"Was that Brianna I saw leaving just a while ago?" Lizzy looked up.

Grace nodded. "Yes. She seems to be doing really well."

"Daniel said she's doing great. You must be so relieved."

Grace released a slow breath. "I just hope it lasts."

"I know what you mean. I used to get my hopes up with Daniel all the time." Lizzy let out a heavy sigh before brightening. "But he got there in the end, and so will Brianna."

"I hope so." Grace toyed with her napkin. If anyone knew what she was going through, Lizzy did. Her's and Daniel's marriage had almost fallen apart because of his addiction to alcohol. "She asked if I wanted to go hiking with them tomorrow."

Lizzy's eyes widened. "You should go, Grace. You'll love it."

"I was thinking I might. Some exercise might do me good."

"Cup of tea?" Lizzy held up a teapot and raised a brow, an amused smirk sitting on her face.

Grace ignored the smirk. "Yes, please, that would be lovely."

LATER THAT EVENING, when Grace was preparing her hiking clothes for the morning, she came across the letter Niall had given her before she left Belfast. Sitting on the wing chair under the window, she toyed with the letter. She knew the contents by heart, but opened it anyway. She shouldn't have, because her thoughts were drawn back to the night he'd proposed...

She was twenty-four when they both graduated from Law

School, and to celebrate, Niall had booked a table at the fanciest restaurant in Belfast, on top of the Riverside Tower. Grace would have been happy just to go to the local pub, but he'd insisted. He was paying, so she agreed.

He looked so handsome that night—but he always did. He had such style, and that evening, in his freshly pressed navy trousers and crisp white shirt, Grace was acutely aware she was with the most eligible bachelor in town. Her heart skipped a beat when he placed his hand on the small of her back and led her into the elegant dining room.

As the waiter directed them to a window seat, Grace's gaze was automatically drawn in the direction of Londonderry, almost a hundred miles away. Would there come a time when she didn't think about the events of that afternoon and evening? She doubted it, but Niall would never know. No one would.

"Spectacular, isn't it?"

Grace blinked. She had to focus on Niall and on the present, and not on events of the past. Turning towards him, she planted a smile on her face and nodded. "Yes, it is."

All through dinner they chatted easily, talking about life after University, and the jobs they were going to. Niall was going to work in his father's practice, defending the innocent. She'd be working for the Department of Public Prosecution, prosecuting the guilty. It was highly likely they'd cross each other in court some day in the future. They laughed when they discussed who'd be most likely to win.

After dinner, Niall took her hand, squeezing it and looking deeply into her eyes. A quick and disturbing thought flashed through her mind as he reached into his pocket, drawing out a small red box and placing it on the table between them. She gulped.

"Grace, you know how much I love you." Niall's voice, strong and deep, sent a quiver of excitement through her, but she couldn't go there. She steeled herself as he continued, rubbing his thumb gently along her hand. "You won't agree to live with me, so I'm hoping instead that you'll agree to marry me." His Adam's apple bobbed as he swallowed, and his eyes, filled with hope, remained locked on hers. Her stomach churned. He squeezed her hand tighter. "Grace, will you marry me?"

Tears slipped down Grace's cheek as a deep ache grew in her heart. Niall was the perfect man and she loved him, but she could never be his wife. She had to live with her past, but she couldn't expect anyone else to. Looking at him now, she wished she'd never gotten involved with him. She could never commit to a permanent relationship, with him, or anyone.

Sniffing, Grace wiped her tears with a napkin and lowered her gaze. She was about to break his heart, and there was nothing she could do. If only things had been different. Taking a slow breath, Grace looked up and met his quizzical gaze. "Niall..." She gulped. "I can't marry you. I'm so sorry. Not now, not ever." She swallowed hard. If only she could have said "yes".

Niall's face paled. He leaned closer, gripping her hand. "Grace... why not? Please tell me. We can work through whatever the problem is... please don't do this." His voice was shaky, pleading, distraught.

Grace shook her head and fought back her tears. "No, Niall. We can't." Images of bloodied bodies strewn on the pavement flashed through her mind. There was no way they could work through that together.

"Grace... please tell me." He gripped her hand. She couldn't bear the pain in his eyes, but there was nothing she could do. *Nothing.* The suffocating sensation of loss gnawed at her, overwhelming her. This was the end for them. She had to make a clean break. She couldn't allow him any hope.

She squeezed his hand and forced her tears back. "Niall, I can't marry you, not now, not ever. I'm sorry." Tears streamed down her cheeks as she pushed her chair back and stood. "I've got to go, I'm sorry." She could barely speak. She fled towards the elevator, and when she got home, she drank a whole bottle of gin and cried herself to sleep.

Sitting in the chair under the window in Lizzy's cottage, tears streamed down Grace's cheeks. She'd tried to bury the pain and despair of that night in her work, but nothing had changed. Niall coming back into her life had proven that. She still loved him, but she still couldn't marry him, or anyone else. Those innocent people's lives were on her head, and would be until the day she died.

SLEEP ELUDED GRACE AS USUAL. Memories circled in her head like vultures, each eager to take a piece of her. But that was nothing new, and so the following morning, she was ready to leave by half past eight.

Grace shivered as she walked the short distance along the path that joined the cottage and the mansion. Mist hung in the air like a damp blanket. Why had she agreed to go? Right now, a courtroom held way more appeal.

As Grace rounded the corner and approached the main entrance, her breath caught. Ryan was leaning against the centre's minibus, his arms folded and one ankle crossed over the other as he chatted with Danny. He was a good-looking man, and her heart quickened, not only at his ease and self-confidence, but also at the muscles bulging under his ribbed khaki sweat shirt.

Since Niall, she'd only had casual liaisons, and the thought of a casual dalliance with Ryan appealed. It wouldn't have to be serious, just a short fling. And it might help rid her of Niall's lingering memory.

Ryan lifted his gaze as Grace approached, his eyes sweeping over her face approvingly. "You decided to come?"

"Yes." She tilted her chin, but her heart pounded.

"It's a great day for a hike." An easy smile played at the corners of his mouth.

"You could have picked a better one." Grace glanced at the mist hanging over the mountains. "It'd better not rain."

"A bit of rain never hurt anyone." He chuckled, his eyes twinkling.

Grace raised a brow.

"Ryan's right, Grace, you get used to it." Leaning forward, Danny placed a kiss on her cheek.

"We'll see..."

Ryan winked at her as he began loading the students' backpacks into the bus.

Shortly after, sitting in the middle beside Brianna, surrounded by Brianna's new friends, Grace felt like a fish out of water, but she fixed her eyes on the broad shoulders and the curly reddish-blond head of hair in front of her.

As Ryan drove skilfully along the single-track winding its way above the eastern shore of Loch Linnhe, the mist began to lift and Grace glanced out the window at the rugged, bare hills dotted with sheep and the occasional herd of highland cattle. She had to admit it was kind of beautiful in its own way.

Ryan stopped the bus on a heather covered meadow on the crest of a hill and everyone piled out. Ryan and Daniel handed out the packs, and when Grace took hers from Ryan, her fingers brushed his. Lifting her gaze, she angled her head and looked into his blue eyes, once again wondering what a man like him was doing in a place like this.

They set off in single file, Ryan in the lead and Daniel at the tail. Grace chose to walk with Daniel—she'd make her move later when it was more appropriate, and besides, from the back, she could keep her eye on Ryan.

The winding path led across bare foothills dotted with rocks, heather and sheep. Below, to the right, the loch reflected the grey of the sky, and the remains of an old castle sat on the far side, bearing witness to times gone by.

Up ahead, Brianna chatted with her new friends. Grace knew she should be happy for her, and she was, but it only highlighted her own unhappiness. Brianna might be able to shake off the shackles of the past in religion, but Grace could never do that. She needed to return to work, immerse herself in it. That was the only way she could survive, by prosecuting scum, because in some cathartic way, every case she took, she was prosecuting herself...

"You're very quiet, Grace. What's up?" Daniel asked from behind.

She shrugged. "Nothing, just enjoying the view."

CHAPTER 19

$\mathcal{A}$ fter hiking for an hour, Ryan stopped on a grassy knoll, removed his back-pack, and turned around, pleased to see that everyone had kept up, even Grace. He looked at her with a heavy heart. She needed the freeing power of Jesus's love in her life just as much as these drug addicted kids did, she just didn't know it. It didn't matter that she was a wealthy barrister, or gave the appearance of someone who had it all together, he'd seen through her facade the moment he'd laid eyes on her. Maybe it was his training, but he had a gift of knowing what made people tick, and Grace O'Connor had a ticking time bomb inside her. He sent up a quick prayer for her.

Brayden stopped behind him. Ryan smiled at the troubled young man. "Keep up okay?" Brayden's face was still deathly pale and disengaged, but it was early days. Ryan was sure that the enthusiasm of the others would rub off on him in time, and that the Holy Spirit would touch the young man's heart, softening it, drawing him slowly but surely to the Healer of broken lives.

Every night the staff prayed for the students, and the guests, like Grace. In the two years he'd been with the Elim Community, Ryan had witnessed miracle after miracle as God's healing touch changed the lives of those who came. Something wonderful happened when troubled youth distanced themselves from the hustle and bustle of city life and came face to face with the raw beauty of God's creation. He expected the same would happen for both Brayden and Grace, just like it already had for Brianna.

Brayden shrugged, barely giving a grunt.

Squeezing the young man's shoulder, Ryan gave him an encouraging smile. He was going to be hard work, but God was able to break through his barriers, it might just take time.

Everyone else stopped and took out a snack—oatcakes made by the students, and water. Ryan had several flasks of coffee, and after offering some to the students, held out a mug to Grace. "Like some?"

"Thought you'd never ask." She let out a small chuckle as she took the mug. Throwing her pack onto the ground, she lowered herself gracefully onto a rock, stretching her long, slender legs in front of her, and took a sip.

"Mind if I join you?"

She looked up, her hazel eyes travelling lazily up his body. "Please do."

He ignored her play-acting and sat on the ground beside her. "So, Grace O'Connor, what do you think of the Highlands so far?"

Tilting her head, she met his gaze and took her time in answering. "They have their good points."

He chuckled. "They certainly do." He held out a container full of oatcakes. "Like one?"

She shook her head. "No thanks."

"Come on Grace, you're not watching your weight, are you? And besides, your sister made them."

Grace grunted, and reaching out, picked out one of the cookies. "I don't normally snack."

"Too busy, huh?"

Grace shrugged. "Something like that."

"Well, if you stay out here long enough, you'll not only develop a good appetite, but you'll feel better. Maybe you need to slow down a little."

"I'm perfectly fine, thank you."

He studied her before speaking. She was a beautiful woman, there was no doubt about it. Her rich auburn hair lay thick on her shoulders, and although her profile was strong and determined, underneath that facade lay a soft heart, of that he was sure, otherwise, why would she have brought her sister here? "Are you really fine, Grace?"

She took another sip of her coffee and lifted her chin. "Yes." Her eyes flickered as she dug her heel into the ground.

He gave her a warm smile. "If you ever want to talk, I'm a good listener."

Grace angled her head. "And what about you, Ryan MacGregor? Are you fine? What are you really doing here?" She raised her brow, an amused look on her face. "Hiding from something? *Or someone?*"

Ryan laughed. "I can see why you're good in the courtroom." He held her gaze as his expression sobered. "I'm here because I want to be." He drew a breath and released it slowly. "I love these kids, and I want to help them." Her gaze didn't waver… she was assessing him, just as she'd assess a witness in one of her high-profile cases. He had nothing to hide. Not any longer, anyway. His past was just that—his past. God had cleansed him and forgiven him, praise the Lord.

Grace's eyes narrowed. "That's a very glib answer."

"It may be, but it's true. I love it here. It's peaceful and it's rewarding. And I'm not hiding from anyone or anything."

"Everyone has something in their past, Ryan, including you."

"Perhaps, but when you have God in your life, He gives you a clean start, and your past can be left where it belongs… in the past."

She went silent.

Something had happened to Grace, and it still haunted her. He'd say an extra prayer for her tonight. "Well, it's time we made a move." He jumped up and held his hand out. The touch of her skin triggered an unexpected response, one he hadn't felt for a long time. Her hand remained in his a moment longer than necessary. She was still flirting with him, but this time he looked at her with fresh eyes. He could easily fall for her… but not until God did a work in her heart.

GRACE WALKED beside Ryan until they stopped for lunch. She was tempted to quiz him, to ply him with questions about his past, but refrained. Instead, she quizzed him about the highlands and about the countryside they were walking through, anything that wasn't personal or about God.

"We're all going to the Highland Games on Saturday. Will you still be here then?" Ryan asked as they walked along the grassy trail with plenty of room for two high above Loch Linnhe. The mist had lifted completely, and the loch shimmered in the bright sunshine.

"I was thinking I'd go home since Brianna seems settled."

"Why don't you stay, Grace? At least until after the weekend. You can't come to Scotland and not go to a Highland Games."

"That's what Lizzy said." Grace shrugged. "I'll give it some thought."

"You'd enjoy it. It's a really fun day, and there's a Ceilidh in the evening... you can't miss that."

"I can't dance, Ryan." She chuckled at the very thought of doing a Highland Fling.

"I can teach you."

Grace turned and looked at him. If things were different, she could easily fall for this man. His easy, relaxed manner was so refreshing, but nothing had changed in her life, and all she could offer him would be a few fun times together and then she'd have to walk away. But maybe she could go to a Ceilidh with him... and then afterwards.... who knew what might eventuate?

"You're very convincing. Okay, I'll stay."

His face broke into a wide, open smile, lighting up his eyes that were as blue as the loch below them.

When Grace returned to the cottage later that afternoon, Lizzy and the children were sitting on a blanket out on the grass having a picnic. Lizzy waved her over. "Come and join us, Grace."

Dillon's face lit up. He jumped up and ran towards Grace, throwing his arms around her waist. "I missed you, Auntie Grace."

Grace couldn't help herself, and a laugh bubbled up from deep within. Dillon's infectious enthusiasm warmed her heart. It really was nice being wanted, even if it was only by a child. "And I missed you, too, Dillon." She bent down and gave him a hug before he grabbed her hand and led her to the rug.

"Sit down, Auntie Grace, and have a gingerbread man. I helped Mummy make them."

Grace caught Lizzy's amused look and grinned. "They look lovely, Dillon, but I don't know if I could fit one in."

The expression on his little face fell.

Grace let out a breath. She'd said the wrong thing. "On second thought, I'd love one."

His smile returned and he quickly picked a gingerbread man out of the container and held it out to her.

"Put it on a plate for Auntie Grace, Dillon," Lizzy said in a stern voice.

He giggled. "Sorry." He picked up a small plate and after placing the gingerbread man on it, handed it to Grace with a sparkle in his eye.

"Thank you, Dillon, it looks great." Grace took a bite just to be polite, but it actually tasted so good she took a bigger bite. Maybe Ryan was right and the highland air had given her an appetite.

"So, how was the hike?" Lizzy leaned back, resting her hands on the ground behind her.

"It was actually much easier than I thought it'd be, but I think I could do with a rest. I'm not used to all this physical activity."

Lizzy gave her a warm smile. "Plenty of time before dinner. Oh, I almost forgot to tell you... there was a phone call for you. I wrote the number down inside."

Grace's face fell. It couldn't be Caleb, because Lizzy would have said so. *It had to be Niall.*

SHE FINISHED her gingerbread man and managed to ease Clare off her lap. For some reason, the little girl had taken a liking to her and took whatever opportunity she could to sit on her lap. Grace thought it cute, in fact, everything about Clare was cute, from her big round eyes and adorable blond hair cut in a bob, to the thumb that perpetually lived in her mouth. "Auntie Grace has got to go, Clare. I'm sorry. I'll see you at dinner, okay?"

The little girl nodded.

Grace walked into the cottage and found the note Lizzy had taken. Yes, it was Niall's number. She glanced at her watch. He'd called more than three hours ago. Strange he'd be calling on a work day. Something must have happened—perhaps to his father. Why else would he be ringing? Nothing had changed between them, and he knew that.

She dialled the number, and he answered within two rings.

CHAPTER 20

"Grace, thanks for calling back." Niall's voice sounded so familiar, so calm, so steady.

"I only rang because I thought something must have happened to your father."

"No, nothing like that... sorry to have caused you worry. I was just ringing to let you know that O'Malley's appeal has been scheduled for next week. I know you said you wouldn't be back for it, but I just thought I should let you know, in case you changed your mind."

Grace held the receiver tighter against her ear. Her heart rate increased. The pull of the courtroom was strong, and hadn't she been thinking about returning anyway? It was tempting... very tempting. She let out a slow breath. "I'll think about it, Niall. Thanks for letting me know." She paused, her eyebrows furrowing. "Would we be against each other again?" How would she ever convince him they had no future together if they kept seeing each other?

"Yes. Come back, Grace. I've missed you." His voice had lost its calmness, and had grown thick and unsteady.

Grace slumped against the wall and held her hand against her head. There it was... the real reason... She exhaled slowly. "Nothing's changed, Niall."

He didn't reply. Most likely he'd be sitting at his desk holding a photo of her. If only he'd let go of her. She wasn't any good for him, and he deserved better. *Way better.* He was a good man. A lovely man. A caring man. Grace closed her eyes as the acute sense of loss overwhelmed her again. Maybe she could live with him and keep her secret hidden? No, he'd find out somehow. He was a barrister, and he'd whittle it out of her eventually. She couldn't drag him down with her if ever she was discovered. She had to stay strong, keep her walls up. Even going back for the appeal would be asking for trouble... but then, she'd have to go back sometime. She'd just have to learn to live in the same city as him without allowing him back into her life. Difficult, when they'd meet in court every other day.

"How's your father?" She had to say something.

"Doing okay. How's Brianna?"

"Good." She swallowed hard.

Silence.

"I'll think about the appeal. I need to go."

"I love you, Grace." His words came out quickly.

"Niall... don't..." Tears pricked her eyes and she could barely speak. "I have to go..." She hung up and made her way to her bedroom. Falling onto her bed, she sobbed into the pillow until she fell asleep.

SOMETIME LATER, Grace woke to soft knocking on her door. Her head felt thick like concrete, heavy and lifeless.

"Dinner's ready, Grace." Lizzy's voice came to her through her fog.

Grace struggled to lift her head. There was no way she could drag herself to the table. "I'll be down later, Lizzy." Her voice belonged to someone else. Not to Grace O'Connor, Barrister.

"Are you all right?" Lizzy's voice held concern.

Grace forced herself to reply. "Just tired."

"Okay. I'll keep your dinner warm."

Rolling onto her back, Grace lifted her hand to her forehead and stared at the ceiling. What did she have to live for? Brianna no longer needed her, now she had Danny and religion. She couldn't marry Niall, she could never have children, not that she wanted any, hadn't even thought about it until being with Lizzy and Danny's kids, but maybe if things had been different... all she had was work. Which meant she needed to go back. Only work would provide the answer to her deep despair and loneliness. But then she'd have to see Niall... she had no choice—she'd just have to learn to ignore him. She'd have that fling with Ryan MacGregor, and then go back.

THE NEXT COUPLE of days passed. Grace put up her walls and pretended everything was fine. She was good at that. She even feigned joy when Brianna told her that she'd given her heart to Jesus. Grace hugged her and wished her well, but she didn't know this new Brianna. In some ways, she was more comfortable with the old Brianna. At least she understood her then, but now? It was like Brianna's past had never existed. Grace doubted it would last. It had happened too quickly. How could Brianna forget about being raped and the death of her baby just like that? Grace guessed she hadn't told anyone about either, and it would only be a matter of time before she was back on drugs. But then, she'd be Danny and Lizzy's problem, not hers.

Grace had told everybody she'd be leaving on Monday to attend the appeal—she had no doubt the guilty judgment would be upheld, but it was an excuse to leave. She was tempted to go earlier, but everyone insisted she go to the Games on Saturday. Besides, spending the day with Ryan still held attraction. She might get to have that fling with him yet.

The morning of the Games, Grace went with Danny, Lizzy and the children—Ryan said he'd meet her there as he was transporting the students in the mini-bus. The light, misty rain, which Danny told her was called *smirr*, didn't seem to worry the crowd already filling the football field.

As Grace stepped out of the van, Dillon took her hand. "Can you take me to the rides, Auntie Grace?" His little face was full of excitement and expectation. Grace swallowed hard. As much as she tried to pretend she wouldn't miss the children, she would. They'd broken through her walls with their innocence and honesty, *and love*. The sooner she could return to work, the better.

"Dillon, leave Auntie Grace be. Daddy will take you a little later, okay?" Lizzy ruffled Dillon's dark, wavy hair and raised her brow.

"It's all right, Lizzy, I can take him."

Dillon jumped up and down and whooped without letting go of Grace's hand.

Grace couldn't help herself and let out a laugh. If only she could wind the clock back...

"Can we go now?" He was still bouncing, and his little face pleaded with her.

"All right, Dillon. But what about James and Clare?"

"They're too little. Come on, let's just you and me go."

Ryan appeared from in front of the van, looking as relaxed and handsome as ever in his faded blue jeans and red, white and blue checked shirt. He met Grace's gaze, his eyes twinkling in amusement. "And where is this young man taking you?"

Grace chuckled, but Dillon replied before she could. "To the rides. You can come too." Dillon grabbed Ryan's hand and tried to drag both Grace and Ryan away from the van.

"Whoa, little man. Let's see if that's okay with your mum first."

"I said I'd take him, Ryan, it's okay." Grace's heart quickened as she looked into his blue eyes.

"Okay then, let's go. We'll meet up with you later, Liz."

"Thanks Ryan. Good luck with him. And you behave, Dillon... okay?" Lizzy chuckled as she raised her brow again, shooting Dillon another warning look.

"Okay, Mummy." His voice was so cute, Grace's heart came close to melting.

IT SEEMED SURREAL, walking through the food stalls where delightful aromas of freshly baked treats filled the air, rubbing shoulders with burly Scotsmen proudly wearing their Clan's tartan, and listening to the bagpipe music blaring from the hill, but what was more surreal was that she was holding a little boy's hand and Ryan held the other. Grace fought the overwhelming sense of loss which had been surfacing more every day she stayed. She needed to go home, away from this place that just served to remind her of the life she might have had if only things had been different.

"Would you like a coffee, Grace?" Ryan asked as they passed an area set aside with tables and chairs at the far end of the food stalls.

"I'd love one, but we'd better take Dillon on a ride first."

"You're right. We'll come back."

They headed for the children's rides and let Dillon pick which ride he wanted to go on. He chose the merry-go-round, and he wanted both Grace and Ryan to go with him.

Grace laughed. "I've never been on one of these."

"Well, it's time you did!" Ryan dragged her onto the merry-go-round, and after he'd helped Dillon onto a dark brown horse with a cream mane, he helped Grace onto the horse to Dillon's left, a white one with a bright pink mane. Ryan took the horse to Dillon's right. As the music began and the horses rose and fell while circling the carousel, Grace almost forgot herself. How many times as young children had she and Brianna looked with envy at the other children riding the carousel at the local fair? Mam could never afford for them to go on any rides, and Aunt Hilda never let them go. Joy welled in her heart at the pure excitement on Dillon's face, but when her eyes met Ryan's smiling ones, warmth trickled through her body from the tips of her fingers to the bottom of her toes.

"Can we ride it again?" Dillon asked, his little face fully animated.

Laughing, Ryan ruffled Dillon's hair. "Maybe later. Auntie Grace would like a drink, and so would I. Would you like one, Dillon?"

"Can I get a milkshake?" His eyes sparkled, just like his dad's.

"Of course." Ryan smiled and took Dillon's hand.

It was tempting to slip her hand into Ryan's, but she refrained, and instead, took Dillon's spare one.

Seated at a table covered with a red and white checked plastic tablecloth and a vase with a sprig of heather sitting in the middle, Grace found it difficult to look Ryan in the eye, instead, she paid attention to Dillon. There was something unnerving sitting here with Ryan, almost like they were playing happy families. Nothing was further from the truth.

"I like you being here, Auntie Grace. Why can't you stay?"

Grace sighed, clasping her hands together and staring at them before slowly lifting her eyes. "You know why, Dillon. Auntie Grace has to go back to work."

Ryan raised his brow. They'd already had this conversation, and she guessed Ryan knew she was running away, and that she didn't really need to go back.

"I'm going to miss you."

Grace swallowed hard. "I'm going to miss you, too, Dillon."

Lifting her gaze, she met Ryan's magnetic blue eyes and her heart pounded. His mouth twisted in a grin that told her he knew exactly how she was feeling and what she was thinking. She held his gaze for a long moment before tearing her eyes away. He was the most infuriating man. She hated that he had the uncanny knack of seeing through her.

"We should go find our seats. The events will be starting soon." Ryan toyed with his coffee mug.

"Good idea." Grace downed her coffee and stood. "Come on Dillon, let's find your parents." She took his hand and didn't wait for Ryan. She needed the safety of numbers. It was foolish to think she could flirt with a man like Ryan and not get hurt. She was falling for him, and fast, and she couldn't let herself go there.

THE STADIUM WAS a-buzz with anticipation as the massed pipe bands prepared to enter the grounds. Sitting with Lizzy on one side of her, Ryan on the other, and Clare on her lap, Grace should have been happy. Brianna was sitting with her new friends, including Brayden, and looked happy and relaxed. Happy faces were everywhere. Happy faces belonging to happy people. She didn't belong amongst them.

Somehow she got through the day. Bagpipes, drums and Highland flings gave way to caber tosses and hammer throws. Grace laughed and clapped and chatted, but inside, she was empty. It was all meaningless. None of them had any idea of the weight she was carrying. How could they? She'd told no one, not even Brianna. Why it had resurfaced of late, she didn't know, but her nightmares had increased, especially since being here with such good, kind people. *And Ryan.*

"Coming to the Ceilidh tonight?" Ryan asked her as they all made their way back to their vehicles after the main events had finished. He held an umbrella over her head as the *smirr* grew heavier, and she had to fight the overwhelming temptation to slip her arm through his. If only she could welcome his friendship, let everything go. All day her swirling emotions had tormented her, as all her loneliness and guilt welded together to the point she just had to get away or else she'd explode. One more day... she took a deep breath and put on a bright face. "Yes, I'm looking forward to it."

"Great! And I'm looking forward to seeing you in tartan!" His eyes sparkled as he opened the door of the van for her.

Grace's forehead puckered. "I don't have any tartan."

"I'm only joking. You can wear whatever you want."

She let out a small laugh. "Okay, I'll see what I have. See you tonight."

As she settled into her seat beside the children, Grace let her gaze linger on Ryan as he walked around to the mini-bus and chatted freely with the students as they all climbed in. He was so relaxed and happy—something she could never be.

"Have you had a good day, Grace?" Lizzy asked as she finished buckling up Clare.

What could she say? *"No, it's been torture...?"* She couldn't say that. She smiled at Lizzy. "Yes, it's been great."

"And you're going to the Ceilidh with Ryan, I hear?"

"So it seems." Grace gave a small chuckle. How had she gotten herself into this situation?

"He's a nice man, Grace. You could do worse for yourself."

Grace shrugged. "I'm not interested."

Lizzy laughed. "Yeah, right."

Grace met Lizzy's gaze. "I'm not interested in him, Lizzy. In him, or anyone."

Lizzy's expression slipped. "Okay, sorry. I was only having a bit of fun."

"Well, don't." Why was she talking to Lizzy like this? It was like someone else had taken over her tongue and words she didn't mean tumbled out. She had to get away. She didn't mean to snap at Lizzy of all people.

Thankfully, the children's chatter filled the van on the short drive home. When they arrived, Grace excused herself and began packing.

∼

"WHAT'S UP WITH GRACE?" Lizzy asked Daniel when they sat down for a cup of tea after dinner before getting ready for the Ceilidh. David and Rosemary were putting the children to bed, having offered to mind them so Daniel and Lizzy could attend the dance.

"What do you mean?" Easing back onto the sofa, Daniel angled his head, and slipping his arm around her shoulders, pulled her close.

"I don't know, but she seems kind of... troubled, I think that's the word. She snapped at me in the car." Lizzy ran her hand slowly along Daniel's leg.

Daniel straightened. "Grace snapped at you? What on earth made her do that?"

Lizzy shrugged. "I just told her she could do worse than Ryan."

Daniel laughed. "You should know better than that, Lizzy. I remember a time when you told me off for asking her if she had anyone special in her life."

Lizzy let out a sigh. "Yes, you're right. I shouldn't have said anything. But even without that, she seems on edge more than normal."

Daniel rubbed her arm. "We just have to keep praying for her, Liz, you know that. We don't know what's going on inside her, but God does."

"You're right, Daniel." Lizzy straightened. "Maybe we should pray for her now?"

He smiled. "Good idea. Let's do it." Taking Lizzy's hand, Daniel bowed his head. "Dear Lord, we bring Grace before You. We'd hoped that by being here, amongst those who love You, and amongst Your great creation here in the Highlands, that she might have let her walls down and opened her heart to You. We feel saddened that this hasn't happened yet, but Lord, we trust You to continue working in her heart, drawing her to Yourself, chipping away at the walls she's put up. Lord, we pray that she'll open her heart to Your love and peace, and that she'll give whatever's troubling her over to You, the great Comforter and Healer. Open the eyes of her heart to the truth of the gospel message; may she embrace the sacrifice Jesus made for her when He gave His life on the cross so that she might live. Lord, bless her this day, we pray, in Jesus' name, Amen."

"And Lord," Lizzy cleared her throat, "give us wisdom to know what to say to Grace, especially as she's planning on leaving soon. I'm sorry for being so thoughtless with her this afternoon. And Lord, we thank You so much for the change in Brianna's life. Thank You for healing her hurts, and giving her hope for the future. We're so glad she's opened her heart to You. Continue to strengthen her on a daily basis, so that she won't succumb when temptation comes knocking on her door, as it's bound to do. Amen." Lizzy let out a slow breath as she brushed tears off her cheeks.

"We have to leave her in God's hands, Liz."

"I know. I just wish He'd hurry up."

"Patience, Lizzy, patience."

"You know that's not my forte."

Daniel lifted his hand and brushed her cheek. His blue eyes twinkled, sending her senses into a tailspin. "Yes, but you've come a long way, Lizzy O'Connor."

Lizzy chuckled. "I guess I have, but He's still got a lot of ·work to do on me."

"As He does on me."

Lizzy smiled at him. "I love you, Daniel. And I love that God brought us to this place. It's hard to remember what life was like before we were here. I feel like we've come home."

"Home is wherever you are, Liz."

"You're such a big softie, Daniel." She chuckled as he lowered his lips against hers, but she pulled away before he could kiss her properly. "If we're going dancing, we need to get ready."

"I guess we do." He gave her another quick kiss and then fixed his eyes on hers as he traced her hairline with the tip of his finger. "Later?"

Nodding, she stretched up and gave him a slow kiss.

CHAPTER 21

$\mathcal{W}$hen Grace asked Lizzy what she should wear to the Ceilidh, Lizzy suggested jeans and a comfortable top, but in her designer jeans and soft cream silk shirt, Grace knew she would still turn eyes.

Ryan ran his eyes over her when they all met up outside the main building before leaving. Despite not wanting to go at all, Grace found it hard to take her eyes off him too. Wearing black trousers and a long-sleeved black shirt with the cuffs rolled up, he was devastatingly handsome. His compelling blue eyes and confident set of his shoulders, coupled with the tantalising smell of his after-shave, sent her pulse racing.

"Would you like to sit up front with me, Grace?" Ryan held his hand on the sliding door and looked at her as she stood beside Lizzy and Daniel. Danny had his arm around Lizzy's waist, and she got the impression they didn't want to be separated.

"Go on, Grace, it's fine." Danny said, giving her a nod.

Grace let out a breath. Why not? She smiled at Ryan. "Okay, thanks."

The students were already in the back, and Ryan slid the door closed after Daniel and Lizzy climbed in, and then held the front door open for her. "You look lovely tonight, Grace."

As she lifted her eyes to his, a ripple of excitement flowed through her. She gave him a grateful smile, but didn't trust herself to speak as she climbed in as elegantly as she could.

The Ceilidh was being held in the local hall, and even as they pulled up, the sounds of accordions, drums and fiddles filled the air. Grace had to admit that the music was stirring, possibly even more so than the Irish music that often floated out of the hotels near Chambers. Despite not expecting to enjoy herself, her heart quickened in anticipation.

The drizzle had stopped, and people gathered inside and out while they waited for the official start, but some eager couples were already dancing to the music. Ryan's light touch on her back sent tremors through her body. "Can I get you a drink?" He had to shout as he guided her through the crowd.

Turning her head, she lifted a brow. "Gin and tonic?"

He shook his head and chuckled. "We've been through this before, Grace. Water, soft drink or tea..."

Grace raised her other brow. "Whisky?"

He chuckled again. "Sorry."

She let out a sigh. "Guess I'll have water."

He handed her a glass. "I need to check on the students. I'll be right back."

She smiled at him. "Okay. I'll stay with Lizzy."

Ryan left with Daniel and headed towards the students who were all standing together in a huddle. The old Brianna would never have been seen dead or alive at a gathering such as this, but what would the new Brianna do? Grace kept her eye on the two men as they stood with their arms folded talking with the group. Half of the students looked like they didn't want to be there. Brianna was talking with Brayden, who had a sullen look on his face.

Daniel and Ryan returned just as the band stopped playing and someone blew into the microphone.

"Welcome everyone to tonight's Ceilidh. Take your partners for the first dance of the night, a Gypsy Tap."

Ryan held out his arm. "May I have this dance, Madam?" His eyes twinkled, warming Grace's heart.

"Thank you." She took his arm, as solid and firm as a tree trunk. The smell of him made her flesh tingle.

"Do you know this dance?" he whispered into her ear.

"No."

"Don't worry, it's easy." They joined the circle of other couples before an older man wearing a kilt stood at the microphone and gave instructions. Within moments, Ryan slipped his arm around Grace's back and his left hand took her right one. His face was close enough for her to feel the warmth of his breath on her cheek. Against her better judgment, she allowed herself to relax. The music played, the man called the steps, and the dance began. Ryan was right—it wasn't difficult, and within a couple of sequences, Grace had it sorted. He hadn't told her it was progressive, and too soon she found herself with men she'd never met, each paying her a compliment. She was sure they said the same thing to all the women, but it boosted her spirits, nevertheless. When she came to Brayden, she tried to jolly him along. She was surprised he was up dancing at all. She glanced around the circle and found Brianna. She was laughing, and it looked like she was having the time of her life. The change in her was still so hard to believe.

Once the Gypsy Tap finished, Strip the Willow was called. Ryan headed straight for Grace, and taking her elbow, placed her opposite him in a long row that stretched all the way from the front of the hall to the back. She had no idea what she was letting herself in for, but by the time it was hers and Ryan's turn to "Strip the Willow", she had a good idea she was going to embarrass herself in front of everyone, but Ryan's arms were so strong, and he made sure she didn't fall over, and every time she swung out into his arms, he steadied her. By the time they'd finished stripping the willow, she was breathless, but couldn't stop laughing.

"You did well, Grace," Lizzy stepped close to her and shouted into her ear.

"Thanks!" Grace's chest heaved as she tried to catch her breath. On the other side, Ryan winked at her, and a warm fuzzy feeling surged through her.

The rest of the evening passed all too quickly. Grace had never danced so much in all her life, nor had so much fun. Before she was ready, it was time to leave.

As she sat beside Ryan on the way home, instead of after-shave filling her nostrils, masculine body odour oozed from him, but she didn't find it offensive, in fact, it had the exact opposite effect on her. She found it intoxicating, and had to fight her overwhelming desire to be close to him.

When he stopped the bus in front of Lizzy and Danny's cottage, her hopes for a romantic evening flew out the window. He jumped out, jogged around the front, and opened the door for her. Instead of sweeping her up in his arms and kissing her as she'd hoped he would, he just took her hand and smiled. "I enjoyed myself tonight, Grace. I hope you did, too."

She forced a smile. "Yes, I had a lovely time, thank you."

"Will we see you in church in the morning?"

She fought her automatic response of "no", and instead answered "maybe."

"You'd be welcome." His smile widened, and her heart once again fluttered as his eyes twinkled at hers.

"I'll think about it." But she'd already thought. If he was there, she'd go.

"Thanks for coming, Grace. I'll look forward to seeing you tomorrow." He leaned forward. She held her breath as he placed the lightest kiss she'd ever had on her cheek. But just the touch of his lips was enough to send her heart into a spin.

As Lizzy, Daniel and Grace waved good-bye to Ryan and all the students, Grace's throat clenched. Nothing could happen between her and Ryan, but seeing him drive away just accentuated her loneliness. It would have been nice just to talk with him, if nothing else.

"Come inside and have a cup of tea, Grace." Danny placed his hand gently on her back. "Did you enjoy yourself tonight?"

She let out a sigh and nodded, turning her head slightly to smile at him. "Yes, it was fun, thanks."

"It was good to see you laughing." He left his hand on her shoulder as they walked inside.

Rosemary and David greeted them with tired smiles as they all entered the kitchen.

"How were the children?" Danny stepped to the stove and picked up the kettle.

"No problem at all. They're all sound asleep in bed, which is where we should be." Rosemary chuckled.

"Sorry we're so late, Rosemary." Lizzy hurried over and gave Rosemary a big hug. "Thanks so much for looking after them."

"Our pleasure, Lizzy. Hope you all had a good night."

Lizzy beamed. "The best. It was so much fun."

"Ceilidhs always are."

"You'll have to come next time."

"Not sure about that." Rosemary chuckled. "I don't think I could strip the willow any more than I could climb Ben Nevis! No, we were happy to mind the children so you could go."

"And we appreciate that, we really do."

"As I said, it's our pleasure, but we really must be going. We have to be up early in the morning to prepare the flowers for church."

After Rosemary and David left, Danny pulled out a chair for Grace and they both sat while Lizzy began making tea.

Grace toyed with the spoon that had been left sitting on the table. The feeling of loneliness that had crept through her after Ryan drove away still sat heavily inside her.

"So, one more day..." Danny angled his head and looked at her.

"Yes. One more day."

"The kids will miss you." He paused. "We'll miss you."

Grace swallowed hard, her shoulders sagging under the

weight of her loneliness and confusion. She finally lifted her head and met Danny's gaze. "And I'll miss you all, too." Her words caught in her throat.

Danny leaned forward and squeezed her hand. "You don't have to go, Grace. You're very welcome to stay as long as you want."

His kind eyes unnerved her further. She glanced down at her lap and tried to compose herself.

Finally, she lifted her head and met his gaze. "I don't know, Danny. I don't know what I want to do."

"Why don't you stay, then? Surely somebody else can step in for you."

Shaking her head, Grace sucked in a slow breath before releasing it. Her shoulders slumped. "I really don't know." She swallowed hard. And that was the truth. She didn't know. If she went back to work, it would all be the same. She'd get caught up with high profile cases that might help her forget for a while, but seeing Niall on an almost daily basis would be a constant reminder of what she could never have. If only she'd never got tangled up with Samara and Fergus. The only real way out was to confess and pay the penalty. But could she really do that now, after all this time? And how would she cope being in prison with those she'd put there? Grace shuddered at the thought. She was caught between a rock and a hard place. The only way forward was to push it all away again and not think about it. Bury it. Hide it. Pretend it had never happened. She could do that. She'd done it before, she could do it again. *But staying a while longer was tempting.*

Danny squeezed her hand again. "Think about it?"

She shrugged. "Maybe."

Lizzy placed three steaming mugs of tea on the table and sat down opposite. "Dillon would love it if you stayed longer." She lifted her eyes and smiled. "And so would I, Grace. It's been lovely having company."

Tears sprung to Grace's eyes. If she ever wanted a friend, Lizzy would be a great choice. Oh, blow it! She'd stay. Sniffing, she let out a small chuckle. "Okay, you talked me into it."

Lizzy's eyes popped. Jumping up, she threw her arms around Grace's neck. "That's fantastic, Grace."

Grace laughed. "I didn't know I was so popular."

"You'd better believe it." Smiling, Lizzy took her seat and touched Grace's wrist lightly. "The kids adore you, Grace."

"I don't know why."

"Oh, I think it's because you look like their dad, and they love him to bits." Lizzy's eyes shone with love and devotion as she slipped Danny a smile.

Once again, the pain of knowing she'd never share such a moment with anyone special tore at Grace's heart. But being loved by Danny and Lizzy's children was some compensation at least... *or was it?*

"Well, now that's sorted, let's drink our tea." Danny winked at Grace as he lifted his mug. Did he ever miss drinking anything stronger? She knew she did... but she'd have to do without while she was here.

Taking a sip of her tea, Grace leaned back, and wrapping her hands around the mug, angled her head towards Danny. "Do you think Brianna's going to make it?"

His expression grew serious. She'd caught him off-guard with her direct question. He cleared his throat and steadied his gaze. "Yes, I think she will."

"What makes you so sure? She's stayed off drugs before for weeks at a time, and then she's gone back onto them. What's different this time?" She raised her brow. "And don't tell me it's because she's found God."

Danny drew a slow breath, put his mug on the table and folded his arms. "I can't guarantee she won't go back on them at all, Grace, but I do know that she's sincere about wanting to stay clean. I know you won't want to hear about her conversion experience, but you should ask her someday. I believe it was real, and that God has filled the hole in her heart that's been there all her life. He's given her a new start, Grace. He's washed away all the dirt from her previous life, and cleansed her from the inside out. She's still going to face challenges, as we all do, but she's got God in her heart now, and He'll give her the strength to get through whatever comes her way."

Grace remained silent. It was a lot of rubbish as far as she was concerned, but she couldn't deny Danny's sincerity, and the change in his own life. "Has she told you what happened to her?" Grace's eyes narrowed as she angled her head.

Danny leaned back in his chair. "No, she hasn't, but I can see she's been hurt in the past." He turned his head and met Grace's gaze. "Was it terrible for you at Aunt Hilda's, Grace? I've always wanted to know, but you've never wanted to talk about it."

Grace shook her head. "You really don't want to know."

"I feel guilty that you and Brianna were sent away when Mam died, Grace. I wished you could have stayed in Belfast with Caleb and me. I'm sure there would have been room for you at Aunt Moira's."

"But you didn't have such a good time either, from what I hear."

Danny sucked in a big breath. "No, you're right. I messed up badly."

Lizzy reached out and squeezed his hand.

He looked up and smiled at her, causing Grace to gulp. He shifted in his seat and turned back to Grace. "Would you like to hear about it?"

Grace shrugged. "Okay. I've only heard bits and pieces from Caleb, so I may as well hear it from you."

He drew a slow breath, as if he was steeling himself. "You already know Aunt Moira and Uncle Desmond took Caleb and me in."

Grace nodded.

"I was fourteen, and angry about Mam dying, and even more angry about the way Da had treated her." He shrugged. "I started drinking when I was sixteen, but then one night I got so drunk I ended up in hospital. I was given an ultimatum, either start going to church with the family, or move out. They'd had enough of me." He paused. "I wasn't ready to move out, so I started going to church, and I met a girl… her name was Ciara."

Danny's eyes moistened. "She was beautiful. She had long, flowing hair, and she was always smiling. For some reason, she liked me, and we started dating." His expression grew serious and he wiped his eyes. "She got pregnant, and her parents made us get married. We lived in a room at the back of their house. It was hard, but we loved each other." He closed his eyes and sucked in a deep breath.

Grace reached out and touched his arm. "You don't have to tell me if you don't want to..."

He opened his eyes. "No, it's okay. I want to."

As she gave him a smile, her heart went out to him.

"The baby was born. A little girl... we named her Rachel. She was the most precious little thing, and we loved her so much." He swallowed hard. "Having a baby to look after made me grow up. I got a job, Ciara and I moved out into a place of our own, and everything was great for six months, until one night, Rachel died in her sleep." His eyes moistened again, and his body shuddered. "I can still remember that night..."

Lizzy rubbed his back.

Grace pushed back tears of her own as memories of the night Brianna's little baby boy died flooded back. But she couldn't tell Danny about that. It was up to Brianna to tell him if she wanted to.

"I couldn't handle it and started drinking again, heavily. I went on binges, and one night when I came home, my cousin Liam had his arms around Ciara. I lost it, and beat him until he was almost dead. I went to prison for it." He lifted his head. "Ciara left me after that. I don't blame her. But this is the worst bit, Grace." Tears flooded his eyes. "A few years later, Ciara took her life." Tears rolled down his cheeks. "I should have been there for her when Rachel died, instead of beating Liam up and landing in jail."

Tears streamed from Grace's eyes. She reached out and pulled him close. She'd had no idea. Why hadn't Caleb told her? Maybe he had but she just hadn't listened. "I'm so sorry, Danny."

He sucked in some big breaths and released them slowly.

"It's okay. It's part of my past, and it doesn't haunt me anymore. Meeting Lizzy was the best thing that happened to me. Well, the second best. She led me to Jesus, and He changed my life. I know you don't believe in Him, Grace, but I can testify for a fact that He's real. The gospel message is real. Jesus died for my sins so that I can live with Him forever, and while I'm here on earth, He's given me peace, joy, purpose, and forgiveness. That's what Brianna's found, and I pray that you'll find it too."

Grace didn't know what to say. She couldn't deny Danny's experience. But how could Jesus ever forgive her of murder?

CHAPTER 22

The following morning, Grace rose and dressed for church, something she hadn't done since Mam died, almost twenty years ago. Danny's story had haunted her all night. Something about it had stirred her heart. If God had relieved him of his guilt over Ciara's death, maybe there was a way of getting rid of her own. Maybe she didn't need to tell anyone, other than God, what she'd done. Brianna hadn't. She'd go and hear what they had to say, because if there was a way out of this hole, she was starting to think she should look for it. Anything had to be better than the hell she was living in.

The children were already sitting around the table eating breakfast when Grace entered the kitchen. Lizzy smiled brightly and the children all called out for her to sit beside them.

Grace laughed. She really had no idea why they liked her, but she had to admit it felt nice to be wanted. She just hoped they'd never find out that the auntie they seemed to love so much was a murderer. She chastised herself. She had to stop thinking like that.

"Let Auntie Grace pick her own seat." Lizzy shook her head at the children but laughed along with Grace, catching her eye as Grace chose a seat at the foot of the table on either side of James and Clare. "Coffee?"

"Yes, please."

Lizzy smiled warmly as she poured Grace's coffee and placed a mug of the steaming brew in front of her before taking her own seat beside Dillon. Lizzy knew better than to ask if she wanted breakfast, but the toast sitting on a plate in the middle of the table smelled good, so she reached out and took a slice.

"How are you feeling this morning? My muscles are really sore after all that dancing."

Grace chuckled. "The same... I could hardly move when I got up."

"Sounds like we need to do more exercise."

Grace grimaced as she buttered her toast. "I'm not sure my body could handle much more."

"Me either, but it was fun." Lizzy glanced at the clock on the wall. "Danny's already left to help prepare for the service, and we need to be leaving shortly."

"I'll just finish this and then help you with the children."

"Thanks, Grace." Lizzy met her gaze, a genuine smile on her face. "I'm glad you're coming."

Grace drew a breath and released it slowly. Going to church was so normal for Lizzy, but for her, it was anything but. The only memories she had of church angered her. Eight children and Mam, sitting all in a row on a hard pew, with

Mam doing her best to keep them all quiet. Why she'd bothered, Grace really didn't know. It seemed more trouble than it was worth, especially since God hadn't stopped Mam from dying. If God had kept her alive, then Grace and Brianna would never have gone to live with Aunt Hilda, Brianna wouldn't have been raped or fallen pregnant, and Grace wouldn't have set that bomb and killed all those innocent people. So really, it was all God's fault. *So what was she doing going back on her vow never to set foot in a church again? What had changed?*

Grace nibbled her toast while the children chattered around her. Could she go through with this? She remembered Da's funeral. She hadn't wanted to go—she hated the man. The way he'd treated Mam was despicable. An abusive drunkard, he'd disappeared when Grace was eight, leaving Mam to look after all eight kids, including a baby. And then when he reappeared years after Mam died, Caleb and Danny had the gall to forgive the man. They said Da had 'found God', and that he was sorry for what he'd done. She didn't see him before he died, but she remembered the words spoken about him at his funeral.... it was like they were talking about a different person, not the Da she remembered. But something had happened inside her that day—a few chinks in her walls had been chipped away although she'd rebuilt them since. *Was she ready if that happened again?* No, she wouldn't let it. It was just emotion. She'd put on her lawyer's hat and assess everything. She wouldn't let herself get caught up in all that like Brianna had.

"Auntie Gwace..." A small voice came to her. How long had Clare been tapping her arm?

Grace blinked. "Sorry Clare, what did you say?"

Clare stuck her thumb in her mouth and giggled.

"Clare, don't put your dirty fingers on Auntie Grace's shirt." Standing, Lizzy grabbed the cloth. "Here, let me wipe it for you, Grace."

"Don't worry, Lizzy, it's fine." Grace waved her off. "It's just a bit of jam."

SHORTLY AFTER, Lizzy and Grace walked with the children into the small chapel sitting on the far side of the main Elim Community building. Built of stone, it had once been a barn, but several years ago it had been renovated and made into a simple place of worship, and now it even had stained glass windows. It wasn't just the students and staff of the Community who attended. People came from miles around as the small church's reputation for preaching God's word without compromise had spread over the years.

The chapel was already half full when they took their seats at the back. "I have to sit back here because of the children," Lizzy whispered to Grace.

Suited her... she could hide back here... well, almost. Her heart quickened when Ryan caught her eye and lifted his hand in a wave. An easy smile played at the corners of his mouth, and in his pale blue jeans and white polo shirt, his toned body looked so masculine and appealing. It probably wasn't appropriate in a place like this, but her flesh tingled at the memory of being in his arms last night as they danced. She nodded and returned his smile.

Brianna and the other students sat towards the front. They had chapel every day, so this would be nothing new for them, but Grace was surprised that as well as a piano, a small band filled the left front of the church. A young girl with a violin, another with a flute, a young man with a guitar, and yet another young man sitting behind a set of drums. At least there wasn't a bagpipe.

Clare climbed onto Grace's lap, but when the music began playing a few moments later, everyone stood. Awkward... what should she do? She glanced at Lizzy. She'd stood and had James in her arms. Grace guessed she should do the same. Standing, she lifted Clare up and positioned the little girl on her hip. It felt strange, but kind of nice. How did Lizzy normally do it on her own? At least Dillon seemed happy to stand on his own, although he jumped up and down on the seat behind Lizzy. *Mam would never have let us get away with that.*

Although the songs were unfamiliar, the tunes were catchy and the band played well, but Grace was determined not to join in. Singing was just one of the ways they got at vulnerable people. Instead, she studied the congregation as her gaze travelled from one side of the building to the other, but her gaze got stuck on Ryan and Danny, who both stood near the front on the opposite side to the band. More masculine men would be hard to find, but here they both were, singing, clapping, and waving their hands in the air. Unbelievable.

Grace drew a breath and smiled at Clare as the little girl played with Grace's earring. She was such a precious little girl, and Grace's heart softened.

The singing continued, probably a little too long for Grace's liking, but then Danny stepped to the front and welcomed everyone, and then he asked everyone to join him in prayer. Grace swapped Clare to her other hip. She didn't know how Lizzy could hold them for so long.

Instead of closing her eyes, Grace kept hers on Danny. Was he play acting? She had to know. After hearing his story last night, she seemed to think he wasn't. Danny's remorse over what he'd done had certainly sounded genuine, as did his belief that Jesus had forgiven him and given him new life, but was he deluded? As he prayed, he held one hand in the air, but it didn't look like he was acting. Grace got the impression he was in awe of the God he was praying to, and His words confirmed that.

"Lord God, our Heavenly Father, we stand in Your presence today, in awe of what You have done, and who You are. You're the Almighty God, the creator of heaven and earth, and we bow before you in humble adoration. There is none like you, oh God. Open our hearts and minds to Your love, and speak to those who don't know You yet. Those who are struggling with things in their past that are weighing them down, those who are carrying guilt over actions and thoughts that have created a barrier between You and them. Let them know the freedom of forgiveness that Jesus bought for them when He died on the cross for them, and the joy of the new life that is waiting for all those who believe. Please be with us today, dear Lord, and be with Ryan as he brings us Your message. In Jesus' precious name, Amen."

Grace gulped. If he was making it up, he was a very good actor.

Danny sat and Ryan took his place at the front. Grace straightened, fixing her eyes on Ryan, mesmerised by his warm, genuine smile and his relaxed demeanour. He radiated a vitality that drew her like a magnet and her whole being waited eagerly to hear what he had to say.

Resting his hands on the lectern, Ryan gazed around the congregation, his eyes soft and caring. Grace's heart quickened when his gaze lingered on hers momentarily.

"Let me start by asking a question." He paused and took a sip of water. "I don't ask this lightly or in judgment, but because it's important. Even if you've accepted Christ into your heart, you might not be experiencing the full freedom that Jesus came to give you. Jesus came to this earth to free you from the bondage of sin and death, to give you new life here and now." He paused, casting his gaze around the congregation. "But are you experiencing that new life and freedom, or are you chained to the past? Is there something you've done, something you've thought, or has something been done to you, an insult, a slur, a put down, or even worse, have you been rejected or abused, that's set like some immovable dead weight in your soul and every time you try to move forward in your life, spiritually or emotionally, this incident just chains you to the ground?"

Grace shifted uncomfortably in her seat. Ryan's question pierced her heart like an arrow. Had he planned this just for her? She gulped. *Did he know about her past?*

Ryan continued. "If you're carrying guilt over something, or if you feel you're unworthy of love because of the shame of what might have happened to you, or you believe you're a failure for whatever reason, let me tell you, *Jesus is your freedom.* He has the power to break the bondage of the past, whatever you've done, or whatever has happened to you. *He can free you from it.*

"You might be asking how He can do that, especially if you've already asked Him into your life and you still feel the weight of that bondage. Firstly, if you're in bondage because of something you've done, you need to receive the Lord's forgiveness. Come to the cross of Jesus, and realise afresh, or perhaps for the first time, the power of the cross in your life. The cross is our freedom. It doesn't matter what you've done, it doesn't matter what's in your past, how ugly, how brutal, or how violent it is, it doesn't matter how badly you've messed up, the cross can set you free. Let me read from Colossians chapter 2, verses 13 and 14: "… God made you alive with Christ. He forgave us **all** our sins, having cancelled the charge of our legal indebtedness, which stood against us and condemned us; he has taken it away, nailing it to the cross." Do you understand what God's saying here? *All* our sins are forgiven—not just some, but *all*. We stand holy and blameless before our Lord because of the cross. Jesus died for **all** our sins."

A hush fell over the chapel. Grace couldn't take her eyes off him—he really meant this stuff, and her heart pounded.

Ryan's voice softened. "If you're chained by something that was done to you, you might need to be healed at a deeper level, but know that as you have a new identity in Christ, you're not chained to whatever happened to you, because Jesus buried your past forever and has given you new life. You're in a new place, and you're no longer a slave to anything in your past. I want to encourage you today to take God at His word. If He says you're a new creation because you've accepted Jesus as your Saviour, that's what you are. The old has gone, the new has come. The bondage of your past is broken, and you can live in the freedom that Jesus bought for you on the cross. If you

SECRETS AND SACRIFICE

don't know that freedom, come to the cross today. While we sing the last song, come, but before we sing, please join me in prayer." He held his hand up as he bowed his head.

"Lord God, thank you that Jesus died on the cross for all our sins, not just some of them. There is nothing that any of us can't be forgiven of, and there's nothing that's been done to any of us that can't be healed by the love of Jesus. Help us to grasp the fact that the cross is our freedom, and that Jesus came so that we might have new life, here and now. In Jesus' precious name, Amen." He looked up slowly and smiled. "Let's sing, and while we sing, come forward if you need to do business with God."

The band started, and everyone stood. Grace's heart continued to pound. Ryan had been very convincing, and she was almost tempted to go forward, but she wouldn't. How did she really know it wasn't just some kind of emotional manipulation? But she had to agree that it certainly sounded good. To be free of guilt, how would that feel? Instead of going forward, she'd talk to him about it. She had to do something.

The song mimicked Ryan's sermon...

WOULD you be free from the burden of sin?
  There's power in the blood, power in the blood
  Would you o'er evil a victory win?
  There's wonderful power in the blood.

THERE IS POWER, power, wonder-working power
  In the blood of the Lamb

There is power, power, wonder-working power
In the precious blood of the Lamb

TEARS STUNG GRACE'S eyes as Brianna and Brayden, along with some others walked forward and knelt down on the steps at the front. Danny, Ryan, David and Rosemary knelt with them, placing their hands on their shoulders.

Grace glanced at Lizzy... her eyes glistened. Lizzy reached out her hand and Grace took it.

Lizzy squeezed it and then slipped her arm around Grace's shoulders, pulling her close. Clare touched Grace's cheek with her chubby fingers.

"What's wrong, Auntie Gwace?"

"Nothing, sweetheart. Auntie Grace is fine." Grace pulled Clare closer and hugged her. She wasn't fine, and she knew it.

The song continued, and Grace's heart still raced. The weight of her burden was so heavy, and growing heavier by the minute. But she couldn't do it. She drew in a slow breath and steadied herself as the song came to an end. She was a barrister, and she wasn't going to be drawn in unless she could prove it all true, but deep in her heart, she prayed that it was. But could she really expect God, *if He existed,* to forgive her of murder?

THE SERVICE ENDED. Grace dabbed her eyes with a tissue and hoped her mascara hadn't run. Many people remained in their seats while the band continued playing, a lot of them with bowed heads. Others hugged each other, and others walked out quietly.

Lizzy gathered the children's books and placed them in a bag, and then stood, giving Grace a warm smile. "Are you ready to go?"

Grace nodded. Standing, she lifted Clare back onto her hip and followed Lizzy and the other two children outside. Yesterday's *smirr* had returned, but nobody seemed to mind. It was so fine it was barely noticeable.

Lizzy stopped and turned to Grace. "We normally have lunch with the students after church. Do you want to do that, or would you rather go home for lunch?"

Grace was in two minds. She needed to talk with someone, but who? Lizzy, Danny, Ryan? Could she face being amongst all the students and pretend everything was fine, or should she go back to the cottage with Lizzy? She'd rather talk with Ryan, but he was still busy with other people. Maybe talking with Lizzy was the thing to do now. She could talk with Ryan later.

"Can we go back to the cottage? Would you mind?"

Lizzy rubbed Grace's arm. "Not at all, Grace. Dillon will probably want to stay—he loves Sunday lunch at the Hall, but we can take these two." Lizzy glanced at James and Clare and smiled at them.

"Thanks, Lizzy. I appreciate that." Grace was struggling to speak.

Shortly after, Grace and Lizzy settled into Lizzy's comfortable and homely living room with mugs of hot coffee and a sandwich each. Lizzy put a children's programme on the television for James and Clare to watch, and then turned her attention to Grace.

"I'm a good listener, Grace. I can see something's going on inside you, but I also know how hard it can be to talk about things. I hope you'll trust me enough to share what's on your heart, but just tell me what you want, nothing more, nothing less. Danny and I would just love to see you free from whatever's troubling you."

Tears pricked Grace's eyes. She drew a deep breath. Now the moment had come, she really had no idea where to start. Her pulse raced. So many years of building walls, and now they were crumbling around her. But Lizzy was the first real friend she had, and so there really was no better time to start.

She let out her breath. "I don't know where to start, Lizzy. There are things in my past I've never told anyone, and I still can't." She looked down at the bright red mug in her hands. "The service was moving, and Ryan spoke well... he was very convincing." She looked up and smiled. "He could almost be a barrister. I was tempted to go forward, but I need to know that what he was saying is true. I'm not just going to blindly believe."

"Nobody would expect you to do that, Grace." Lizzy sat forward and smiled. "There's plenty of proof that Jesus existed, that He really did come to earth and lived here amongst us. There's also plenty of proof that He died on the cross and that He rose again, but the main proof is in the lives He changes and their testimonies. Believing is one thing, but accepting and following is another. It's not until you take that step of faith that you really know, because something changes in your heart that nothing can explain. It's spiritual, and it's like nothing you've ever experienced before, but I can understand where you're coming from." Lizzy straightened. "How about you and I do a study of John's gospel? We can take our time, and you can ask as many questions as you want, and we can do research as well as we go. I've also got some other books you might like to read. Apologetic type books that provide arguments for and against God's existence and Jesus's death and resurrection, as well as a lot of other issues that people ask questions about. How does that sound?"

"I think I'd like that, Lizzy. I need to do something, because I don't think I can go on like this much longer." Grace covered her face with trembling hands as tears streamed down her cheeks.

Lizzy moved swiftly and sat beside her, wrapping her arms around her, comforting her. "It's okay, Grace. I'm here for you... God's here for you."

Grace sobbed until she could sob no more. Her heart felt constricted, heavy. She felt ill.

"Can I pray for you, Grace?" Lizzy brushed Grace's forehead with her fingers as she peered into her eyes.

Grace nodded. She couldn't speak.

Lizzy took her hand and squeezed it. "Dear God, You know what's in Grace's heart. You know the hurt that's in her life, the despair she's feeling. Lord, I ask that You gently draw her to Yourself. Wrap her in Your love, and give her freedom from the burdens that are weighing her down. Let her know it's between You and her, and no one else. Touch her in her deepest parts, dear Lord, heal her, make her whole. She's your precious daughter and You love her so much. Let her know that You love her in a truly personal way, dear Lord. Open her heart and mind to You. Thank You for her life, and for the care she's taken of Brianna. So many hurts from the past, dear Lord, but we know that the cross of Jesus provides freedom, no matter what's in the past, the cross of Jesus is enough. Lord, please bless us as we study Your Word, open Grace's eyes to the truth of the gospel message. In Jesus' precious name, Amen."

Grace drew a steadying breath, and opening her eyes, squeezed Lizzy's hand. She gulped and let her breath out as she dabbed her eyes. "Thank you, Lizzy. I needed that."

"You're welcome, Grace. God's going to do a mighty work in your life, I just know it." Warmth flowed from Lizzy's eyes as she gave Grace a hug.

"We'll see about that." Grace let out a small chuckle.

"Do you want to start now? We've got time before Danny gets back."

Grace shrugged. "I guess so."

Lizzy stood and pulled a Bible from the bookshelf behind the couch and handed it to Grace, and then picked up her own Bible from the lamp table beside her as she sat back down. "Guess you've never opened one of these before?" Lizzy's brow lifted as she leaned forward, an amused but friendly grin on her face.

Grace shook her head. "Never."

"Okay, John was one of Jesus's disciples, and he gives a first-hand, eye-witness account of Jesus's life. He wrote it so that people might believe that Jesus is the Messiah, the Son of God, and that by believing they might have life, so it's a great place to start. It's the fourth book of the New Testament, about two-thirds of the way through... "

Grace opened the Bible and flicked through until she found it.

"That's it. Shall I start reading?"

Grace shrugged again. "Okay."

"Stop me whenever you want." Lizzy smiled before lowering her eyes to the book on her lap. "John Chapter 1... 'In the beginning was the Word, and the Word was with God, and the Word was God. He was with God in the beginning. Through him all things were made; without him nothing was made that has been made. In him was life, and that life was the light of all mankind. The light shines in the darkness, and the darkness has not overcome it.'"

As Lizzy continued reading, Grace interrupted occasionally and asked a few questions, but she was mainly happy just to listen. Somehow the words soothed her spirit, and the questions could wait. Grace had never heard such words before, and she was hungry to keep reading, but the programme finished on the television too soon and James and Clare wanted her to play.

"We can pick up again later, Lizzy, besides, I'm going to need time to digest all of this." Grace chuckled as Clare tried to drag her off the couch.

"Okay, to be continued." Lizzy smiled warmly as she stood and gave her a hug.

CHAPTER 23

For the rest of the afternoon and evening, Grace devoured not only the gospel of John, but dug into the Apologetic books Lizzy had given her. She was used to reading fast, and always read with an analytical mind. She approached the Bible and these books no differently, but there was something different about the Bible—when she read it, her heart quickened, as if it wasn't just words she was reading. Lizzy told her it was because the words came from God, and that God was speaking into her heart. Grace was starting to believe that Lizzy was right.

Grace telephoned Niall on Monday morning and told him she wouldn't be coming back for the appeal. The disappointment in his voice ripped her heart apart, but she couldn't give him what he wanted. She also called the Prosecutor's Office and told her boss she didn't know when she'd be returning.

Lizzy set aside as much time as she could to spend with

Grace, but on Tuesday, Lizzy suggested Grace attend Daniel's evening class.

"I'm not sure I'd fit in, Lizzy. Are you sure it'd be all right?"

"Absolutely. Daniel's a great teacher, and it'll be good for you to be amongst others who are also seeking. Besides, I'm sure Brianna would be excited to have you there."

"I'll think about it." Grace closed her Bible and drained the remains of her cup of tea.

"Do that, Grace. I'm sure you'll enjoy it. But now, I've got a trip to town. Would you like to come?"

"I'll pass, if you don't mind. I think I'll take a walk."

"No problem, Grace. Enjoy your day." Bending down, Lizzy gave her a hug and then left.

THE DAY WAS warm by Scottish standards, and Grace was eager to get out amongst the hills and have time to think by herself. There was something magical about the wide open spaces, so different from the hustle and bustle of downtown Belfast with its heavy traffic and constant noise. Out here amongst the hills of heather, the only sounds came from the occasional bleat of a sheep and the squawk of red kites as they soared in the air.

Sitting on a rock above Loch Linnhe, Grace breathed in the clean, fresh air and tried to settle her heart and mind. As she gazed out at the hills in the distance, one of the verses she and Lizzy had studied that same morning came to mind. John chapter 5, verse 24: "I tell you the truth, whoever hears my words and believes Him who sent me has eternal life and will not be condemned; he has passed over from death to life." She drew a breath and shook her head. *God, I find that really hard to believe. How could you not condemn me for murder?* The old battle surfaced, and tears streamed down her cheeks. *All those people, blown to shreds. God, I don't deserve your love and forgiveness.* Drawing her knees up under her chin, she wrapped her arms around them and rocked back and forth and began to sob. The sobbing increased the more she remembered. *All those people. God... I'm so sorry...* Gut wrenching sobs that had been building for so long rose from deep inside her. *I didn't mean to kill them. You know that...* She rolled onto the grass, curling into the fetal position as tears spilled down her cheeks. Deep, guttural weeping rose from her innermost being until she could cry no more, but neither could she move. Maybe she should stay here and let the buzzards fight over her body—that was all she was good for.

RYAN WAS out for his afternoon walk when he saw someone lying on the grass up on the hill above the loch. If it hadn't been for the deep agonising wailing coming from that direction, he would have missed seeing the person altogether, but he immediately hurried up the hill in case the person was in trouble.

As he approached, he gasped. It was Grace! He bent down on one knee and brushed the hair off her face. "Grace, what are you doing here?"

Her face was damp, and when she opened her eyes, pain and anguish filled them. His heart ached for her. *Lord God, please bless dear Grace. Whatever's going on with her, help her to give it to You, dear Lord.* "Grace, can you hear me?" Sitting down beside her, he stroked her hair. Her body shuddered with deep, heart-wrenching sobs.

She lifted her head slowly and looked into his eyes. "God will never forgive me for what I've done." Her voice was raspy and weak, and her head flopped back onto the ground.

"That's not true. It doesn't matter what you've done, nothing's too big for God to forgive."

She shook her head and began weeping again.

Ryan looked at her shaking body. God was working on her, that was for sure, but what had she done that was so bad? *Lord God, please give me words that will reach her heart.* He continued stroking her hair. "I thought that once, too, Grace, but God's offer of forgiveness covers all sin, no matter how big or small. Can I tell you my story?" He swallowed hard. Very few people knew the full details of his past, but he wanted to tell Grace. In the short time he'd known her, something had been happening inside him, and he wondered if this might be the beginning of something special. If he wanted her to trust him, he had to start by trusting her.

Grace sniffed and nodded weakly.

He sucked in a breath. This wasn't going to be easy… "I didn't leave the army by choice."

Grace's head jolted up. "What do you mean?"

He blew out his breath. "It all started when I was sent to Aden. Do you know where that is?"

She nodded.

"It was 1964, and I was in my second tour of duty. I'd never wanted to join the army, but it was expected of me. My family has a military background, and my father encouraged me to join as an Officer. I joined when I was eighteen, straight from school. Aden was like something I'd never seen before... hot, dry, and full of families living in the most basic of houses, if you could call them that. I would have much preferred to have been sent there as an aid worker, not as a combat soldier, but I did what everyone else did, and put on a stiff upper lip, and did my job. Whenever I was faced with a kill or be killed situation, I never looked the person in the eye before I pulled the trigger. I could never come to terms with taking someone's life, but it was him or me, so I had no choice.

"My family was proud of me. I was promoted, and offered a position in the Special Services, but I was living someone else's life, not mine. I kept it hidden. My father, in particular, would have been devastated if he knew how I felt.

"When I was sent to the Falklands in '82, I snapped. I'd kept everything bottled up all those years, but I just couldn't do it anymore. I had a breakdown, and was sent to hospital. It was the most humiliating time of my life. I'd let myself down, my family down, my country down." He squeezed his eyes shut and shuddered. "I was medically discharged. Pensioned out, as my father calls it."

Grace straightened and touched his wrist. She'd stopped crying, but her eyes were etched with red. "I'm so sorry, Ryan. That must have been awful."

Ryan shrugged. "Yeah, it was at the time, but I got to talking to the chaplain while I was in Rehab. A guy by the name of Rob." He smiled and gazed out at the mountains. "Rob was a cool dude. He talked to me about God, and how He could help me to forgive myself. I felt like I was a failure, and I felt guilty about all the people I'd killed, even though I was just doing my job. That guilt weighed me down for so many years. Over several months, Rob helped me put the pieces of my life together, and I was finally able to forgive myself when I asked God into my life.

"Rob explained to me about Jesus dying on the cross for my sins, and that if I believed, and asked Him into my life, He'd forgive all my sins, and would give me a new heart and a new mind, and free me from all that guilt." Smiling, Ryan looked down at Grace. "So I did. I can't explain what happened, but it was like a load was lifted from me, and in that moment I was finally free from the guilt and despair that had been with me for years. My recovery after that was quick. I was discharged from Rehab within three weeks, and went home to my family a changed person. My father still doesn't understand, but I don't judge him for that." He paused, and looking into her eyes, brushed tears from her face.

"You can trust Him, Grace. He promises to forgive all sins, even the big ones, because in His eyes, they're all the same. No sin is any different or worse to God. We're all sinners in need of His saving grace. He sees what's in our hearts. If we truly believe in Him, and we're truly sorry for our sins and ask Him for forgiveness, He wipes our slates clean and gives us brand new beginnings." Ryan paused again and looked deeply into her eyes. He prayed her heart would be open to God's cleansing love. "Will you do that, Grace? Will you take Him at His word and give your heart to Him?"

Tears gathered in the corners of her eyes and one by one rolled down her cheeks as she nodded. "Yes." Her voice was soft and barely audible. She straightened further, and shuffled to sit beside him. "Yes, I will, Ryan." Her voice grew in strength and conviction.

"That's wonderful, Grace, you won't regret it." His whole face spread into a smile as he took her hand. "Just say this prayer after me, okay?"

～

GRACE NODDED her head as Ryan bowed his head and began the prayer. "Dear Lord, I know I'm a sinner, but I also believe that You sent Your Son, Jesus Christ to this earth for one purpose, to die a sinless death on the cross to bridge the gap between God and man."

Grace repeated Ryan's words in a quiet but sincere voice. It was like someone else praying, but she knew it was her, and something was happening deep inside her.

"Lord God, I repent of my sin, and ask You to forgive me for all my sins." Her voice caught in her throat as tears trickled down her cheek. "I want to take Jesus as my Lord and Saviour, and to live with You as my Lord and King." She took a slow breath. "Please fill me with your Holy Spirit, and give me a new heart and a new mind. Thank you, Lord Jesus. Please help me to live my life in a way that will bring honour and glory to You. Amen."

Ryan pulled her close as tears streamed down her face. "You're now a child of God, Grace, forgiven, clean, and perfect in God's sight. He's living in your heart, now, and you don't need to carry that burden anymore." He released her and peered into her eyes. "How do you feel?"

Grace sucked in a breath and let it out slowly. How did she feel? Lighter? Certainly different. It was like a load had been lifted from her... something inexplicable had happened, something she'd never expected. She wiped her face and returned Ryan's smile. "I feel strange... different. It's like you said, I don't know how to explain it." But it was true. God had taken the load of guilt off her, and she was cleansed and new. "I need to tell Lizzy and Danny. They'll be so excited."

Ryan smiled at her as he gently took her hand in his, his gaze holding firm. "Brianna will be excited, too."

"Yes, of course." Grace made no effort to retrieve her hand. Her heart pounded. Was it wrong to hope he'd kiss her moments after she'd given her heart to the Lord?

"Grace, I've been waiting for this moment since the day you arrived. I can't tell you how happy I am that you've given your life to Jesus. It's just the beginning of a whole new life for you. God has great things in store for you." As he paused, he rubbed his thumb gently along the top of her hand. "We've only known each other for a short time, but there's a connection between us. Do you feel it too?"

Swallowing hard, Grace nodded. She didn't trust herself to speak.

"If you're willing, I'd love to get to know you better, and see where God might lead us." His eyes were sincere and gentle, just like his voice.

Was she hearing right? Ryan wanted to get to know her better? This strong, handsome man she thought she'd like to have a quick fling with, wanted to get to know her? To spend time with her? She gulped. That was all very well, as long as he didn't expect her to give up her secret. God may have forgiven her, but what would Ryan do if he found out what she'd done? He might understand she hadn't meant to do it, but he was a soldier, and she'd been in one of the radical groups they were fighting against. In fact, he might even have been there that day the bomb went off. She gulped, and then she remembered... God had forgiven her, and she had no need to think about it ever again.

A smile trembled over her lips. "I think I'd like that."

He squeezed her hand and gave her a smile that sent her heart racing. If only he'd kiss her...

CHAPTER 24

*N*either Grace nor Ryan were in a hurry to return that afternoon. For Grace, it was a magical time of new beginnings, and for the first time ever, she felt blissfully happy and fully alive. The colours in the sky and the hills and the loch seemed so much brighter, the air so much fresher. She was wrapped in a silken cocoon of euphoria as she clung to Ryan's warm, strong hand.

Several times they stopped, and just sat and talked. One time, as they sat beside a bubbling brook, Grace asked him more about his family, about where he'd grown up, and what had brought him here to the highlands. He told her his family lived in the south of England, but they had Scottish heritage, which is what had drawn him to this place.

Grace angled her head to study his profile as she twiddled a piece of heather between her fingers.

"After Rehab, I was ready for a new life, and to be honest, I've never had any regrets about being here. I get to help people who are struggling just like I was, and I get to go hiking, abseiling and rock climbing as much as I want. I love these highlands." He smiled at her as he chuckled. "I think they're in my blood. I should have been born here, not in southern England."

"It *is* lovely countryside, and there's so much history."

"You're not wrong. I'll have to take you exploring."

"I'd like that."

She dreaded him asking about her childhood. He didn't... instead he asked why she'd become a lawyer, but that was almost as difficult to answer without giving away hers and Brianna's secrets.

She leaned forward and hugged her knees, her thoughts filtering back to those days when she and Brianna survived on next to nothing, just so she could get through her course and become a lawyer. *Why had she done it?* Why had she put herself through such stress and pressure? Grace knew the answer, but could she tell Ryan? She drew a breath. He'd entrusted her with things from his past he'd probably rather not have shared, so she probably should share a little... just a little...

"Things happened to Bibi and me when we were staying at our aunt's and uncle's place in Londonderry after Mam died." She lifted her head and stared at the water gurgling down the brook's narrow path. "It wasn't good. I can't really say what happened unless Bibi has already told you..."

Ryan put out his hand and touched Grace's arm. "I know part of it, Grace. She opened up last night at her inner healing session."

Grace's eyes widened. "Did she tell you she'd been..." she couldn't say it...

Ryan angled his head. "Raped?"

Grace nodded.

"Yes, she did." His eyes were as soft as a doe's.

"Did she tell you who did it?"

Ryan shook his head. "No, but she said she had a baby who died."

Tears pricked Grace's eyes and she lowered them. It was one thing talking about it with Bibi, but totally different talking about it with Ryan...

"It must have been so hard on you both."

Nodding, Grace pushed back her tears and swallowed hard. "It was so sad. And that's what made me determined to become a barrister. To put people like..." she stopped mid-sentence. She couldn't disclose who'd raped Bibi without opening herself up to questions about why they hadn't reported their cousins. About Aunt Hilda's threat to expose her secret if she ever told anyone who'd raped her sister.

"You've done well for yourself, Grace. I looked you up... the youngest female to work as a barrister for the DPP. Impressive."

She shrugged. "It seems kind of surreal sitting here talking about it. It's like a different life."

"Are you missing it?"

She turned her head and looked at him. His blue eyes were compelling, magnetic. Her heart pounded. *Not when I'm with you...* She gave him a small smile. "It's been good to have a break."

"How much longer have you got?" His soothing voice gently probed.

"As long as I want." She could hardly lift her voice above a whisper as her heart hammered in her ears. If only he'd kiss her. She longed to be wrapped in his arms.

"Well, let's make it count." He put his arm around her shoulder and drew her close, kissing the top of her head. "I think I'm falling for you, Grace O'Connor."

Ryan's words sent waves of joy through Grace's body—she thought she might burst. In his arms, she felt safe, secure and loved, wrapped in an invisible warmth. Tilting her face, her heart lurched as she gazed into his eyes. "And I think I'm falling for you, Ryan MacGregor." His face was so close, his breath warm.

He lifted his hand and traced her hairline slowly with the tip of his finger. "You're very beautiful, Grace."

She raised her brows playfully. "You're not bad yourself."

"I shouldn't do this, but I really want to kiss you."

Her heart beat wildly. "You have my permission."

His kiss was slow and tender, and she never wanted it to end. When he lifted his mouth, her lips were still warm and hungering for more, but somehow she knew she'd have to wait. This wasn't going to be the quick fling she'd hankered after, instead, it was going to be a relationship that grew slowly, with purpose and control. *How would she cope?*

"We'd best get back." Ryan stood and held his hand out to her. Drawing her up, he wrapped his arms around her and held her tight as he whispered into her hair. "I'm looking forward to getting to know you, Grace."

Her heart steadied as a warm glow of content flowed through her. Somehow, this felt right.

SOON AFTER, as the sun slipped behind Ben Nevis, Grace and Ryan returned to the cottage. Stepping inside, Grace's hand shook a little as she walked down the hall towards the back of the house where the children's happy chatter came from. Two momentous events to tell Lizzy about, and for some reason, Grace felt a little nervous. Ryan's hand on the small of her back as he walked beside her helped steady her nerves, but she couldn't help but wonder what Lizzy would think about her and Ryan. Yes, Lizzy had been encouraging it, but now it had actually happened?

Lizzy glanced up as Grace entered, her eyes popping as her gaze shifted to Ryan and then back to Grace. She left her grocery bags on the table and stepped forward, taking Grace's hand. "Grace?"

Grace's eyes misted over and a lump appeared in her throat as she gave Lizzy an enthusiastic nod. "I gave my heart to Jesus, Lizzy."

Lizzy's eyes widened further and her whole face lit up. "Really? That's wonderful news, Grace." Lizzy threw her arms around Grace and hugged her, jumping up and down on the spot like an excited schoolgirl.

Grace laughed.

Lizzy finally stopped jumping, but left her hand on Grace's arm. "We'll have to tell Daniel... he'll be so excited." She glanced at the clock. "He should be home any time now."

"I thought I might go to his class tonight."

"Great idea, Grace. Now, let me get you both a cup of tea..." Her gaze travelled to Ryan again, her eyebrows arching.

Crossing his arms, Ryan leaned against the door-frame. "Guess you're wondering how I came to be with Grace?"

Lizzy nodded. "Yes."

Grace's hands twisted nervously in front of her, but Ryan flashed her a grin that dismissed any concern she might have held.

"I came across her while we were both out walking."

"Yes... and is there more you want to tell me?" Lizzy's eyes held an amused glint.

"Maybe..." He reached his arm out to Grace, and slipping it around her shoulders, drew her to his side. "We might just be an item." His face split into a broad grin.

Squealing, Lizzy jumped up and down again on the spot. "No! That is the second best news of the day!" She threw her arms around them. "That's wonderful. I'm so happy for you both."

"Mum, what's so exciting?" Dillon raced in from the play room and looked up at her and then at Grace and then at Ryan.

Grace laughed at the innocence in his eyes and leaned closer to Ryan, cocooning herself against his strong body.

Ryan chuckled. "Auntie Grace and I have become good friends, Dillon my mate."

As Ryan pulled her closer, Grace had never felt so contented and loved.

Lizzy made tea, and soon after, Daniel walked in. Lizzy told him about Grace coming to the Lord, and like her, he was overjoyed. "This is amazing. Two sisters, both coming to the Lord. How special is that?" As he hugged her, Grace felt his body tremble. Tears rolled down his cheeks, but his eyes were filled with joy. "Can I pray for you, Grace?"

Grace smiled as she let out a small laugh. "If you want to."

He smiled. "I'd love to." Leaving his hand on her shoulder, he bowed his head. "Lord God, we rejoice that both Grace and Brianna have given their hearts to You. Thank You that they know Your love in a real way, and that you've cleansed them and given them hope for a bright future with You as Lord and King. Be with Grace in the days ahead as she learns more about You, and as she grows closer to You. Guide her as to what You would want her to do with her life. Thank You so much, Lord, I'm just so excited and grateful that both Grace and Brianna have come to know You. You are indeed a mighty God. In Jesus' precious name, Amen."

Grace wiped the tears off her face and then gave Danny a hug. "Thanks, big brother."

"My pleasure, Grace." He smiled at her. "You know who we need to call?"

Grace angled her head. "No... who?"

Danny chuckled. "Caleb. He's been praying for you for so long."

Grace smiled. She could just imagine the look of shock on Caleb's face when he heard.

"I've already told him about Brianna. He won't believe you've finally given in, Grace." Danny chuckled again.

"No, he probably won't."

Danny draped his arm across her shoulder. "Come, let's call him now."

"Okay..." She cast a backward glance at Ryan as Danny led her out to the back room where the phone was and chuckled. *Wait until Caleb hears I'm seeing someone...*

As expected, Caleb was just as over-joyed as Danny. "That's

great news, Grace. Welcome to the family. I can't wait to tell Caitlin."

"Thanks Caleb. Thanks for praying for us both for all those years."

"It was nothing, Grace. We knew it would happen one day. This is really special." The sincerity in Caleb's voice warmed her heart and made her miss him. "So when do you think you'll be coming home? I thought you were coming back for the appeal?"

Grace's grip on the receiver tightened. She'd been dreading that question... what could she say? "I... I changed my mind, Caleb. I'm not sure what I'm doing right now, but I'll let you know, okay?"

"Okay... but you might need to call Niall. He's been coming around to visit a lot. He's like a lost kid without you here, Grace."

Grace's heart fell. She lowered her voice. "I've told him countless times it's over between us, Caleb." For some reason she couldn't bring herself to tell Caleb about Ryan. Not that she was embarrassed, but all of a sudden she felt coy.

"Well, he doesn't think it is. He's determined to get you back."

She let out a heavy sigh. "I'll call him again."

"Good... you do that."

"I will." How could she tell Niall she'd taken up with someone else? It'd break his heart.

"Thanks for calling, Grace, it's been great talking to you, and I'm so glad about your news."

"You're welcome, Caleb. Give my love to Caitlin and the girls."

"Will do."

Grace hung up the receiver and slumped against the wall.

Looking at her with drawn brows, Danny placed his hand on her shoulder. "What's wrong, Grace?"

She let out another heavy sigh and rolled her eyes. "Men problems."

Danny laughed. "What do you mean? I didn't know you had anyone in your life."

Danny's laugh cheered her and she let out another small chuckle as she glanced at Ryan in the other room. "There's two, actually. One's right here in your kitchen, and the other's back home." She spoke quietly so Ryan couldn't hear—she'd tell him about Niall later.

Danny's eyes widened. "You mean…? You … you and Ryan?"

A coy grin grew on her face as she nodded slowly.

"When did that happen?"

"This afternoon. It was Ryan who led me to the Lord."

Danny ran his hand through his hair. "Wow. I had no idea. And who's the other?"

"Niall. You don't know him, but I've known him since university days. He's a barrister, and he asked me to marry him years ago. We met up again recently."

"Why didn't you accept him?"

She shrugged. "It just wasn't right. I didn't want to get married." She couldn't tell him the truth.

"But he's not taking no for an answer?"

She shrugged. "Seems like it."

"Well, you'll just have to tell him about Ryan."

"Guess I will."

Lizzy came out and slipped her arm around Danny's waist. "What's going on out here? Can I join?"

Danny kissed the top of her hair. "Course you can. Grace is just telling me about her men problems."

Grace glared at him before glancing towards the kitchen. She breathed a sigh of relief... Ryan was engrossed with Clare and James, colouring at the kitchen table.

Danny lifted his hand to his mouth. "Sorry."

"What's this about *men problems*, Grace," Lizzy whispered, her brows drawn. "I didn't know there was someone else."

Grace let out a breath. "I was just telling Danny about this barrister friend of mine—he asked me to marry him recently, and I turned him down, for the second time.... seems he's not taking no for an answer."

"Oh dear... what are you going to do?" Lizzy's eyes softened.

"I'll have to call him. And I'll also have to tell Ryan about Niall."

"Good idea."

"But not now—I'll call later. I couldn't handle it right now."

"Let's get some dinner, and then it'll be time for Danny's class... if you're still going?" Lizzy raised her brow.

"Are you coming to my class, Grace?" Danny's face lit up.

"Thought I might." A playful grin grew on her face.

"Sweet."

CHAPTER 25

*T*hat evening, Ryan stayed for dinner, and then held Grace's hand as they strolled to the main building for Danny's class. Being late summer, it was still light, even though it was almost half past seven. Grace shivered as a cool breeze came off the loch, and Ryan put his arm around her.

"This still feels really strange, Ryan, but I like it." She snuggled closer to him.

He chuckled. "I know what you mean... I do, too." Turning his head, the beginning of a smile tipped the corners of his mouth.

Brianna's eyes popped when Grace followed Ryan into the classroom a few minutes later. She was sitting between Brayden and one of the girls. Jumping up, Brianna hurried towards Grace, holding her arms out. "Good to see you, Grace! What made you come?"

Steering Brianna to the back of the classroom, Grace told her quietly about giving her heart to the Lord that afternoon.

Brianna's eyes glistened as she threw her arms around Grace. "We can both leave the past behind us now and start afresh. I'm so excited about it all." Stepping back, she grabbed Grace's hands and met her gaze with eyes full of excitement. "I had prayer and counselling last night, and you know what?"

"No. What?" Grace angled her head.

Brianna's voice lowered to a whisper. "I think I can almost forgive those boys for what they did to me."

"Oh Bibi..." Tears sprung to Grace's eyes. "I'm not sure I can do that yet, but that's good for you. Do you feel better?"

She nodded. "I don't know why we didn't listen to Caleb years ago."

Grace lifted her hand to Brianna's face and tucked a stray piece of hair behind her ear. "We both coped in our own ways, Bibi."

"I guess so." She glanced down quickly before lifting her eyes again. "And you know what?"

Grace shook her head. She hoped Brianna wasn't going to say that something was going on between her and Brayden. He still seemed like such a lost soul, even though he'd walked forward at church the other day.

"I don't even want drugs anymore."

Relief flowed through Grace's body as she smiled at Brianna. "That's great, Bibi."

"I know I've still got a long road ahead, but so far, so good."

Danny cleared his throat. "Would you two at the back like to take your seats?"

Spinning around, Grace caught his amused gaze and grinned. It was such a strange situation—to be in a classroom with her brother as her teacher and her sister as a fellow student, but it felt good. And what was even better? Ryan would be waiting for her outside.

Grace took her seat behind Brianna and her friends, and was surprised when Ryan joined her. Angling her head and arching her eyebrows, she leaned close to him. "What are you doing here?" She kept her voice low.

His eyes sparkled, radiating a vitality that drew her to him like a magnet. "Thought I might learn something from your brother."

Already her feelings for him were intensifying, and she couldn't stop the warmth spreading through her body when he winked at her.

She tore her gaze from his and forced herself to focus on Danny. That's what she was here for, after all.

"Welcome, everyone, and a special welcome to our newest student, my sister, Grace." As Danny held his arm out in Grace's direction, a grin stretching from ear to ear grew on his face.

Grace forced herself to smile when everyone turned and looked at her, but she wished he hadn't done that. *Brothers.*

"Okay, let's open in prayer, and then we'll begin."

Everyone returned their attention to the front and bowed their heads. Danny prayed a short prayer, asking God to open their hearts and minds to His Word and to the truths it held.

Grace shifted in her seat. Ryan's presence beside her was unnerving. How could she focus on God's Word with him so close? She felt like a school-girl with her first crush. *Take some breaths, Grace... focus...*

Danny cleared his voice. "Tonight we're looking at the two commandments that Jesus said were the most important, and how they apply to our lives here and now. Let's open our Bibles to Matthew chapter 22, verses 36 to 40."

Grace panicked. She had no idea where the book of Matthew was—she'd been reading John. She began flicking through the pages when a hand touched hers. She looked up and met Ryan's gaze. He didn't have to say anything... he took the Bible and opened it for her and smiled.

"Okay, Matthew 22, verses 36 to 40: ""Teacher, which is the greatest commandment in the Law?" Jesus replied: "Love the Lord your God with all your heart and with all your soul and with all your mind. This is the first and greatest commandment. And the second is like it: Love your neighbor as yourself. All the Law and the Prophets hang on these two commandments.""

Danny leaned forward in his chair. "For many of you, love is a foreign concept. I get that. You might have felt unloved by your parents, or maybe you were moved around between foster parents, and there was never anyone you could really call a parent. You might have been abused, or you might have been told you'd never amount to anything. Your concept of love has been tainted by this world and the experiences you've had."

Grace couldn't meet Danny's gaze... he was too close to the truth.

"Jesus came to show what true love really is. In I John chapter 4, verses 7 and 8, we read: "Dear friends, let us love one another, for love comes from God. Everyone who loves has been born of God and knows God. Whoever does not love does not know God, because God is love." To understand true love, we have to know God.

"There's no better way to get to know God than by studying Jesus's life here on earth. Jesus showed love and compassion to all people—not just those who were nice. He loved the unlovely; He loved the weak; He loved the sick; He loved the hurting; He loved those who'd been shunned because of their backgrounds or lifestyles; He loved sinners. He didn't judge them; He didn't tell them to clean themselves up before He would love them—He loved them as they were, and that's what He asks us to do—to love not only our friends and those people who are easy to love, but also to love our enemies, for want of a better word."

Looking up, Grace raised her brow. *I hope he doesn't mean I have to love Aunt Hilda...*

"In Matthew Chapter 5, verses 43 to 48, Jesus says: "You have heard that it was said, 'Love your neighbor and hate your enemy.' But I tell you, love your enemies and pray for those who persecute you, that you may be children of your Father in heaven. He causes his sun to rise on the evil and the good, and sends rain on the righteous and the unrighteous. If you love those who love you, what reward will you get? Are not even the tax collectors doing that? And if you greet only your own people, what are you doing more than others? Do not even pagans do that? Be perfect, therefore, as your heavenly Father is perfect.""

Grace's shoulders slumped. *That's exactly what he means... I can't do that...*

Danny shifted in his chair and began gesticulating with his hands. "We can't do this in our own strength—it doesn't come naturally. We must call on the power of the Holy Spirit living in us to grow the fruit of the spirit—love, joy, peace, patience, kindness, goodness, faithfulness, gentleness and self-control, inside us, so that we can love like Jesus."

He paused and took a deep, slow breath. "The more we love God with all our hearts, souls and minds, the more we'll love our neighbours, even the unlovely ones, like Jesus commands us to. Love is laying down your life for your friend, like Jesus did for us when He died on the cross." He let out a small chuckle. "We're not expected to do that literally, but by putting other's needs before our own, we're effectively laying down our lives for them. We become focused on the well-being of others instead of concentrating on our own. God blesses those who care for others, who treat others with kindness and compassion, who go out of their way to make sure they have food, shelter and feel loved and wanted."

A genuine smile grew on his face. "This journey we're on is an exciting one. There's so much hate in the world because people have turned their backs on God. They don't know Him, and they don't love Him, and therefore they don't love with His love. As His people, let's commit to loving God with all our hearts, all our souls, and all our minds, and to treating each other how we'd like to be treated ourselves. Let's be kind to each other, and let's find ways to bless each other... maybe we can do something nice for someone without letting them know who did it, and we can speak nicely with each other, respecting each other, uplifting not tearing apart. The more we can practice that here, surrounded by friends, the easier it'll be to do out there amongst people we don't know."

Pausing, his gaze travelled around the room. No one made a noise. "I hope this has given you some idea of what it means to be a follower of Jesus. There aren't any rules or regulations apart from loving God and each other, but if we truly want to follow Him, we need to follow His example, and do it gladly." He smiled. "Let's pray." Raising his hand, he closed his eyes and bowed his head. "Lord God, help each of us to love You with everything we have, and to love both our neighbours and our enemies alike, just as you commanded. This doesn't come easily, as most of us have been bruised and battered by this world, but we come to You, the author and finisher of our faith, and we ask You to help us to love like You do. In Jesus' precious name, Amen."

Grace brushed tears from her eyes as Ryan reached for her hand. Where had Danny learned to speak like that? Amazing. But it wasn't only *how* he said it, it was *what* he said. After having such a challenging childhood and youth, to be able to talk about loving your enemies like he had was almost too much. It could only be God working in his life, and now she had God in her life too. Although she was excited about what He was going to do in her, she wasn't ready to love Aunt Hilda or those cousins yet, but maybe, in time... who knew?

At supper a short while later, Grace sat down with Brianna and had the best talk they'd ever had. Brianna had a clear head, and Grace had a soft heart. Brianna apologized for all the trouble she'd caused Grace and Caleb over the years, and Grace apologized for being so impatient with her. They hugged and cried, and then hugged and cried some more. Danny joined them after a while, and for the first time ever, the three of them talked about Mam and remembered just how much she'd loved them all and how much she'd given up for them.

Ryan joined them, placing his hand lightly on Grace's shoulder.

Brianna's eyes widened, her gaze travelling between the two of them. Finally, she fixed her gaze on Grace, angling her head and asking the question with her eyes.

Nodding, Grace let out a small chuckle as she lifted her face and smiled into Ryan's eyes that were caressing her with softness, sending a gentle stream of warmth through her body.

Shortly after, Ryan walked Grace back to the cottage. Darkness had set in, but the moon was trying its best to peek through the wispy clouds overhead, causing the surface of the loch to shimmer whenever it came out. His fingers were laced through hers, and his hand felt strong and firm. Gravel from the path crunched underfoot, and in the distance, a curlew called.

When they reached the cottage, Ryan turned Grace to face him and rubbed his hands on her upper arms as he gazed into her eyes. "I have to work tomorrow, but I have the following day off. I'd love to spend it with you, Grace. We could take a drive and see where we end up." He raised a brow, his grin irresistibly devastating. "Deal?"

She broke into a smile and laughed. "Deal." She couldn't think of any better way of spending a day.

His blue eyes twinkled before his expression sobered. She held her breath. Would he kiss her again? His nearness made her senses spin and her heart lurched madly. She was tempted to reach up and pull his face towards hers, but something held her back. Whilst she longed for his kiss, she'd allow him to take the lead, and she'd be patient. *Even if it killed her.*

He brushed the hair from her neck as he gazed into her eyes. Her body tingled at the touch of his hand.

He smiled into her eyes. "I'll look forward to it." He lowered his face slowly and pressed his lips against hers before gently covering her mouth in a slow, tender kiss. She longed for more, but she would not spoil this.

When he pulled away, he gazed into her eyes before kissing her forehead and turning away.

GRACE SNUCK INTO HER ROOM, flopped on her bed and closed her eyes, lifting her finger to her lips, still tingling from the sweetness of Ryan's kiss. She sighed contentedly before sitting up and bowing her head. *Lord God, thank you for bringing me into Your family. I don't deserve Your love and forgiveness, but I'm extremely grateful for it. Help me to be all that You want me to be. And thank You for Ryan. Help me not to mess it up. Amen.*

THAT NIGHT, Grace fell asleep with Ryan on her mind and warmth filling her heart.

CHAPTER 26

The next morning, Grace rose early to telephone Niall before he left for court. She hesitated as she picked up the phone. Would it be fair to call him on the morning of the appeal? Even though he wouldn't win, he'd need a clear head, and it wouldn't be right to upset him. No, she'd wait until later in the day.

She put the phone down and climbed back into bed, plumping her pillows so she could lean against them, and picked up her Bible. She flicked it open, but so many thoughts flitted through her head it was hard to focus. She should be in court today—O'Malley was her case. He was unlikely to win his appeal... he was as guilty as they came, *but what if he did?* Niall wouldn't have encouraged the appeal without some new evidence.

And then there was Ryan. A sense of anticipation flowed through her. She still had to pinch herself... but where would it lead? It was still early days, but would she marry him if he asked? She'd turned Niall down, but that was because marrying him could have jeopardised his career if her past was ever discovered, but could she, in all honesty, marry Ryan without telling him what she'd done? Could she even encourage their relationship without telling him? Would it be fair on him not to? But what if she did, and he decided to end it before it really began? Already she was lost in his charisma, good looks, and strength of character. A tumble of confused thoughts and feelings assailed her.

She let out a heavy sigh and closed her Bible. *God, what should I do? I have no idea what's ahead... but I guess You do. You're the only one I can talk to about this, so please show me what I should do. I don't think I've told you this, but I'm really sorry for what I did. I feel so bad for all the people I killed, and all their families.* Her throat thickened as tears stung her eyes. *Lord, I didn't mean to kill them, You know that.* Her breathing grew heavier as she squeezed her eyes shut and tried to rid her head of the images bombarding her mind. Images she'd been trying to erase for so long without success.

Curling into a ball, she sobbed herself to sleep.

SOMETIME LATER, Grace woke to soft knocking on the door. She glanced at the clock. Her eyes sprung open. *Midday... how did that happen?*

"Grace, are you okay?" Lizzy sounded slightly worried.

Grace sat up and pushed her hair back off her face. "Yes... sorry, I slept in. I'll be out in a minute."

"No problem. Just checking to make sure you were all right."

Grace smiled. It was nice having someone care. "Thanks. I'll be out soon." She slipped out of bed and opened the curtains. No wonder she'd slept. Rain tumbled down and a thick mist hung over the loch, giving it a kind of ethereal look. Ben Nevis was invisible. A great day to curl up with a good book. Or to sleep.

She dragged herself out of bed and stepped into the shower, turning the heat up slowly until the water was hot on her skin. She stood there for a few moments longer than she should, but it felt so nice. She still had no answer as to what she should do, but the hot water flowing over her body helped calm her thoughts. God would show her. Wasn't that a perk of being one of His children?

Shortly after, Grace entered the kitchen where Lizzy was preparing a lunch of toasted sandwiches for the children. They all looked up with eager faces, each wanting her to sit beside them.

Grace laughed. "I think it's James's turn."

Clare and Dillon both let out a wail.

"Clare, Dillon, stop it." Lizzy turned around and glared at them. "Auntie Grace might decide to go home if you keep that up."

The two children quietened momentarily as Grace took her seat beside James, opposite Clare and Dillon.

"Where's your home, Auntie Grace?" Dillon asked in his cute little voice.

"You know where Auntie Grace lives, Dillon."

"No I don't." He flashed Lizzy an annoyed look.

Grace chuckled. "I live in Ireland, where your daddy comes from."

"Is that why you speak funny?"

Grace laughed again. "I guess so."

"Dillon!"

Grace smiled at Lizzy. "It's okay, Liz. I don't mind."

"Okay…" Lizzy glared at him again as she placed a plate of steaming sandwiches in the middle of the table and took her seat at the end. "Dillon, it's your turn to give thanks."

"Okay." He held out his hands and took Lizzy's and Clare's before bowing his head.

"THANK you for the world so sweet,
    Thank you for the food we eat,
    Thank you for the birds that sing,
    Thank you God for everything."

"AMEN", everyone said in unison. Grace let go of James's and Lizzy's hands, and sat back in her chair and smiled. The children were so sweet.

Lizzy began handing out sandwiches, and the children began chattering, even Clare.

Lunch passed, and the children went into the living room to play before taking a nap. Lizzy made a pot of tea and returned to the table where Grace was still sitting.

Folding her arms, Grace angled her head. "Liz, how does God talk to you?"

Lizzy's brows lifted as she took her seat. "Interesting question, Grace. What makes you ask?"

"Oh... I've just asked Him something, and I'm wondering how He'll answer."

Lizzy leaned forward, her eyes bright. "Is it about Ryan?"

Grace chuckled. "Not directly. But I'd rather not say... I just want to know how He'll answer, that's all."

"All right..." Lizzy poured two mugs of tea and handed one to Grace. "You probably won't hear a physical voice, rather, it'll most likely be a quiet assurance that one answer is right and the other, wrong."

"Kind of like your conscience?"

"Kind of, except that you'll hear God better the more You know Him, and come to understand His ways. Answers will often come when you're reading His word, so spending time studying the Bible is a great way to learn to hear His voice. When you spend time with Him, don't just talk with Him about what you want or need. Be still before Him and listen."

Lizzy paused and sipped her tea. "I hope this is helping."

"Yes, it is. Thanks." Grace smiled at her as she replaced her mug on the table.

"Also, He'll never want you to do anything that goes against His principles, so often, all we need do is ask ourselves what Jesus would do in a particular situation, and we have the answer, because if we're honest, we probably know what He'd do."

Lizzy leaned back in her seat. "Other times it might not be as clear cut as that, but basically, if we pray for His guidance, and if our hearts and minds are committed to doing what He wants us to do, we then just have to make the best decision possible, and trust that that's His answer. Often our own needs and desires get in the way, and we don't see things from God's

SECRETS AND SACRIFICE

perspective, and we end up making wrong decisions. God is just, and He's kind. He wants the best for people, so if we use that as a guide, chances are we'll do the right thing. Sometimes you might get a real sense that He's leading you, and other times you just have to trust that your faith and understanding of what He wants will ensure you make the right decision." Lizzy paused. "Does all this make sense?"

Grace let out a sigh. It wasn't as easy and simple as she'd hoped. If only God would give her a straight answer. "Yes, it does. I guess I was just hoping He'd just tell me."

Lizzy chuckled. "Don't we all! Is it something we can pray about, Grace?"

Grace swallowed hard. This was getting a little too close for comfort. "Not really... I think it's something I have to work through on my own."

"Okay, but if you want to chat about it or pray about it together, let me know."

"Thanks, Liz." Grace sipped her tea, her hands wrapped around the mug as she gazed out the window at the mist. This thing was going to haunt her all her life. God may have forgiven her, but would Ryan ever forgive her if he found out after it was too late, presuming their relationship developed? Maybe Lizzy was right and she already knew what she had to do. Jesus would never have kept such a huge secret from someone He loved—not that she loved Ryan yet, but she might come to love him soon. He deserved honesty, even if that jeopardized their relationship and she might end up in jail. She felt ill in her stomach. "I think I need some time alone, Liz." Grace pushed her chair back and stood.

"No problem. I'll be praying for you, Grace." Lizzy rubbed

Grace's arm and then hugged her. "Whatever's troubling you, God will help you through it. Okay?"

"Okay. And thank you." Grace gave Lizzy a grateful smile and then left the kitchen, sneaking past the living room to avoid attracting the children's attention. As much as she loved them, she needed to sort this thing out.

BACK IN HER ROOM, Grace opened her Bible randomly at the book of Ephesians and began reading from the beginning. Sometime later, when she reached Chapter 4, verse 25, her eyes popped. "Therefore each of you must put off falsehood and speak truthfully to your neighbor, for we are all members of one body." Her heart thumped, but she knew... the answer was clear. She had no choice. She had to tell Ryan.

For the remainder of the afternoon, Grace read the Bible and prayed. Her senses were heightened, because for more than fifteen years, she'd vowed she'd tell no one what she'd done. She'd even chosen not to report Brianna's rape so she wouldn't be found out, and sacrificed marriage with Niall because of it. And now she was potentially sacrificing a relationship with Ryan. But she had to. She had no choice. God had spoken. No more secrets. She had to speak truthfully with Ryan before they got serious. She gulped. *While he had time to back out...*

Ryan would have to report her. If he was the honest Christian he professed to be, he'd have no choice. She suppressed the urge to vomit as her stomach heaved at the prospect of being charged with murder. Grace O'Connor, Barrister, Prosecutor, *murderer*. Why had she thought she'd get away with it?

Even after all these years, she constantly expected a knock on her door, but it had never come, and now here she was, about to give herself up. Maybe she could ask Niall to represent her. Then he'd know the reason she'd turned him down. *Niall!* She'd planned on calling him.... she couldn't do it now. *Tomorrow...*

She fell to her knees. "God, I feel so sick. I know this is the right thing to do, but why is doing the right thing so hard? Please help me to tell Ryan tomorrow about what I've done. I know he'll understand how I'm feeling, but he won't understand why I did it. Give me strength to face the consequences of my actions, even if that means going to prison. God, steady my heart, and help me do what's right in Your eyes. Amen."

If she had any cigarettes left, she would have smoked one, but as she hadn't bought any since arriving, that wasn't an option. Instead, she told Lizzy she was going for a walk, put on a rain jacket and wellies, and stepped outside. What did it matter if she got wet? She had to do something to get her mind off what was about to happen.

THE GROUND WAS MUDDY, sodden and slippery as she made her way along the track beside the loch. The rain was a grey blanket around her, but at least she could see the foothills of Ben Nevis, and the sheep still grazing as if the rain didn't matter.

Even though she knew what she was about to do was right, a heaviness hung in her heart. Maybe this was how Jesus felt when He knew His time on earth was coming to an end, not that she could compare herself to Jesus, but at least He would know how she was feeling. *But He hadn't done anything wrong.* She had, and she deserved her punishment.

She walked for more than an hour. When she came to a fast flowing burn, she stopped—it would be folly to try to cross it. But then, maybe dying out here would be better than going to prison. She sucked in a breath. *Where did that thought come from?* She sunk to her knees and sobbed. *I'm sorry, God. I didn't mean that.*

She half expected Ryan to come along like he had yesterday. Had it only been a day since he'd led her to the Lord? It seemed much longer. He didn't come. She pulled herself back up and retraced her steps. The words from one of the songs they'd sung at church on Sunday played through her mind... "What a friend we have in Jesus, all our sins and griefs to bear, what a privilege to carry everything to God in prayer." She sang the words out loud as she stepped over rocks and logs, and tried to stay upright on the slippery grass. The words began to cheer her, and she prayed about the conversation she'd have tomorrow with Ryan, and decided to leave the outcome with God.

THAT NIGHT she didn't need to put on a happy face. She had confidence that God would sustain and bless her because she was doing what He wanted, even if it might mean losing Ryan and going to prison.

CHAPTER 27

*D*espite having peace in her heart, Grace had trouble sleeping, so sometime during the night she rose and wrote Niall a letter. She owed him that much at least. When she confessed to the Police, as no doubt she'd be doing in the next few days, she'd make sure he got it then. At least then he'd know why she hadn't agreed to marry him. She also read more of her Bible, clinging to the comfort it provided that God would uphold and bless those who did right in the sight of the Lord.

Morning finally came. When Grace drew back the curtains, instead of a grey, misty morning, the sky was bathed in a glorious blue, and below, the loch shimmered in the early morning sunshine, warming her heart. It was going to be a lovely day, but how would it end? Grace's heart pounded once more, but as she gazed out at the beauty of God's creation, she reminded herself that God was with her, and would uphold her. Calmness returned to her soul.

As much as she loved Lizzy and the children, Grace breathed a sigh of relief when she entered the kitchen to discover it empty. She turned the kettle on and made her herself a strong coffee. A note on the table caught her attention, and she picked it up.

Dear Grace,

Sorry we missed you—I didn't want to wake you... I've taken the children into town to see the doctor. I hope you're okay and that you have a nice day. We'll see you tonight.

Lots of love and God bless,

Lizzy

A nice day... Closing her eyes, Grace gripped the edge of the table and drew a long, slow breath. *If only...* Releasing her breath, she sat, resting her head in the palm of her hand. How many times had she played over in her mind how she'd tell Ryan, and imagined the look of shock in his eyes when she did? But she had to do it, and God would be with her. Maybe they could have a nice *morning...* and then she'd tell him.

Grace drank her coffee and poured another. Taking the mug back to her room, she placed it on her dresser while she showered. Ryan was picking her up at nine, so she had less than twenty minutes to be ready. She chose a pair of dark blue designer jeans, a red collared shirt, and matching red ballet flats. She threw in a denim jacket just in case.

Looking in the mirror, she applied a light coat of foundation, some blusher, and some red lipstick to match her shirt. She decided to leave her hair down. She peered into the mirror. Would anyone pick her as a murderer? She'd looked into the eyes of many a killer, and they all had a look about them. *Did she?*

She closed her eyes and swallowed. *God, please be with me today. I need Your strength more than ever to do this.*

If they were to have a few hours of enjoyment before she dropped the bombshell, she needed to pull herself together before Ryan arrived. She'd done it before, and she could do it again. Drawing a deep breath, she steadied herself and opened her eyes, downed the rest of her coffee, picked up her bag, and went outside to wait for him.

HE TURNED up on the dot of nine in an old, olive-grey Land Rover. Not quite the car she was used to, but then, this was the Scottish Highlands, not downtown Belfast. Pulling up in front of the cottage, he jumped out and jogged around to where she stood in front of the white, picket fence.

Grace's heart skipped a beat. So ruggedly handsome in blue jeans and white polo shirt, she struggled to tear her eyes away from Ryan's powerful, well-muscled body.

He stopped in front of her and gave her a smile that sent her pulses racing. At the same time, her heart was crumbling. Taking her hands in his, he smiled into her eyes. *The eyes of a murderer.* "It's great to see you, Grace. Are you ready for today?"

She swallowed hard and returned his smile. "Absolutely. Where are you taking me?"

A mischievous look came into his eyes. "You'll have to wait and see." He chuckled. "Come on, let's go." He let go of one of her hands and led her with the other to his truck before opening the door.

He must have seen her raised eyebrows as she clambered

inside. "Don't you like it?" He wore an amused grin as he climbed in beside her.

She cast her gaze over the basic dashboard, the long gear stick, the torn seat, and the metal floor in the back. "What makes you think that?"

He shrugged as he let out another chuckle. "I have no idea."

Their eyes locked. Grace's heart pounded. Leaning towards her, he lifted his hand to her cheek. "You look lovely today, Grace." His voice was soft, tender. He leaned closer, brushing his lips gently across hers, teasing her.

"Thank you." She could hardly lift her voice above a whisper. She so desperately wanted him to kiss her. His nearness was overwhelming.

He pulled back but left his hand on her cheek. "We'd best go."

Her heart fell as he straightened and turned the key in the ignition. She studied his profile with sadness. They'd have so little time together.

Ryan pointed the Land Rover northwards on the A82 towards Inverness, but soon after turned right onto the A86.

"So, where are we going?" She had to speak loudly to be heard over the engine, and she didn't really care where they were going. It was just nice sitting beside Ryan, watching his strong arms handling this beast of a truck, but she guessed she should have some idea.

Turning his head, Ryan leaned towards her. "Thought we'd take a drive into the Cairngorms, stop at Aviemore for a coffee, and then decide where to from there."

"Sounds good." Grace smiled at him and then returned her

attention to the countryside, all the while praying for strength for the conversation they'd soon be having.

Half an hour later, Ryan pulled off the road and headed onto a smaller track.

Grace angled her head and laughed. "Is this the right way?"

He chuckled. "I know a short cut."

She raised a brow. "I hope it doesn't turn into a long cut."

"We'll be all right. Don't you worry."

They bounced along the rough track, climbing steadily until they reached a plateau. Ryan pulled over and killed the engine. "Come on, I want to show you something."

Grace climbed out as gracefully as she could and took the hand Ryan offered. The clean, crisp air took her breath away. All around were mountains dotted with sheep and heather, craggy rocks and the remains of old stone buildings. So peaceful, so quiet, so beautiful. "Where are we going?"

"I found the remains of one of my ancestor's cottages a while ago. There's not much to see, but it's still interesting."

"Do you still have family around here?"

"Some. Distant relatives, but they've made me feel part of the clan, even though I'm a Sassenach."

Grace laughed. "What would they think of me?"

"They'd love you, Grace." His eyes flashed warmly as he wrapped his arm around her.

She chuckled, but the heaviness in her chest was growing. *They won't when they know all about me...* But with Ryan's arm around her she felt safe, and she tried to push away the impending situation and just enjoy the present. "Tell me about them."

She listened eagerly as he talked about the clan MacGregor,

the most famous member being the one and only Rob Roy MacGregor.

"The outlaw?" Grace laughed.

"Yep."

She looked more closely at him. "Ah, I see the resemblance..."

He hit her playfully, and then stopped all of a sudden, gathering her in his arms. He flicked some hair off her shoulder and gazed into her eyes.

Her heart thudded noisily.

"I enjoy being with you, Grace. We understand each other." His voice was soft and warm, and sincere.

His look was so galvanizing she almost melted in his arms. "Yes, we do." Her voice caught in her throat. An undeniable magnetism was building between them, and the mere touch of his hand against her cheek sent a warming shiver through her.

Her knees weakened when he lowered his face and pressed his lips against hers. His kiss was slow and gentle, and she savoured every moment of it as if it were the last kiss she'd ever receive. When they parted, it was as if they'd entered a whole new world together. *If only she didn't have to spoil it...*

He took her hand as they continued along the track in comfortable silence.

When they reached the pile of rocks which Ryan told her were the ruins of a crofter's cottage that he believed belonged to one of his ancestors, she laughed. "You brought me all the way up here to show me a pile of rocks!"

"They're special rocks. Can't you see that?" He bent down and picked one up.

She looked at the rock in his hand and laughed. "It's just a rock!"

He chuckled. "I guess so. But it's kind of cool to think my ancestors used to live up here." He turned around and gazed out at the bare mountains that stretched into the distance.

"It must have been a hard life." Grace's tone sobered.

"They were a tough lot, but yes."

"Ryan..." Grace's heart pounded.

As Ryan turned to face her, his expression changed. "What's wrong, Grace?" He stepped closer, placing his hands on her shoulders.

"I... I need to tell you something." Her pulse raced. She swallowed the lump in her throat.

"What is it?" His eyes held concern as they peered into hers.

Her shoulders slumped. "I wasn't going to tell you until later, but I can't wait any longer. Can we sit?"

"Sure. How about over there?" He pointed to a flat grassy patch to his right.

Once seated, she took his hand and looked into his eyes. "I don't know how to tell you this, Ryan, but I need to, because once you hear it, you may not want to be involved with me."

"Grace, it's okay. I don't get shocked easily."

She grimaced. "No, but this might be the exception." Her bottom lip quivered as tears stung her eyes.

He wrapped his arm around her shoulder and tilted her face towards his with his fingers. "You don't have to tell me, but if you feel you need to, I'm not going to judge you. Okay?"

Blinking back tears, Grace's body shuddered as she drew a big breath. "Okay." Her voice was barely a whisper. She took several more breaths. "When I was sixteen, I did something really stupid." She gulped. "I got involved with a radical group." She gulped again. How could she do this? Her chest heaved.

"It's okay, Grace. Take your time." Ryan stroked her hand and pulled her closer to him.

She sucked in a steadying breath. Now she'd started, she had to continue. "I... I think I was just looking for something to be part of." She blew out her breath. "Being at Aunt Hilda's was horrible for Brianna and me, and I was angry we were there. I was just looking for something. *Anything.*"

Her body shuddered. "A friend introduced me to this group." She lifted her eyes and met Ryan's gaze. "It was exciting, and I jumped in head first." She gulped again, but held her gaze steady. "I went to bomb making classes without Aunt Hilda or Brianna knowing, but then I was given my first assignment." She swallowed hard as tears stung her eyes. "I had to place my bomb at a bus stop. Maybe I was naive, but I'd never really thought it through properly. I didn't think I'd be planting a bomb that would kill anyone. There was no way out if it, I had to place the bomb, otherwise who knows what would have happened to me, but I left a wire loose so it wouldn't go off. Only, it did." Tears streamed down her cheeks.

"Ten people were killed, including three children." She wiped her cheeks with her fingers. "Somehow I got out of there without being picked as the one who'd planted it. I guess being in a school uniform helped. When I got home, that's when I discovered Brianna had been raped by our cousins. I was going to report them, but Aunt Hilda had found the piece of paper I'd stupidly thrown in my bin that had the time and place of the bombing on it." Grace sucked in a breath as the smug smirk on Aunt Hilda's face flashed through her mind.

"She knew it was me who'd placed that bomb, and she vowed that if I ever reported her boys to the police, she'd report me." Grace clenched her fists. "Brianna and I fled, and we've never been back since. I changed my appearance and kept a low profile. Nobody other than Aunt Hilda knows, not even Brianna. She only knows something happened, but still doesn't know what." Grace lifted her gaze again. "But now that I'm a Christian, I know it's time to face the consequences." Her hands shook and her body felt cold. "So if you don't want to have anything more to do with me, I understand. And I'm ready for you to take me to the police."

~

RYAN WAS UNABLE TO SPEAK. He'd known Grace was holding things back, but he'd never in his wildest dreams imagined anything like this. And he knew about the bombing... he'd been in Londonderry when she was sixteen, having been sent there as part of a special task force to help combat the Troubles.

But Grace? Caught up in that? Grace, Barrister, upholder of the law... maybe it wasn't just Brianna's rape that had motivated her to become a lawyer. Maybe she was putting herself on trial every time she stood up in court.

What should he do? God had forgiven her, but he'd have to report her. If only she hadn't told him... but no, she had to, he could see that. It was better he knew. But he was falling for her... and now she'd given her heart to the Lord... but if what she was saying was true, she was responsible for the deaths of ten innocent people. He knew what that was like... how had

233

she been able to keep it secret all these years without going crazy?

He drew a deep breath. His heart was breaking as he gazed at Grace. *God, please help me. Show me what to do.* He squeezed her hand and then dabbed her cheeks with a tissue he drew from one of his pockets. "Grace, you're not a killer."

Her eyes widened. "Yes, I am."

"No, you might have killed people, but that doesn't make you a killer. You never intended to kill them."

Her body shuddered.

"I find it strange that no one came after you. The police were good at tracking down rebels back then."

She angled her head. "How do you know?"

His voice softened. "I was there, Grace. I was in Londonderry when that bomb went off."

Her face paled even further. "I've been expecting a knock for more than fifteen years."

"I bet you have. It must have been terrible."

She nodded. "I should have handed myself in straight away. The longer I left it, the harder it became."

"Are you sure it was your bomb that went off?"

She nodded again. "The job was given to me. I was the only one there."

He let out a heavy sigh. "We'll have to go the police."

"I know."

"I'll stand by you, Grace."

"You don't have to do that, Ryan. We barely know each other."

"Yes, but I want to know you better."

"Even now?"

"Nothing's changed that. From the moment I met you I felt a bond between us."

"What if I'm sent to prison?"

"We'll cross that bridge if we come to it."

Tears spilled down her cheeks. She threw her hands over her face and burst into tears.

He pulled her close, tucking her head into the hollow between his shoulder and neck as he gently rocked her back and forth, brushing her hair with his hand. "Shh... it'll be all right." He had no idea how, but thank God, He did.

CHAPTER 28

*R*yan suggested they continue with their day out and not rush into anything. "It's been so long already, Grace, another day isn't going to make any difference."

"Are you sure?" Grace couldn't believe what she was hearing. Ryan had said he'd stand by her, and that there was no hurry, and they could continue their day out, almost as if nothing had happened.

"Yes. As soon as you go to the police, they'll take you into custody, you know that."

She nodded.

"We need to think this through, because something doesn't seem right to me. Did you follow the story in the news to see if they arrested anyone?"

"No. After Brianna and I left, we kept our heads down and tried to stay out of trouble. I never looked it up, and I knew Aunt Hilda wouldn't report me because if she did, I'd tell the police about the rape."

"I think that's where we need to start."

She drew her brows together. "Why? What are you thinking?"

"I'm not sure. We just need to do some digging, that's all."

"Okay. How do we do that?"

"You're the lawyer…"

"Yes, you're right… but not for much longer."

Ryan squeezed her hand. "Don't say that, Grace. Don't give up hope." He smiled at her as he traced her hairline with his finger. "I think we should pray about it."

"That's all I've been doing."

"Another prayer won't hurt."

"You're right. Thank you." She gave him a grateful smile before bowing her head, squeezing tears from her eyes as Ryan prayed for her.

"Dear Heavenly Father, we come to You with heavy hearts. I thank You that Grace has come to know You, but as a result, she now has to face the consequences of her past. Please give us guidance and wisdom to know how to handle this, and if there's anything we need to know, please guide and direct us, but most of all, I pray that You'll bless Grace's honesty, and that she'll feel Your loving arms around her, no matter what happens. In Jesus' precious name we pray, Amen."

Sniffing, Grace gave Ryan a weak smile. "Thank you."

"You're welcome." He pulled her tight and gave her another hug as he kissed the top of her head. "Now, let's leave these rocks and grab a coffee. I sure need one, and I bet you do."

"Where are we going to get one of those? I don't see any cafés around here." Grace chuckled. She felt lighter somehow, as if the weight she'd been carrying for so long had lifted. It was strange to think that after all these years of hiding it, her secret was finally out.

"Oh, I have my secret places."

"Really?" She chuckled again. "Did you bring a flask?"

"No, but I should have." He jumped up and held his hand out to her. "Come on, there's a place not far from here."

"I'll believe you when I see it."

'You'll just have to trust me."

Tucking her hand into the crook of his elbow, she smiled up at him. "I will, won't I?"

"Yes."

As she walked, Grace thought about what Ryan had said. Never had she doubted it was her bomb that had gone off... no one else had been there. But it might be worth doing some research. Easier said than done, out here in the middle of the Scottish Highlands. Niall. *Niall!* She hadn't called him... Her stomach churned and she let out a sigh. Well, at least now she could tell him why she hadn't married him rather than letting him read it in a letter. And surely he'd help her... but maybe not if he knew about Ryan... Only one way to find out.

"I know someone who can help."

Ryan turned his head. "Who?"

"A lawyer back home. He fights for the bad guys."

"You're not a bad guy, Grace."

"So you say, but I guess we'll see when everyone finds out."

They reached the truck and climbed in. Ryan pulled back onto the heavily rutted track.

"I really hope this leads somewhere."

"Don't worry, it does."

He was right. In less than five minutes they reached a cross road, and directly in front, on the main road, sat an old stone building with a 'Café Open' sign hanging out front. Ryan pulled up in front of the building and jumped out, running around to open the door for Grace. "I told you I knew somewhere."

"Okay, you win..."

Ryan took her hand and pushed the door open. The café doubled as a souvenir shop, and the front section was filled with all things Scottish, from postcards of Edinburgh Castle and Fort William, to Tea Towels adorned with Scottish recipes and pictures of Ben Nevis and Loch Lomond, to miniature pipers, complete with bagpipes and kilts, but in the back, the café was warm and friendly, with a view to die for.

The waitress directed them to a table beside a huge picture window and handed them each a menu.

Ryan glanced at the menu and then looked up. "I think we should have lunch... there's no hurry."

"Okay. What do you suggest?"

"There's a Haggis Lasagne on the menu." He raised a brow.

"Absolutely not. You'll never get me to eat it."

"Never?"

"Never."

He leaned closer and lowered his voice, a grin forming on his face. "Even if that's all you'll get in prison?"

Grace's eyes widened. "Don't joke about things like that!"

He looked bashful. "I'm sorry. It really was just a joke."

She let out a sigh. "It's okay. I'm sorry I got upset."

"I won't do it again."

"Thank you."

"So, will you try it?"

"No!"

He snickered as he lowered his eyes to the menu. "Okay, I guess that's a no for Haggis. How about a Smoked Haddock Crepe?"

Holding his gaze, she didn't say anything, she just sat there with folded arms and a raised brow.

"Okay, what about Crumbed Scampi and chips?"

She smiled. "That sounds better."

"At last." He chuckled. "I can see why you're a good barrister."

She gave a small shrug. "And I can see why you're so good at your job."

He angled his head. "How's that?"

"You're easy to be around."

His face softened. "That's nice of you to say that, Grace."

"It's true. I like being around you."

"And I like being around you too."

She drew a breath. "It's such a pity we're going to be separated." Her bottom lip quivered. "I'll have to go back to Ireland."

He leaned forward and took her hand. "Don't look too far ahead. A day at a time. Okay?"

She nodded. "Okay."

Ryan gave the order to the waitress and then returned his attention to Grace. "This friend of yours... when can you call him?"

"As soon as we get back."

"Could you call him from here?"

"How?"

"I'm sure they have a phone. We can tell them it's urgent, and pay extra."

"I thought you said we weren't in a hurry?"

"We're not, but the sooner we can get some information, the better."

"I guess you're right. Okay, let's ask, but he might be in court, I don't know how the appeal went."

"Wait here, I'll see if I can find the owner."

She smiled at him. "I'm not going anywhere."

While Ryan was gone, butterflies appeared in Grace's stomach. Could she really tell Niall everything after all these years? Would he understand? And would he help? She felt ill. *Oh God, please still my heart. Give me the words to say.*

Moments later, Ryan returned and gave her the okay sign. "She said yes—the phone's in the back room."

Grace gulped as she stood and followed Ryan to a poky little office filled with overflowing bookshelves and benches littered with paperwork. The telephone sat on the wall, an old fashioned one that Grace doubted would even work.

"Do you want me to stay?"

Grace drew a breath. She'd love for Ryan to stay, but what she had to say to Niall was for Niall's ears only. "I think I need to talk to him alone. Do you mind?"

"Not at all. I'll wait outside."

She smiled. "Thanks."

She drew another steadying breath as she picked up the hand set and dialled the number for Niall's office.

His receptionist answered.

"Mairie, this is Grace O'Connor. Is Niall available?" She held her breath.

"You've just caught him, Miss. I'll put you through."

Grace's pulse raced.

"Grace, this is unexpected. Are you calling about the appeal?" His voice was so familiar.

She drew another breath. "No. This is personal. Can you talk?"

She could imagine him leaning forward in his large swivel chair, eager to hear what she had to say. She was about to break his heart... again.

"Yes, what's up, Grace? Have you changed your mind?"

"No, but I'm about to tell you why I can't marry you."

Silence.

"Niall... are you there?"

"Yes... you threw me, that's all. What's going on, Grace?"

"It's a long story, and you may not believe it, but it's true. Remember when you met me at University and you always said you thought I was hiding something?"

"Yes..."

"You were right." She gulped. "I was involved in a bomb blast that killed ten people when I was sixteen."

"No..."

"Yes. And I'm about to go to the Police."

"No..."

"Yes. I need you to do something for me, Niall. Can you help me?"

"Of course. I'll do anything."

"Can you look into it for me? After Brianna and I fled Londonderry on the day it happened, I was never game to read anything about it. All I heard was that ten people were killed, and they were looking for those responsible. Nobody has ever come knocking on my door, even though I've been waiting all these years. So we just want to know if anything was ever found. Can you do that for me, Niall? I can't do it easily from here."

"Give me the details."

"Friday the thirteenth of November, 1969. That's all you need to know."

"I'll get right onto it. Where can I call you?"

"At Danny and Lizzy's. You have the number."

"I'll call as soon as I have something. When are you going to the Police?"

"Tomorrow. We'll be back at Danny and Lizzy's late this afternoon, best not to call before then. They don't know yet."

"You said *we*. Who are you with?"

Grace gulped. "A friend."

Silence.

"Niall…"

"Yes…"

"Thank you, and I'm sorry. You can see now why I couldn't marry you."

"I guess so. How could you have done something like this, Grace? The media will have a field day."

"I know." She bit her lip. "I was young and stupid, but the bomb shouldn't have gone off."

"I don't understand."

"I chickened out, Niall, and I left a wire loose, or I thought I had… it shouldn't have gone off."

"I don't understand, but I'll do it anyway. By the way, O'Malley lost his appeal. They wouldn't even look at it."

"I'm sorry."

"Not sure why you're sorry, Grace. You won."

"I'm sorry for you, Niall."

"Yes, well, such is life." His voice was clipped.

"I guess so."

"I'll talk to you soon."

"Thanks." As she hung up, her heart ached for him as she pushed back tears. Niall didn't deserve this. *God, please bring someone special into Niall's life, and help him to move forward.*

She wiped her face and took another moment to steady herself before opening the door.

Ryan was sitting at an old table reading a newspaper, and looked up when she stepped towards him. "Okay?"

"Yes. He'll do it."

Ryan held his hand out. "You've been crying."

She dabbed her eyes again and nodded. "Years ago, Niall asked me to marry him. I turned him down, and he never knew why. He does now."

"The poor guy."

"I feel sorry for him."

"He must still be a good friend if he's prepared to help you out."

"I hope so. He was my best friend, *my only friend*, at University."

"I'm sorry, Grace."

She shrugged. "It's okay. It's just what happened. I hope he can move on."

The waitress popped her head around the corner. "Sorry to interrupt, but your meals are ready."

Ryan lifted his hand in acknowledgment and smiled. "Thanks."

He stood and squeezed Grace's hand. "Come on, let's eat."

THE REST of the afternoon passed in a blur. So many mixed emotions ran through Grace. The joy of being with Ryan, knowing they shared a connection that was real, but unsure of what would happen if and when they went to the police. She tried not to think about it, but it was impossible not to. Her whole life was about to change. And then there was Niall... he'd sounded so desolate on the phone, as if his whole world had also been shattered. Her heart ached for him. They could have been happy together, if only...

Ryan ran his thumb along Grace's hand. "What are you thinking about?"

Taking a slow breath, Grace tore her gaze away from the window she'd been staring out. "Just everything."

"It'll work through, Grace. Whatever happens, God's with you, and I'll be there for you."

She released her breath and gave him a grateful smile. "Thank you. I know I shouldn't, but I can't help thinking about it all."

"It's understandable, but you need to get your mind off it for a while. There's nothing we can do until we hear back from Niall."

She angled her head. "What do you have in mind?"

He chuckled. "A game of mini golf might be fun..."

She drew her brows together. "And where are we going to do that?"

"There's an old course just outside. Hasn't been used for a while, but I asked Sheila, and she said we could use it."

"Who's Sheila?"

"The owner."

"Is she a friend of yours?"

"She is now."

Grace laughed. "Okay, you win. Mini golf it is. But I can't play…"

Ryan's eyes twinkled. "It doesn't matter. I'll have fun teaching you." He raised a brow, a playful look on his face.

"I get the picture." Grace's heart fluttered at the thought of Ryan standing behind her helping her hold the golf club.

SHORTLY AFTER, once Ryan had paid for the meal, they ventured outside with a golf club each and several golf balls. Ryan was true to his word and showed Grace how to hold the club and how to swing. Competitive by nature, Grace took it seriously, although several times she had to tell herself to focus on the ball and not on Ryan, leaning back with his arms crossed, studying her with an amused grin on his face. When it was his turn, she admired his easy style and his ruggedly handsome good looks. She just wanted to wrap her arms around him and stay here forever.

But finally they had to go. Ryan chose the circuitous route through the quaint town of Aviemore and then through to Inverness, where they stopped at a small traditional café for an afternoon tea of scones with clotted cream and mouthwatering pastries. Grace tried not to think it might be her last meal out before being incarcerated. She was in no hurry to return to the cottage—they'd agreed she should tell Danny, Lizzy and Brianna, but the thought made her ill.

The whole way back, Grace had her hand on Ryan's leg, and when he could, he held it. They chatted easily about lots of things, but when they arrived at the cottage just before dinner time, and Danny was coming through the gate, waving to them, Grace's butterflies returned.

She forced a smile and returned his wave as she climbed out.

Danny strode towards them, and when he reached Grace, gave her a hug. "Enjoy your day?" He winked at Ryan.

"Yes, it was fun, thanks."

"Staying for dinner, Ryan?"

Ryan shrugged. "If there's enough."

"I'm sure there will be. Come inside."

Ryan took Grace's hand as they walked inside with Danny.

Dillon, followed closely by James and Clare, raced down the hallway. Danny swept Clare into his arms and kissed her. Clare clung to him and put her thumb in her mouth as she looked down at Dillon and James with a smug look. Ryan swept James up into his arms, and Dillon tugged on Grace's hand.

It was all so surreal. Happy families. Her news would shock them.

Lizzy appeared, looking flustered.

Danny bent down and kissed her. "Got enough food for Ryan?"

"Always." She blew some hair off her forehead. "Oh, Grace, that friend of yours called a few minutes ago. I told him you'd be back soon."

The blood drained from Grace's face. Ryan placed his hand lightly on her shoulder.

"Thanks. I'll go call him."

"Okay. Dinner will be ready in ten minutes."

Grace extricated herself from Dillon's hold, and Ryan

placed James back on the floor and followed Grace into the back room and closed the door.

"They'll know something's going on." Grace's hands shook as she picked up the receiver.

"We'll tell them after dinner. I'll call the centre and ask Brianna to come over." Ryan held her gaze, his voice softening. "Are you okay, Grace?"

Grace shook her head. Her chest felt constricted and she could barely breathe.

"Take some slow breaths." He breathed with her. "That's the way."

Her heart still pounded, but she tried to steady herself with her breathing. "I'm scared to hear what he's found out."

"Do you want me to talk to him?"

She sucked in a long breath. "No, I need to do it. But thanks." Her hands shook as she dialled the number.

With each ring, her heart rate increased. Maybe he wouldn't answer. She gulped when he answered on the fifth ring. "Niall..."

"Grace, thanks for calling back. I made some enquiries, and no one's been charged... they didn't find the bomber."

Grace's heart plummetted. "Because it was me."

"I did come across something that might be of interest. The reports suggest there might have been two bombs, but looks like only one went off. Might be worth pursuing."

"Two bombs? I only planted one."

"I don't know, Grace. I'll keep checking. Is it possible some-body else planted one as well?"

"I guess it's possible, but I wouldn't have thought so."

"What will you do?"

Gripping the receiver, she sucked in another breath. "Go through with it."

"You'll need a lawyer. I know a good one."

"Are you offering?"

"Of course. I'll do whatever I can. I'll be there in the morning."

Grace gulped. "You don't have to do that, Niall."

"I want to."

Grace's throat burned, and she could hardly get her words out. "Thank you."

"You're welcome."

WHEN GRACE HUNG UP, she lifted her gaze slowly to Ryan's. "Did you hear?"

He placed his hands on her shoulders and returned her gaze. "Yes."

"He's coming."

"I know."

CHAPTER 29

*A*fter dinner, Ryan made the call to the Centre and asked Brianna to come over. Ryan and Grace were still sitting at the table when she arrived within ten minutes of the call.

"You look like somebody's died." Her gaze travelled between Ryan and Grace as she took off her coat and joined them. "What's happened?"

"We need to wait for Danny and Lizzy. They're just putting the children to bed." Grace was glad Ryan answered, because she couldn't. What would Bibi think after all these years? If it hadn't been for the bombing, she would have prosecuted those cousins and they'd still be in prison. Would Bibi ever forgive her?

Ryan made small talk. Grace said the occasional word, but her heart thumped so loudly it was a surprise Bibi didn't hear it.

She offered to make tea, but Ryan took over. Finally, Danny and Lizzy returned.

"Brianna, good to see you." Danny smiled warmly, but his forehead was puckered. It wasn't usual for Brianna to be here after dinner. "What do we owe this to?"

It was Brianna's turn to look puzzled. "Ryan called me over."

All eyes turned to Ryan as he cleared his throat and squeezed Grace's hand. "Grace has something she needs to tell you."

Lizzy and Danny both took a seat.

"Sounds serious, sis. What is it?" Danny's voice softened.

Tears stung Grace's eyes. How could she tell them? She wrapped her hands around her mug of tea, and inhaled slowly. She lifted her gaze to Danny's. "It is."

As she relayed the story, silence filled the room. Three sets of eyes looked at her in disbelief.

"I'm sorry." She swallowed hard and shifted her gaze to Bibi. "I'm sorry Bibi. I should have told you." Tears streamed down Grace's cheeks.

Brianna pushed her chair back and stormed out.

"I'll go." Ryan stood and followed her.

Grace fiddled with her hands. Seconds passed. *Why weren't they saying anything?*

Tears streamed down Lizzy's cheeks. Reaching for the tissue box, Lizzy handed one to Grace and kept one for herself.

Danny ran his hands through his hair. "You've been hiding it all this time? Does Caleb know?"

Grace shook her head. "Nobody knew until today."

"And you're going to hand yourself in?"

Grace nodded. "I have to." She swallowed hard, forcing down the lump in her throat.

Standing, Lizzy walked around to the other side of the table, and slipping her arms around Grace, gave her a big hug. "What you're doing is very brave, Grace, and God will honour it."

Grace swallowed again as she dabbed her face. "I hope so."

Ryan re-entered with Brianna.

Grace lifted her gaze and held her hand out to Bibi. "Will you forgive me, Bibi?"

"Yes, but I wish you'd told me." Tears welled in the corners of her eyes.

Grace stood and hugged her. "I'm so sorry, Bibi. Please believe me."

"If only we hadn't gone to Aunt Hilda's." Brianna's voice caught in her throat and tears streamed down her cheeks.

Grace closed the gap between them and hugged her. "Everything would have been different, but we can't change what's happened, and I'm prepared to face the consequences of what I did. And you know what this means?"

Brianna pulled away and shook her head.

"Aunt Hilda won't have anything over me anymore, and we can report those boys for what they did to you."

Bibi's bottom lip trembled. "I… I'll have to think about that. I don't know if I want to go through it all again now I'm moving on."

Grace squeezed her shoulder. "Just think about it?"

Bibi nodded and then looked up. "Will you really be sent to prison?"

Grace drew a breath. "Unless Niall can get me off. But I did it, so that's where I deserve to be."

Tears streamed down Brianna's cheeks again. "I can't believe it, Grace."

"I know. It seems like another life, but I can't live with it anymore. I have to hand myself in."

"I'll be praying for you."

Grace choked. To hear those words come out of Bibi's mouth was too much. The tables had been turned. God had changed her little sister so much.

"I think we all need to pray." Ryan slipped his hand onto Grace's shoulder.

"Good idea," Danny agreed.

Everyone gathered around Grace and took it in turns to pray for her, even Brianna. Grace knew she was doing the right thing, and peace settled in her heart, slowly replacing the anguish that had threatened to overwhelm her. Whatever happened, God would be with her.

NIALL BOARDED the plane for the flight from Belfast to Inverness with a degree of hope. If he could help Grace, maybe she'd agree to marry him after all. He didn't really care what people thought, or if being associated with her damaged his career. He loved her, and that was all there was to it. Besides, with the information he'd gathered, he felt confident he could get her off. He couldn't get there soon enough.

Grace and Daniel had agreed to meet him at the airport, and they'd go on from there to the Police Station.

He still couldn't believe that Grace had been involved with terrorist activity. What was she thinking? And then to hide it all these years? And then to take the oath as a barrister? He shook his head as he gazed out the tiny window. What made her decide to hand herself in now? She'd obviously been hiding it well... in fact, she probably could have gotten away with it forever... if she'd done it, that is. He opened his folder and pulled out his notes. There was certainly room for doubt. He'd make it difficult for any jury to convict her, if it got that far.

Before he could finish his cup of tea, the plane began its descent into the small city of Inverness. He should have been looking at the magnificent scenery, but only one thing held his interest, and that thing was meeting up with Grace O'Connor.

Holding his chin up, Niall stepped into the Arrivals Hall and scanned the waiting crowd. He felt a little overdressed in his dark, tailored suit, but impressions were everything. He was meeting Grace as a client for the first time.

Grace stood with a man he assumed was Daniel. As she lifted her hand in a wave, a ripple of excitement flowed through him. Grace needed him, even if she wouldn't admit it. As he stepped closer, his gaze travelled over her face and then searched her eyes. His heart went out to her. She was different. Gone was the confident barrister. Her face was pale, and dark circles sat under her eyes. She mustn't have been sleeping. Not surprising, really.

Placing his brief-case on the ground, he reached out his arms and drew her close. His heart warmed when she returned his hug. "Good to see you, Grace. And don't worry... I'm going to get you off."

Pulling away, she gave him a warm but slightly shaky smile.

"Thanks for coming, Niall." Turning to the man beside her, she extended her arm. "This is my brother, Daniel."

NIALL TOOK Daniel's hand and shook it. "Good to finally meet you. I've heard a lot about you."

"All good, I hope." Daniel let out a small chuckle, lighting up his eyes which were the same as Grace's, mesmerizing.

"Of course." Niall tried to be jolly, but he just wanted to hold Grace and talk with her, not with her brother. He returned his focus to Grace. "Are you sure you want to go ahead with this?"

"Yes, I am."

"Okay. We need to go through some things first. Can we grab a coffee while we chat?"

"Yes, but not in here, it's too noisy. Let's find somewhere quieter."

"Good idea."

"I know a place," Daniel said.

"Okay. You lead the way."

Niall walked beside Grace as they followed Daniel to the car park. Niall raised his brow as they stopped beside an old van with 'Elim Community Centre' plastered over it.

Daniel chuckled. "It's not quite a sports car… sorry…"

Niall chastised himself. "It's fine, Daniel. I've been in worse."

Grace drew her eyebrows together. "Have you? When?"

It was Niall's turn to chuckle. "You don't know everything about me, Grace."

"I guess I don't." Grace's expression sobered. "You'll have to tell me some day."

"It's a deal."

Daniel unlocked the van and held the passenger door open. "We can all fit in the front if you like."

Niall motioned for Grace to go in ahead of him. He climbed in beside her. He longed to put a protective arm around her. There was something fragile about her, something vulnerable, and he just wanted to be there for her. Instead, he asked her about Brianna.

"She's doing well, thanks to Danny and the others." Grace's voice lifted.

"So it was a good move?"

"Absolutely. She's a different person."

He smiled. "I'm pleased to hear it."

Danny pulled up outside a row of shops, one of which was Aggie's Bakery. A few people sat inside, but it was much quieter than the airport café. They ordered a coffee each, and Daniel insisted on getting some pastries.

Once seated at a table away from the other customers, Niall pulled out his folder and opened it. "Grace, I need you to tell me everything. Right from how you got involved until when the bomb went off. The more you can tell me, the more prepared I'll be."

She drew a slow breath and gave him a nod. "Okay, I'll start at the beginning…"

~

RELAYING the whole sordid story to Niall was hard, but Grace had to do it. She also had to tell him about Ryan. She'd seen the look of hope in Niall's face when their eyes met at the airport.

The way his gaze travelled over her face... but her heart now belonged to another, and she'd have to break that news to him sooner rather than later. *After she finished telling him what she'd done.*

She felt ill relaying it all in minute detail, especially with Danny listening. The meeting with Fergus, the elation she'd felt when she'd been accepted into the group. The challenge and secrecy of the bomb making classes, the sinking feeling when she realized what she'd gotten herself into. The nerves she felt when she decided to leave a wire loose. Vomiting into the toilet on her way to the bus stop to plant the bomb. Planting it... and then watching in horror as it exploded. *It shouldn't have gone off. How had it happened?*

"There was another bomb, Grace. Somehow we have to prove that yours wasn't the one that went off. You need to give me every minute detail about it. And you need to be prepared to disclose the details about Fergus and anyone else who was involved."

Grace gulped. She'd expected to be going to prison, why hadn't she thought about the implications? Could she betray Sammy, wherever she might be? And would Fergus come after her if she testified against him? Probably, but wasn't she a barrister, and hadn't she lived with the possibility of that happening with every case she prosecuted? Niall had done his homework. He'd raised her hopes... maybe she hadn't been responsible for all those deaths after all.

"Okay, I think I've got enough to make a start." Niall closed his notepad and drained the last of his coffee. "Are you ready to do this, Grace?" His voice was gentle, and his gaze as soft as a caress.

Grace drew a long, slow breath and nodded. Now the moment had come, she just wanted to get it over with. To face whatever was before her. But she still had to tell Niall about Ryan. The longer she left it, the harder it would become. She could see the longing in Niall's eyes, and she felt so sorry for him. If he decided not to represent her, she wouldn't blame him.

She put out her hand and touched his wrist lightly. "Niall, there's something else I need to tell you before we go."

He angled his head. "What is it, Grace?"

She swallowed hard. "I don't know how to tell you, so I guess I should just come out with it…" She swallowed again. "I… I've been seeing someone."

The colour drained from Niall's face.

Pain squeezed Grace's heart as a muscle clenched along his jaw. "I'm sorry, Niall, I really am. If you decide not to help me, I won't blame you."

"I don't understand, Grace. If you couldn't be with me because of this, how can you be seeing someone else?" The hurt in his voice tore her apart.

"It just happened, Niall, I'm sorry… I told him it'd be best if we weren't together with all of this happening, but he wouldn't listen. It won't hurt his career like it would have hurt yours."

His eyes narrowed. "Shouldn't you have let me decide that?"

Grace gulped as tears stung her eyes. He was right. She'd decided for him. She hadn't even told him why she couldn't marry him. Maybe if she had, he would have stuck by her, just like Ryan was. What kind of person would do that? It was all such a mess. Her chest heaved as her breathing grew more laboured. It was too late for them… she couldn't turn the clock back. Guilt and sorrow flowed through her. "I'm so sorry, Niall. You're right. I should have trusted you."

"Yes, you should have." His voice was short and filled with pain.

She squeezed his wrist. "If you decide to leave, I'll understand."

He shook his head. "I'm man enough to see it through, Grace. But I have to say I'm disappointed."

"I know. I'm sorry."

He lifted his chin. "So, who is this person you're seeing?"

Grace glanced at Danny. He hadn't said a word, which was unusual for him, but as he caught her glance, he sat forward and gave her a supportive smile.

Grace shifted her gaze back to Niall. How she hated hurting him. He didn't deserve this. "He's... he's one of the leaders at the centre. He used to be in the army... and he was actually in Londonderry when all this happened. He was the one who said we needed to find out more."

Niall straightened, his eyes narrowing further. "So you told him, but you wouldn't tell me?"

"It was different, Niall. I had to tell him... I couldn't go through the same thing I went through with you." She squeezed back her tears. "You don't know how hard it was. I wanted to marry you, to say yes, but I couldn't. I just couldn't do it to you."

He let out a heavy sigh. "I guess it's too late?"

She nodded slowly. "Yes. I'm sorry."

"Okay. We'll do this professionally, and I'll treat you like any other client." He reached for his brief case and stood. "Shall we go?"

"Yes." Standing, she met his gaze and then reached up and placed a gentle kiss on his cheek. "I'm sorry, Niall."

His eyes moistened. "And so am I. Let's go." Placing his hand on the small of her back, he followed behind her as she weaved through the tables now bustling with lunch time diners, to the door and then outside to face whatever lay ahead.

CHAPTER 30

The desk sergeant's eyes widened as Niall told him that Grace wanted to confess to a serious crime that had occurred fifteen years ago in Londonderry. He made a phone call and then ushered Grace and Niall into an interview room. Danny was asked to wait outside.

It was like many a room Grace had been in—they were all much the same, cold and impersonal, but it was the first time she'd been the one being interviewed. The interviewing officer quizzed her and she answered all his questions. Niall had told her to be cautious with what she said, but she'd told him she just needed to be honest. She didn't want to hide anything. After hours of interrogation, she was charged with being involved in an act of terrorism and was remanded in custody. A bail hearing was scheduled for the following morning.

Sitting in her cell after Niall and Danny left, Grace determined to be strong, but the reality of what she'd done sat heavily in her stomach, making her feel ill. What if Niall couldn't get her off? Could she survive in a cell like this for perhaps the next twenty years? Bile rose from her stomach and she vomited into the toilet. Wiping her mouth, she fell onto the floor and sobbed. It was too much... what had she been thinking? How could she survive in a tiny cell like this?

Her panic slowly subsided, and she pulled herself up off the floor and sat on the hard, narrow bed. She'd known this would happen, but the stark reality of it was worse than she'd ever imagined. Inhaling slowly, she closed her eyes. Right now she needed to hear from God, to know that He was with her. What had Lizzy said? Learn to listen... be still before God.

She bowed her head, resting her forehead on her upturned hands. *Okay God, I'm here, and I'm listening. Please help me get through this, and help me trust You, regardless of the outcome.* As she hummed the songs she could remember from the Sunday service, peace slowly filled her spirit, and although she didn't hear God's physical voice, she sensed His presence. He truly was close in times of trouble, when everything else was stripped away, and there was nothing else, just her and God. Nothing to get in the way. No television, no one to talk to. She was used to being on her own, but at least at home she had books to read, a television to watch, music to listen to. The silence of her tiny cell would drive her crazy if God hadn't been there with her.

The night passed. She barely slept. Not surprising, really. The guards came for her an hour before the bail hearing and placed handcuffs on her. Not that she was a threat, but they didn't know that. Dressed in drab prison clothes, Grace walked between them down the hallway and to the waiting van.

As she was taken into the court room and placed in the

dock, for the first time ever she knew what all those men and women she'd prosecuted over the years felt like... and it wasn't good. There was nothing good about this. She scanned the court room for Niall. Her mouth went dry. Maybe he'd changed his mind. But Danny and Lizzy weren't there either. *Nor was Ryan.* Had they all deserted her? Her chest tightened. No, they wouldn't do that. Something must have happened.

The clerk stood and walked forward, whispering something to the judge. If only she could hear.

Moments passed. She'd be returned to prison shortly if Niall didn't appear. It was most unlike him. He was always on time or early. Never late. And then she recalled the verse Lizzy had suggested she memorise... "Cast all your care on Him because He cares for You." *Okay, God, I'm casting my care onto You. I'm really struggling here... please help me to trust You. I'm sorry for panicking.*

Moments later, heads turned towards the door and Grace breathed a sigh of relief as Niall entered, looking very professional once again in his smart, dark suit. She caught his eye, but he didn't smile. He just met her gaze and nodded his head before he stood in front of the judge and apologised for being late.

Danny, Lizzy and Brianna followed him in. Grace met each of their glances briefly, but she really only had eyes for Ryan, who brought up the rear. As she met Ryan's gaze, she pushed back tears of embarrassment. How terrible that he should see her like this. Her bottom lip quivered, and her breath stuck in her throat. But his eyes told her what she desperately needed to know. He was there for her.

The four of them took their seats towards the back. The

judge called the prosecutor to state his case. It was all so familiar, but so surreal... like an out of body experience, as if it was happening to someone else, not to Grace O'Connor, Barrister. And then it was Niall's turn. Grace's heart fluttered as he adjusted the buttons on his suit jacket. How many times had she seen him do that? He looked so smart, and as he addressed the judge, his voice was strong and confident. If anyone could get her off, it was Niall.

Niall's argument for bail was strong. She wasn't a flight risk... she'd handed herself in. She was a lawyer, and she knew the penalties for breaking the terms of bail. Plus, there was reasonable doubt that she hadn't actually placed the bomb that had gone off.

She got bail—Ryan put up the security. She left the court a free woman, but only for two months when her case would be heard in Belfast. What a spectacle that would be. Grace O'Connor, Barrister for the Department of Public Prosecutions, being prosecuted by her own department. No doubt she'd be relieved of her position as soon as she told them.

Ryan walked on one side of her, with his arm lightly around her waist, and Danny, Lizzy and Brianna flanked her other side as they all followed Niall out of the court house to face the waiting media. Niall was the spokesperson, and he firmly stated his belief that Grace was innocent, even though she'd handed herself in. Microphones were flung in front of Niall's face as reporters bombarded him with questions, all the while, Ryan, Danny, Lizzy and Brianna huddled around Grace, protecting her from the gazillion cameras flashing in the crowd.

Danny slipped away to get the van, and finally Niall was

able to convince the media that he had no more for them. With his long arms, he shepherded Grace and her protectors away from the crowd and towards the car park exit where Danny was waiting with the van running.

Everyone, including, Niall, climbed in, and Danny took off. He'd very smartly covered the Elim Community sign, so at least the world wouldn't know where she was, for a while, at least.

Danny turned the van onto the road leading to the airport. Of course, Niall needed to return to Belfast—he had work to do. Work for her. Should she go back as well and help? But how could she leave Ryan? She leaned closer into him and gazed up into his blue eyes. No, she'd stay here with Ryan unless Niall needed her to go. Niall would do his job, and she'd pay him. It wasn't what he wanted, but it's all she could offer him.

When they arrived at the airport, Niall opened the front passenger door and climbed out.

Grace squeezed Ryan's hand. "I need to say good-bye."

Meeting her gaze, he returned her squeeze. "Of course."

Grace stood quietly as Niall said good-bye to everyone. When he turned to her, she looked up into his eyes, watching the play of emotions run through them. He was hurting, but he hid it well. Her eyes clouded with visions of the past. They'd shared so much, but in that moment, she knew she didn't love him. Her heart belonged to another. Gulping, she reached out and took his hand. "Thanks for being here, Niall." She struggled to speak.

He remained silent, his face expressionless.

She gulped again. "I'm sorry, I really am."

"So am I, Grace. I hope you'll be happy together."

"Can we still be friends?"

He let out a small chuckle and shook his head. "I'm not sure."

"I hope we can."

"We'll see."

"I'll stay here until the trial, unless you need me before then."

"I'll be in touch." He turned to leave.

She grabbed his wrist, and he turned back. She gave him the best smile she could manage. "Thanks." Her heart was breaking for him, but there was nothing she could do.

When she climbed back into the van, Ryan slipped his arm around her shoulder and pulled her close. Everyone was quiet, even Danny. They understood the awkwardness of the situation. Once they reached the outskirts of the city, Danny glanced around and asked if anyone wanted to stop or just head back. No one wanted to stop.

Grace fell asleep in Ryan's arms and woke to him gently shaking her shoulder as they pulled up outside Danny and Lizzy's cottage. She blinked as she straightened. "I had no idea we were here."

"You slept the whole way."

"I'm sorry."

"It's not a problem. I caught a bit of shut eye too." He kissed the top of her head. "Anyway, it's time to get out." Holding her hand, he helped her out of the back seat.

"Will you stay for a while?" She almost pleaded with him.

"Yes, of course." He placed his arm around her shoulders as they followed the others inside.

Lizzy already had the kettle on by the time they reached the kitchen. "Sit down, Grace, Ryan. Danny's just grabbing the sandwiches Mia prepared for us."

Grace sat at the table between Ryan and Brianna, still in a daze. Lizzy chatted, but Grace barely heard her. Brianna said something, and Grace replied. Danny returned with the sandwiches. Lizzy placed a mug of tea in front of her. Ryan kept squeezing her hand. But none of it was real. It was like a play going on around her, and she was just an observer. She tried to join in with the conversation, but her mind was floating. Eventually she excused herself. "I'm sorry, but I need to rest."

Lizzy's eyes widened as her hand flew to her cheek. "Of course you do, Grace. We're sorry, we should have realised."

"It's okay. I just haven't slept much the last few nights."

"Let us know if you need anything."

Grace pushed her chair back and stood. "Thanks. I'm sorry to have put you all through this."

"Grace! You're family... you don't need to apologise!" Lizzy shook her head.

Tears pricked Grace's eyes. "You don't know how much that means."

"I agree," Brianna said quietly.

Grace placed her hand on Brianna's shoulder and squeezed it.

Ryan stood, and leaning close, kissed her cheek. "I'll come back later after you've rested."

Looking into his wonderful, caring eyes, she gave him an appreciative smile. "Thank you."

CHAPTER 31

When Grace closed the door, she spent a few minutes on her knees before climbing into bed. She didn't deserve to be back here with Danny and Lizzy, amongst family and friends who loved her, she should have been in prison, because, regardless of what Niall said, she was still guilty of being involved in a terrorist activity, and she should be punished. But the memory of that tiny cell sent shivers through her body. If she was found guilty, that would be her life for the foreseeable future. Now she knew what it was like, she'd be better prepared next time, but still, it would only be because of God living in her that she'd survive in there.

Images of a tiny cell and Niall's sad face drifted through her mind, but it was the comfort of being wrapped in God's arms that finally calmed her spirit enough to allow her to sleep.

When she woke later that afternoon, an envelope was sitting

on her floor near the door. Slipping out of bed, Grace picked it up and lifted it to her nose. It held a faint perfume, and on the front, her name was written in an unfamiliar hand. Taking it back to her bed, she sat down and carefully opened it, scanning straight to the bottom to see who it was from. *Ryan...* a smile came to her face as she read.

Grace, I want you to know that I'm here for you. I'm looking forward to spending the next two months with you, getting to know you, having fun together, but most of all, growing together in the Lord. I don't know what God has planned for us, but I know it's something good. God will honour your bravery and obedience, and you have the opportunity to be a witness to the world of how He can change a person. You did so well today, and we're all proud of you. Stay strong in God, Grace, and He'll uphold you with His right hand.

All my love,

Ryan

Grace wiped the tears from her eyes. Yes, she had the opportunity to be a witness to God's amazing love as the case progressed. But to do that, she'd have to be steadfast in her faith. No more anxiety, no more self-pity. She was a child of God, and she was being obedient. Even though in God's eyes she was forgiven, the incident had happened, and many people's lives had been changed forever. The families who'd lost loved ones deserved closure. If she could help Niall and the police discover the truth of that day, she'd be doing them all a service. And if it meant she had to spend time in prison, well, so be it. She'd failed last night, but she'd be stronger next time. Being such a high profile case, she had the opportunity to show that there was a different way... a better way. She'd do it.

She wouldn't wallow in self-pity. Now was the time to be strong.

She threw the curtains open. The weak Scottish sun was sinking slowly over Ben Nevis, washing the sky in soft hues of pinks and oranges. Out on the loch, the students were bringing a number of canoes into shore. Ryan was amongst them, and her heart fluttered with excitement at what the next two months might hold. God was indeed good, and she couldn't wait to see it all unfold.

RYAN DID INDEED KEEP his word. Every spare moment he had he spent with Grace. He took her on long hikes, they went on drives through the countryside, discovering quaint villages and cute cafés. He took her to Edinburgh and to Glasgow and to Inverness, and to all the towns in between. They walked on Culloden Moor, the site of the final Jacobite rising in 1746, where thousands of brave Highlanders fought the English and lost, but they also studied the Bible and prayed together. Ryan told her that if their relationship was going to stay strong, it had to be built with God at the centre, and Grace was more than happy to do that. The more she learned about God, the more in awe she became of His amazing greatness. Not only was He the God who'd created this amazing world, He was the God who lived inside her, giving her new life and hope for the future. She might have lost her identity as a barrister, but she'd gained a new one—she was a child of God, washed clean by the blood of Jesus, loved and cherished as if she were a precious only child.

When the time came to travel to Belfast for her trial, Grace knew with certainty that her strength came from the Lord, and that she would face whatever came her way with God on her side. She'd be a witness to His amazing love as she stood in the dock and testified. She'd be gentle and kind with the media. They wouldn't understand, in fact, Ryan had warned her they'd most likely be sceptical of Grace O'Connor's conversion, and would try to disparage her name. She didn't care. She was standing for the truth, and that's all that mattered.

She'd been in contact with Niall on and off for the entire two months. With the information she'd given him, he believed she'd be acquitted of murder, although she might be found guilty of being involved with a terrorist group, although he was hopeful she might be acquitted altogether. The prosecution maintained that even though her bomb might not have gone off, her intention was to kill.

They hadn't found Fergus, despite Grace providing as much information as she could, all the while knowing he might come after her. The police had been trying to find him and other members of that group for years without success, but armed with the new information Grace had provided, they were hopeful he'd eventually be found. Grace was saddened to discover Sammy had been killed in another bomb blast several years after Grace fled Londonderry. She wasn't surprised she hadn't heard anything from Aunt Hilda or the cousins, but no doubt they'd be worried she'd report the rape some time soon.

As she placed her hand on the Bible and took the oath that day, Grace knew that whatever happened in the days ahead, God would uphold her. Never had she thought she'd be on this side of the court room, but as she listened to the prosecuting barrister's opening speech, one thing she knew for sure, she no longer wanted to prosecute. Yes, for the justice system to work, there was a need for the prosecution, but her heart was no longer there. Her need to punish had been replaced with a heart of love and compassion. The thought crossed her mind that if she was found to be innocent, she could join Niall's firm as a defence lawyer, but then when she looked at him and saw the sadness that still hung heavy in his eyes, she realised that wouldn't work. If he was to ever move on, it was best they didn't see each other after the trial ended. Besides, who knew what God had planned for her and Ryan? But first, she had to get through the trial.

It lasted for three days. The media were relentless, but Grace stayed true to her promise. Unable to speak to them herself, she'd instructed Niall about what to say. He didn't understand either, but she didn't care. She wanted the world to know that truth was more important than self-preservation. That God's forgiveness didn't mean she was exempt from paying whatever penalty she would be handed if found guilty. That providing answers and closure to those family members who'd lost loved ones was more important to her than saving her own skin, and that she was sorry she hadn't come forward earlier.

The prosecution was good, but Niall was better. But that didn't matter. What mattered was that the truth was revealed, and Grace believed it was, although she was stunned as the full realisation that her bomb hadn't gone off finally hit her. All those years believing she'd killed those people. But the evidence was there—they'd found the remnants of a crudely made unexploded bomb amongst the rubble, and it matched the description she'd given. The bomb that had exploded was more complex. Someone else had planted it without her knowing. Had Fergus doubted her ability to follow through? Probably. He was right... how had she ever imagined she could do it?

The jury took just under four hours to find her not guilty. The relief she felt was immense, although she'd been prepared for a guilty verdict. At least now, with all the extra information she'd been able to supply to the police, the actual bomber might be found and brought to justice.

Reporters jostled to get close to her as she exited the courthouse surrounded by Niall, Ryan, Danny, Lizzy, Brianna, and Caleb and Caitlin. The main questions they asked were how she felt and what she would do now. Would she be returning to the bar now she'd been acquitted?

Now she could speak for herself, she was almost tongue-tied, but this was her opportunity, and she needed to take it. A hush fell over the crowd as she lifted her chin and began speaking. "Firstly, I need to thank my lawyer, and *friend*, Niall Flannery, for the superb job he did." She turned and gave him an appreciative smile. Her voice caught, but she quickly regained control. "Niall helped unravel the truth about that awful day, and now the police are a step closer to finding the real culprit. I pray with all my heart that he's found, and that the families of those who've suffered all these years can finally find closure. I've lived for the last fifteen years thinking I'd done it, so I know a little of what they're going through."

A microphone was shoved in front of her face. "So why did you plant it in the first place?"

Grace gulped. The question she'd been dreading. She looked the young female reporter directly in the eye. "I was young and insecure, looking for something to follow. I truly regret my actions."

"So is it true what they're saying? Grace O'Connor has found God?"

"Yes, it's true. Finding God was the catalyst for me coming forward. I didn't want to hide my secret any longer, especially as I believed I was responsible."

"Will you be going back to work for the DPP now?"

"No."

"Will you be staying in Belfast?"

"I'll be considering my options. I don't know at this stage."

Niall leaned in front of her and pushed them away. "That's all for now, folks. Give Ms O'Connor some space."

After the crowd dispersed, the family group gathered at Caleb and Caitlin's house for a celebratory meal. Caleb had invited Niall, and Grace was pleased to see that he'd come, with the blond hanging off his arm. She wasn't sure if the blond was the right woman for him, but she didn't know her, so who was she to judge? But she really wanted the opportunity to share her faith with Niall at some point, and she prayed she'd get the opportunity before she headed back to Scotland, because she was surer than ever that that was where God wanted her.

Niall introduced her formally to Roisin, and Grace discovered she was actually a nice person. Maybe he wasn't dating her just because he couldn't have Grace, maybe he really did like her. Grace prayed that was the case—she didn't want to see him hurt again.

Before dinner was served, Danny gathered everyone together to give thanks. Grace leaned against Ryan's strong, firm chest, with her arm slipped around his waist. It had always been possible she would have been found guilty and sent to prison, but here she was, surrounded by all those she'd come to love and appreciate so much. She brushed back tears of gratitude. God was indeed good.

CHAPTER 32

ix months later, Grace opened the door to her new premises in downtown Glasgow. "Place of Hope" was where rape victims could come for counselling and support. It wasn't flashy by any means, in fact, unless anyone knew it was there, they'd probably just walk straight by. Grace wanted it that way. She wanted to make it as easy as possible for those who needed help to come, and not feel threatened.

After her court case was over, Grace had undertaken an intensive counselling course so she could offer rape victims the best help possible. Brianna had also begun studying a Diploma in Counselling and would be Grace's assistant. But Brianna brought something more than just head knowledge— she brought first-hand experience. She knew what it was like to be raped. The disgust and shame of it all. It had almost killed her, but praise God, thanks to the cleansing power of the cross, she'd come out the other side and was a new person, filled with God's love and compassion for others.

Soon after her court case finished, as part of her preparation for leaving Belfast and moving to Scotland, Grace had written a letter to Aunt Hilda confirming that Brianna was not planning on reporting the rape, and had in fact forgiven the boys. She wasn't surprised she hadn't heard back, but she prayed for them often, because they'd be carrying guilt over what they'd done, and needed God's healing touch in their lives, even if they didn't know it.

As she turned the sign on the door from "Closed" to "Open", a delivery van pulled up in front. The driver jumped out and ran around to the passenger side. He slid the door open, and pulled out a huge bunch of flowers, and then, after looking at the tag, walked straight towards her. Grace chuckled. She knew who'd they be from... Ryan had been sending her a bunch of flowers every week since the court case had ended. It must have been costing him a fortune. But he'd gone all out on this one... it was huge! She thanked the driver and took the bouquet inside. She opened the card and smiled.

Dinner tonight? Pick you up at 6. I love you, Ryan. PS All the best for today.

Her heart skipped a beat. Ryan hadn't planned on coming to Glasgow this week, in fact, she thought he was busy with a new intake of students. She wasn't complaining... dinner with Ryan was something she always looked forward to and didn't do often enough, even though they tried to see each other as much as they could.

The day passed in a flurry. They had four scheduled appointments and two walk-ins. All were women who needed someone to talk to, someone who'd listen without judging, and could offer them hope that one day they'd get through this.

Grace wished Ryan had told her where they were going for dinner so she'd have an idea of what to wear. Casual or formal? She guessed casual, but went smart just in case. She never knew with Ryan. He'd surprised her so often in the past months. They'd had so much fun getting to know each other, but it was hard being apart. He was still the head instructor at the Elim Community, and she'd moved to Glasgow a month after the trial ended…. almost three hours by road each way. It was almost a long distance romance, but in some ways that made the anticipation of their time together even sweeter.

She stood in front of the mirror and checked her make-up. Not that she wore much these days, in fact, she rarely wore more than a lick of mascara and lipstick. She'd even stopped colouring her hair and had returned to her natural light brown. It took her a while to get used to it, but Ryan had told her countless times he loved her regardless of how she looked, and now that Fergus had been found and charged, she had no need to disguise herself any longer.

But she did wonder where their relationship was going. Ryan had never mentioned marriage, and neither had she. She guessed, like her, he was cautious. It was a huge thing for him, especially having lived his whole adult life on his own or with other men. But she felt she was ready to commit. Now her past had been cleared and she didn't have any secrets to hide, she was ready. Or she thought she was. Maybe tonight would be the night he'd ask…

Right on the dot of six the buzzer for Grace's small apartment in a not too salubrious part of town rang. She checked the mirror one last time and then pressed the button to speak through the intercom. "I'll be right down." Grabbing her jacket and bag, she stepped out the door, closed it behind her, and then pressed the lift button. As the lift descended the five floors, she wondered again where he was taking her, and she felt giddy like a breathless girl of eighteen going on her first date.

The lift opened, and he stood there with a beaming smile on his face.

A ripple of excitement ran though her body. She stepped into his arms and lifted her face to his. "I didn't expect to see you so soon."

He cupped her chin and looked deeply into her eyes. "It's a special day, Grace, and we needed to celebrate. It's not every day you start a new career." His eyes sparkled, and she felt enveloped in an invisible warmth.

"That's true." She smiled. "Thank you for the flowers."

"You're welcome."

"You must own shares in a florist shop by now."

Ryan chuckled as he slipped his hand gently behind her neck and drew her face to his. His eyes twinkled. "I can't think of a better investment." As he lowered his mouth against hers, her knees weakened.

"Come on, we'd best get dinner or I might do something I'll regret." Pulling away, he placed his arm around her shoulder and directed her out of the building and towards his Land Rover.

"So, where are we going on this chilly night?" Grace rubbed her arms after she'd done her seatbelt up.

He chuckled again. "I thought you'd be wondering. I've booked a table at The Arthouse."

"You haven't!"

"I have."

She laughed. "And you're going to drive us there in this?"

"What's wrong with my Drover?"

She snickered. "Nothing, but the other diners might raise their eyebrows."

"Let them. I don't care."

She leaned over and kissed his cheek. "I don't either. But can you turn the heat up. It's freezing in here."

"It's as high as it goes, you know that."

"I should have put on an extra coat."

"There's a rug in the back."

As she stretched around to grab the rug, he slipped his hand onto her shoulder and turned her to face him. The only light came from a dim street light, but his eyes still sparkled in the semi-darkness. Her heart raced.

His eyes peered deeply into hers as he took her hands, stroking her skin gently with his thumb. "Grace, I love you so much. I don't want to spend any more time apart." He paused, but his gaze didn't waver.

Grace's heart thudded. For a long moment, she felt as if she were floating, drifting on a soft cloud of euphoria. Was this really happening?

"I want us to do life together, so Grace," his face broke into the most beautiful smile and his eyes lit up, "will you marry me?"

Grace's heart danced with joy. "I thought you'd never ask!"

"So is that a yes?"

"Of course it is!" She threw her arms around his neck, and as his mouth found hers, she gave herself freely to the passion of his kiss. She longed for more. To fall asleep in his arms, to wake up beside him every morning, and to share every aspect of his life. And now, it was about to happen. He'd asked her to marry him, and she'd said yes! It was really happening!

Finally pulling away, he tilted her chin upwards with his finger, as a grin as large as she'd seen grew on his face. "One more thing before dinner." He reached into his pocket and drew out a small box, snapping it open with his thumb and forefinger. Inside sat an elegant sapphire and diamond engagement ring.

Grace gasped and held her hands to her face. "Ryan! It's gorgeous! How did..."

He held a finger to her lips. "Shh... just put it on." He took the ring out of the box and slipped it onto her finger. It fit perfectly.

Grace pushed back tears of joy as her gaze travelled between the ring and his eyes. "Ryan, thank you. I love you so much."

"But not as much as I love you." He smiled as he lowered his lips to hers and kissed her slowly and tenderly.

As they drove to the restaurant a short while later, Ryan turned to Grace and slipped his hand onto her leg. "Now we've got three things to celebrate."

Grace's forehead puckered. "Three? What's the third?"

"Oh, didn't I tell you?" He wore a playful look on his face.

Grace grabbed his hand. "Tell me what?"

He chuckled. "I've got a permanent job in Glasgow... starting tomorrow."

Her eyes popped. "Really? Why didn't you tell me?"

His eyes sparkled. "I wanted to surprise you."

"You certainly did that! Are you going to tell me about it?"

"Over dinner."

"You never cease to amaze me, Ryan MacGregor."

"That's me... full of surprises!" He chuckled again.

RYAN KEPT HIS PROMISE, and over dinner told Grace that he'd been accepted, as a Chaplain, into one of the high schools which had a high rate of troubled youth. He'd be given free rein to implement programmes he felt would benefit the teenagers, and help keep them off the street and out of trouble.

"That's great, but what's Danny going to do without you?"

"Don't worry about that, Grace. He's got a new fellow lined up. In fact, he's starting this week."

"Anyone I know?"

"Maybe." His eye held a glint.

She let out an amused chuckle as she folded her arms. "So, who is it?"

"Just your other brother."

She shot forward. "Caleb?"

He nodded. "Yep, Caleb and Caitlin and the girls have just moved over."

"How come I didn't know?"

"It's just happened, and besides, Danny said he wanted to keep it as a surprise for you and Brianna."

"You're not too good at keeping secrets."

"It's not good to have too many secrets, Grace. You should know that."

Drawing a deep breath, her expression grew serious.

"You're right. Unless they're good ones that are kept for a reason."

"And was this a good one?"

"Absolutely. Does Danny know you've told me?"

"I did mention it would be hard to keep it quiet..."

"So, does he know you were going to propose?"

"Maybe..." She didn't like the mischievous glint in his eye.

"What do you mean by that?"

He pulled a face. "I hope you don't mind, but I asked a few friends to come and celebrate with us."

Grace turned around as a group of people appeared out of nowhere, shouting their congratulations all at once. Danny, Lizzy, Brianna, Caleb, Caitlin. She laughed. So much for a romantic dinner... but she didn't mind. Dinner with her family was always special, and now Caleb and Caitlin were here, it was extra special.

The waiters quickly added more tables, and what Grace had expected to be a quiet dinner with just the two of them turned into a loud, fun-filled evening. They'd all taken the following day off work, and the children were all being minded by Rosemary and David, so the party continued into the wee hours. Grace had no idea how she was going to get up for work the next morning, but she didn't expect to sleep, so it wouldn't be a problem.

Despite the cold, when Ryan dropped her off outside her apartment, she didn't want to get out of the truck. She just wanted to stay with him, encircled in his arms.

"I need to go, Grace—we'll freeze if we stay here, but let's not wait long to get married. We're both sure, and so I propose we get married as soon as we can."

Her eyes widened. "Like in a few weeks?" Her heart raced. Could this be true?

"If you're happy to do that, yes."

"I won't have a dress, or time to do all the normal wedding preparation things."

"I can't imagine you bothering too much with all of that anyway."

She chuckled. "You're right. I can't imagine myself being a typical bride."

"No, you're anything but typical." He brushed the hair off her forehead and looked into her eyes. "So, what say you, Grace O'Connor? Will you become my wife on the first possible date we can make it?"

"Do you need to ask?" She raised a brow.

He chuckled. "Not really... I take that as a yes."

"It's definitely a yes." She threw her arms around him, and knowing she wouldn't have too many more times to do this, tore herself away from him after he'd kissed her thoroughly, and caught the lift to her apartment on her own.

THEIR WEDDING WAS SCHEDULED for midday on the fifteenth of April at The Elim Community chapel. Grace decided it was her turn to surprise Ryan, and found a wedding gown she felt comfortable in, and knew Ryan would like. It fitted her figure perfectly, and although simple in design, it held an understated elegance.

The ceremony was also simple, but she and Ryan planned it to be all they wanted... a committal of their love to each other and to God. They'd both been through so much in their lives, they didn't need all the frills that normally accompanied a wedding.

Danny walked down the aisle with Grace, and then took his place beside Ryan as Ryan's best man. Lizzy and Brianna were Grace's only attendants, but looked stunning in their pale blue suits. Little Clare was her flower girl, and James and Dillon were the page boys. Nothing was too fancy, but the service was perfect in every way.

As Danny stood to pray for them after David pronounced them husband and wife, Grace gazed into Ryan's eyes, still not quite believing that all this had happened. Less than a year ago, Brianna was close to death and hooked on drugs. She herself was hidden behind the walls she'd put up, bitter from the hand that life had dealt her. Yet now, both she and Brianna had new lives, ones full of hope and promise, filled with God's love and forgiveness. They had hope and a future. And Grace had a husband she adored, one she could never have imagined meeting anywhere, let alone in the Scottish Highlands. She had no doubt life with Ryan would be filled with fun and excitement, but most of all, she knew that their marriage would be strong because God would be at the head of it. She smiled at him before bowing her head when Danny placed his hands on their shoulders.

"Dear Heavenly Father, we come to you with joy in our hearts as we witness the joining together of Ryan and Grace in holy matrimony. We're excited for where You're going to lead them, as they both seek to follow You and to live for You. We thank You that they found each other. We love seeing them together, their joy of life is infectious, but their love and compassion for others is what sets them apart. Bless their ministries, dear Lord. Use them to bring hope to those who've lost hope, and let them lead many into Your Kingdom. Bless Ryan and Grace as they start their new lives together as husband and wife, In Jesus' precious name, Amen."

"Amen." Grace lifted her face and gazed into Ryan's intoxicating blue eyes. As their eyes locked, her heart thudded as he lowered his lips and kissed her for the first time as her lawfully-wedded husband, something she had never in her wildest imaginings expected to happen.

"Give thanks to the Lord, for He is good; His love endures forever."
I Chronicles 16:34

❧

NOTE FROM THE AUTHOR

I hope you enjoyed Grace's story as much as I enjoyed writing it. If you have yet to read the first three books of "The Shadows Series", read them now to find out how Danny and Lizzy's story began! The first three books are available in a Box Set which is also free to read on Kindle Unlimited. **Also, keep an eye out for Book 5 in the Series, "A Highland Christmas", coming in November 2017!**

Make sure you don't miss my new releases by joining my mailing list. **Visit www.julietteduncan.com/subscribe** to join, and as a thank you for signing up, you'll also receive a **free short story.**

Finally, could I ask you a favor? Would you help other people find this book by writing a review and telling them why you liked it? Honest reviews of my books help bring them to the attention of other readers just like yourself, and I'd be very grateful if you could spare just five minutes to leave a review (it can be as short as you like).

With gratitude,

Juliette

ALSO BY JULIETTE DUNCAN

The Shadows Series www.julietteduncan.com/the-shadows-series/

Book 1: Lingering Shadows

To her family's consternation, Lizzy deals with heartache by running away with Daniel, a near-stranger. Once they're married, she discovers her new husband has demons he hasn't shared with her. The stresses of marriage will send him back to them.

Book 2: Facing the Shadows

Daniel is locked in a downward spiral, unable to break free of his demons. Though her heart aches for him, Lizzy realizes she must protect herself and their unborn child. She must also face her own past before she turns toward the future. When Daniel is badly injured by his own folly, can this couple who've been divided by pain, embrace God's healing touch

Book 3: Beyond the Shadows

Lizzy and Daniel settle into their new life in the Lake District. As Daniel grows in his faith, they look forward to parenthood. But when Daniel receives news of a family tragedy, his sobriety is threatened. As he and Lizzy travel to Ireland to reunite with his estranged family, can he draw on God's strength and Lizzy's support to remain a steadfast man of faith?

The True Love Series

After her long-term relationship falls apart, Tessa Scott is left questioning God's plan for her life, and she's feeling vulnerable and unsure of how to move forward.

Ben Williams is struggling to keep the pieces of his life together after his wife of fourteen years walks out on him and their teenage son. Tessa's housemate inadvertently sets up a meeting between the two of them, triggering a chain of events neither expected. Be prepared for a roller-coaster ride of emotions as Tessa, Ben and Jayden do life together and learn to trust God to meet their every need.

PRAISE FOR "THE TRUE LOVE SERIES"

"These books are so good you won't be able to stop reading them. The characters in the books are very special people who will feel like they are part of your family." Debbie J

"The story line throughout the books is real, human life portrayed with developed characters, realistic dialogue, interesting settings, well, just the whole package. .. Juliette Duncan sets the bar high for other Christian fiction/romance writers." Amazon Customer

The Precious Love Series Book 1 - Forever Cherished

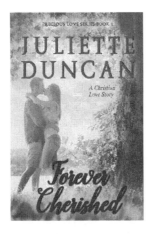

"Forever Cherished" is a stand-alone novel, but follows on from "The True Love Series" books. Now Tessa is living in the country, she wants to share her and Ben's blessings with others, but when a sad, lonely woman comes to stay, Tessa starts to think she's bitten off more than she can chew, and has to rely on her faith at every turn. Leah Maloney is carrying a truck-load of disappointments and has almost given up on life. Her older sister arranges for her to spend time at 'Misty Morn', but Leah is suspicious of her sister's motives.

Praise for "Forever Cherished"

"Another amazing story of God's love and the amazing ways he works in our lives." Ruth H

"This book spoke to me in many ways. Tessa, Ben and Jayden now feel like my friends." Nurmi

Hank and Sarah - A Love Story, *the Prequel to "The Madeleine Richards Series" is a FREE thank you gift for joining my mailing list. You'll also be the first to hear about my next books and get exclusive sneak previews. Get your free copy at www.julietteduncan.com/subscribe*

The Madeleine Richards Series Although the 3 book series is intended mainly for pre-teen/Middle Grade girls, it's been read and enjoyed by people of all ages.

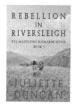  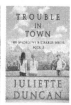

ABOUT THE AUTHOR

Juliette Duncan is a Christian fiction author, passionate about writing stories that will touch her readers' hearts and make a difference in their lives. Although a trained school teacher, Juliette spent many years working alongside her husband in their own business, but is now relishing the opportunity to follow her passion for writing stories she herself would love to read. Based in Brisbane, Australia, Juliette and her husband have five adult children, seven grandchildren, and an elderly long haired dachshund.Apart from writing, Juliette loves exploring the great world we live in, and has travelled extensively, both within Australia and overseas. She also enjoys social dancing and eating out.

Connect with Juliette:

Email: juliette@julietteduncan.com

Website: www.julietteduncan.com

Facebook: www.facebook.com/JulietteDuncanAuthor

Twitter: https://twitter.com/Juliette_Duncan

Made in the USA
Middletown, DE
14 June 2021